IF THE STARS ARE LIT

ARE LIT

SARA K ELLIS

Luna
Press
PUBLISHING

Text 2025 © Sara K Ellis
Cover 2025 © Tara Bush
Editorial Team: Francesca Barbini and Shona Kinsella
Typesetting: Francesca T Barbini

First published by Luna Press Publishing, Edinburgh, 2025

A CIP catalogue record is available from the British Library

www.lunapresspublishing.com

ISBN-13: 978-1-915556-53-0

For Yuka

Contents

Chapter One

Listen!
If the stars are lit,
It means - there is someone who needs it.
It means - someone wants them to be

Vladimir Mayakovski

Like so many things in Joss Carsten's life, this one starts with an explosion.

She's on the passenger ship *Tiktaalik*, paying a week's salary for a pint bottle of Koshu as she tries to talk a woman—Annie, she thinks her name is?—into bed.

Annie is a ship's mechanic, with bright eyes and a carbonated laugh, and she's game it seems, leaning in a little as she lets her hand linger on Joss's arm. "You spent a whole month on that rock? Hope you mean one of Haitch's."

"Nope," Joss laughs. "One of ours, a full thirty-one and change." She lets her gaze drift over Annie's shoulder to the viewport. The bar above Central Hub is crowded tonight, and everyone's here for the same reason. To watch Ross 128 H—or 'Haitch' as the Outer Rimmers call it—recede out of sight and out of mind. As a planet, it's not much to look at, a nubby little orb that spins through its year in a whopping sixteen days.

"You lasted that long, huh?" Annie laughs, her breath fogging the edge of her cocktail glass. "All the more reason to party then."

"You'd think," she says, forcing some cheer into her voice. She really should be ecstatic to get away from Mudtown and the subsistence-level pleasures of that rank, rain-soaked quagmire. She should be celebrating her return home and the swift and, if she says so herself, adept conclusion to the hostage crisis she's just managed, but as Haitch begins to dim in the russet glow of its dwarf star, Joss can't seem to shake a vague but persistent unease.

The job was a straightforward case. A run-of-the-mill hostage negotiation. On-site with no communication lags and a capable strike team at the ready. Just her and the HTs hashing out their terms over the comms.

Not bad for such a brutal start.

Axel Zofia, Haxen Mining Corp's Efficiency Manager had been drugged and strangled, his body strung up like a scarecrow above Mudtown's Tarquin Square, but Joss had gotten the rest of the hostages freed minus further casualties. She'd even managed to land a few of the HTs' very reasonable—in her opinion—demands. Safe passage home and a fair trial under Federation jurisdiction. As one of the Fed's best negotiators, Joss knows the trust you build with your interlocutor is sacrosanct. She keeps her promises, one of them being a secure escort of the prisoners back to Earth.

"Hey," Annie says, her eyes narrowing. "Still here?"

"Sure." She shakes off her unease, tells herself it's just a distraction, a way to keep her mind off that dispatch that blew in on the slow feed just a few days before she boarded for home. The executors of her father's estate had been cheap, sending it on a round-a-bout route—slow to Io, and then bounce assisted to Eridani, then Kestra-Gardis, and from there, a lightspeed snail feed to Haitch. By the time she read those first words of condolence, Hugo Carsten had been dead for over a year.

A heart attack. Much faster than a missive sent through a pulse beacon, and not entirely unexpected. Hugo had been forced to retire early due to coronary artery disease. There wasn't a note in his will, just a notice that he'd left that lonely patch of Nebraska farmland to his one and only and very estranged daughter.

She glances up and spots Aya Deuvim, a member of her strike team, and thinks about flagging her down, but she's too drunk and knows Deuvim might judge her for it. Deuvim sits with her back straight, a lock of blonde hair obscuring her face as she keeps her head cocked to her earpiece. The beer she's ordered sits in front of her untouched like a prop.

Just like Alice, she thinks, taking another pull from her glass. *Never off duty.*

She's getting sozzled but she can't quite seem to stop herself. She nods at Annie's drink, some fizzy citrus cocktail that tickles her nose even from here. It's a mixed crowd here tonight, miners and Haxen execs heading home after doing their time, and the latter never come alone. Their gemels flicker around them like assiduous ghosts, ordering drinks and holding the line, maintaining conversation with potential conquests while their prototypes run off to relieve themselves or do a line of shock powder in the bathroom. One of them, half shadow with a shock of red hair like his progenitor's, flits between Annie and the bartender, signalling for another round. The bartender smiles and bypasses Annie for the gemel.

She clicks her tongue. "Looks like glowboy got the jump on me."

"That's sentientist," Joss says, but if she's honest, she's prickling less at the slur than the sight of Deuvim sliding off her barstool like she's on a combat drop. She scans the credit chip on her wrist, talking at a rapid pace into her implant as she makes to leave. A silencing bubble shields her words from eavesdroppers, but her face is taut, and her gait hurried as she huffs out of the bar. She doesn't even clock Joss as she passes.

Let it go, Joss thinks. *Just tonight. They'll ping you if it's serious.*

Annie's gaze follows the gemel as it floats back over to its sire. A youngish man who's so damned happy to be going home that he's nearing blackout drunk. His cheeks are flushed, and he's reeling a little where he sits, dabbing at his forehead with a monogrammed handkerchief that costs more than Joss's wardrobe.

Annie sighs. "But where's the lie? Those things are going to take over some day. Everyone knows it."

"Don't see how they can," Joss says. It's such a banal statement, she can only muster irritation. "They don't exactly have bodies."

Gemels are sentient holos, 'twins' generated from their owners' subconscious and calibrated to keep that id tightly in check. Only someone desperate or a sociopath would want one of those things, Joss thinks. It'd be like talking to yourself all day. She does that enough as it is.

"Yeah, well, I'm sure they'll figure it out," Annie says. "Only a matter of time."

Annie's pushing it and Joss feels her irritation start to spike into a booze-fuelled pique, enough so that she barely registers the shake when it happens, the wobble of distant stars behind that wall of silicate glass. A few guests halt and glance around, shrugging and chuckling as they move on. Everyone's drunk. Happy to be heading home. So they keep drinking.

Joss downs the rest of her drink and lets Annie's remark go. It's a long trip, after all. Three weeks to Kestra-Gardis, the gas giant in Ross's system and the closest Alcubierre jumpgate, and then a few more stops at Wolf and Eridani, and then Io. Another shake, this time a pall in the chatter lets her know it isn't her. She turns toward a packed table, an uneven swell of nervous grins and scattered laughter as the guests slump back in their seats.

"Someone's brought a pleasure unit onboard," Pink Cheeks yells, but his face doesn't match the levity of his words. He's watching for their reactions, like the universe hangs on their laughter.

It comes. Less enthusiastic this time. Another shake. The revellers trade nervous glances, their smiles listing like melted wax. A few get up, leaning into the thick silicate pane for reassurance as the silence piles on like snow. Pink Cheeks' gemel takes the initiative, floating above the group for a better view. His expression, a full palette of emotion in contrast to his sire, tells the whole story. There's a flicker of brightness at the edges of the viewport, and darkness where it shouldn't be. The stars are obscured, as a fog of smoke stains the sunset hue of Ross 128 into a smog-tinged ochre.

A rumble rises from somewhere beneath the bar, fanning out through the room and setting the glasses to rattling. A few of them slide off the tables. An exec lurches forward, stumbling through the ghostly projection of his gemel, as a high-pitched whine slices through Joss's ear canal. She slaps a hand to her commset.

"Carsten? Respond!"

It's Deuvim. She's not usually the one to give orders, but her tone is curt and choppy.

"Aya? What is—"

"Get to Central Hub! Now!"

Joss shakes her head, the adrenalin spiking her into sobriety. Already, the patrons are rising from their seats and making for the nearest exits; a few run blindly behind their gemels like moths lured to streetlights.

Then someone, it might even be Annie, screams.

✳

Alice did try to warn her. Called her in her hotel room the night before she went up.

"Jack told me you took a contract. Is it true?"

Joss slumped against the wall and stared at the two compact black suitcases already packed and stowed near the door. Of course, this would have to happen.

"You believed him?"

Jack Kenniston was a former Signals Officer on Alice's team and could stretch a story from Florida to Proxima.

"Just be honest with me. For once."

"Always."

But Joss froze at the belligerence in Alice's tone, at that faint hint of ownership that even after years lingered around the edges of their conversations. Alice was slurring her words, but had the drink pushed her to call or had she just downed it in preparation?

"Tomorrow," Joss said. She felt a fresh bloom of anger at what that voice could still do to her. 'Early." The old grooves worn in from their fights had yet to be sanded off. "You know, Jack told me you're just thriving. New place, new life." She was digging for it now, hoping for a reaction, but the only response was a pause, and then a voice, clipped as if Alice had snapped off the words with scissors.

"Jack's not very observant."

"Gosh. You think?" Joss said, and gave a quick glance at the clock, jealous of the boozy lag in Alice's voice and annoyed by this sudden pivot toward vulnerability.

She expected Alice to hang up on her, but her ex-wife grew painfully silent, meting out her punishment in that stillness before she spoke again. This time, her voice was soft.

"I'm going to let that go. Mainly because it's not how I want to remember you."

"What is that supposed to mean?"

"That you don't know what you're dealing with, Joss," Alice said. "You've only worked within Sol and Proxima. You have no fucking idea of what it's like further out."

She was taking on that tone of superiority now, old and familiar and greatly assisted by the alcohol. Before she'd gone into private contracting, Alice had been military, commanding one of the toughest divisions of the Terran Federal Militia. She'd done two tours of duty in the Outer Rim, and had seen things, as she put it, that made Joss's most brutal cases look like arrests for jaywalking. Laborers, forced to ingest thrumweed, the narcotic that allows a person to survive minutes' long exposure to space, sent out repeatedly until their eyesight was gone and their brains were muck. She'd seen hulls torn off ships, their occupants scattered like buckshot into the abyss. When they'd first met, that mask of arrogance had been both a lure and a put-off, a hardness revealing motes of vulnerability beneath its surface. Joss braced herself, prodded by a twinge of that old excitement, even as she looked longingly at her bed. Five hours until she had to be up now. This was just like Alice, sticking the knife in when the timing was right, but this time, her voice was shaking.

"I don't know why you wouldn't tell me." There was fear there. Fear, tinged with a deep love that wormed its way into Joss's ribcage. She closed her eyes. "If you're going to be that fucking stupid, then at least, you could have come to me for advice. You'd have a chance at least. If you'd asked."

"I'm well protected," Joss said. "I'll have a team assigned to me."

"Yeah, well I had an entire platoon."

Joss was about to make a joke at that cocky retort, but the edge in Alice's voice sent a chill through her, one that got colder as she heard the rough intake of breath signalling tears. She turned toward the balcony of her hotel room, peering through the glass to see Hedley's Lift hanging like a braid from the pink cloud cover of the Cape.

Tomorrow, she'd be boxed up inside that elevator, in a first-class compartment that made absolutely no difference during that slow, nausea-inducing climb. She'd be thinking of this moment as she looked down at the world, watching the sea of clouds drift below like her own confusion.

"Are you doing this to punish me?" Alice asked. "Or prove something?"

"You forget they need me out there," Joss said. "Things are getting worse."

"The fucking star."

"What? Ross?"

"You."

There it was again. The spear tossed at Joss's ambition. Always that resentment beneath the surface, at Joss for being good at her job, at Joss for not wanting to settle down, and maybe for being a little better at people than Alice was capable of despite her vaunted leadership skills. Joss had worked her way up Earthside in law enforcement, becoming well-known in her field as a crisis negotiator. She'd saved banks and skyscrapers and packed passenger flights; she'd sweet-talked plenty of terrorists into peaceful surrenders all before moving on to handling more remote negotiations on Mars and Ceres. And it was Joss who'd been the first to develop and test a crisis protocol for working with time delays, now the standard for military and outsourced security whose distance left them isolated and even more vulnerable to attack.

"Ah, flattery?" Joss said, her defensiveness softened by understanding. Alice had never envied her. Not really. This was a tactic, an entry point to get her to hold forth.

"Please," Alice said, but she heard her hitch up in the exertion, and then the thunk of a cork and that trickle of thick, loamy spirit from a bottle.

Joss took in a breath. "Look, I'm sorry. I should have told you, but I've got an early shuttle."

"Alright." Alice was trying for restraint now and Joss felt her stomach knot.

"You take care of yourself, okay?" Joss said, her voice gentle. "Send a message through the ether sometime? Let me know how you're doing?"

"You'll be dead before it gets there."

"Fuck, Al. Why do you have to…" She could see Alice in her mind, that rapid-fire nod whenever she went contrite after a fight. She brought a hand to her ear and tugged at the scarred indentation where an old girlfriend had given her a piercing. That had long healed over. This would too.

More silence. Alice took in a breath like she was building up the courage to speak, to say anything that would make Joss take back her decision, so Joss said a quick, "Bye, Dray" and cut the line, letting herself sink against the wall as the phone powered down. Alice's ID—that five-year-old photo of her—flickered and went black.

They'd spun around that same cold star so many times. It was time for her to break orbit.

✳

Joss opens her eyes and the tracking lights dotting the floor cross her vision like a bright trail of fungi. She's sprawled flat in the corridor of Petal 4, one of the *Tiktaalik*'s passenger mods, her lungs seared with smoke and her head throbbing as the emergency lights flicker and the maddeningly sedate voice of Harbour, the onboard system, reassures her that the atmosphere has stabilized.

Oxygen levels at 60% and climbing. If you are injured, state your location and we will send an evacdrone.

Wait ... how is she here now?

Light flares and subsides beneath her closed lids. Harbour won't shut up.

She was in the bar talking to Annie. She can remember her words slurring, a joke failing to land, then Deuvim barking at her through the comms. She remembers the passengers and service crew, faces expressing mostly irritation, coming at her from the opposite direction as she fought her way out of the bar and down the gangway. The klaxon was blaring, red lights flaring like abrasions across the smooth walls of the corridor. A large man interposed himself between her and the exit ramp, his expression obliging, almost jovial, like he still thought it was just a drill.

"Can't go that way," he said. "They're evacuating Central."

Joss tried to circle around him, but he shadowed her, his smile dropping as another blast shook the corridor. A groan rose from somewhere below as the wall to Joss's right split into a runnel, expunging smoke and wires and graduating the crowd into panic. The big guy stumbled back, his hand slipping against the walkrail, and Joss leaped around him just as the gravity gave out, propelling her upward, the debris whirling around her like swallows.

Then darkness.

So how had she gotten all the way to Petal 4?

She tastes salt and tongues around, relieved to discover that she's only bitten her cheek. No teeth lost. This is good. She pushes herself onto her back, grimacing at the slickness on her fingers. There's something poking from her thigh. Not a bone, thank god, but thin piece of broken pipe.

It's not that far in, so she risks it, fingers damp with sweat as they encircle the metal. She yells as she yanks it out, more from shock than pain. The wound isn't deep. Her trousers are soaked, but that's not her blood she's sitting in. She turns, muscles screaming, to see Deuvim. She's suited up for outside, slumped beneath the manual controls for the external hatch, her lifeless eyes stare through the crack in her visor and there's a piece of shrapnel in her back. Joss seizes up inside, fear compartmentalizing itself into smaller and smaller boxes as she readjusts to the gravity of the situation.

A memory punches its way to the surface.

Deuvim's hand on the back of her neck, firm as a cat's teeth, as they flew through the corridor, the jets in her suit whisking them through the frantic throng of passengers, past flickering lights glinting off a scatter of tumbling debris. She'd been ready for this. How?

She sees Deuvim smack the control panel as the hatch to Petal 4 hisses open, shoving Joss through. The gravity's still functioning here, and Joss twists her body just enough to keep from hitting the tiles face-first. She staggers upright and turns to see Deuvim make a graceful landing, lunging to close the hatch as a flurry of shrapnel flies toward them. On a weightless trajectory, it should skirt Deuvim's head by at least a foot, but the gravity in Petal 4 is active, and while she moves to seal the hatch, a shard of debris arcs down and spears her where she stands. Joss jumps forward, punches in that last command as pain shoots through her leg, and the door drops to crush the encroaching flames. Deuvim had saved her.

She glances over at the body.

"I owe you one, friend."

She doesn't, didn't, really know Deuvim that well. Like Joss, Aya was efficient and closed off, and she could be passive-aggressively insubordinate. But she had a life and a teenage son back on Earth, and she was paying his way through school by keeping Joss safe as she shuttled from crisis to crisis.

Joss clenches her jaw as the guilt washes over her, receding just as quickly into the background noise of survival. Then, one hand pressed to her wound, she grabs the walkrail and forces herself to stand.

The command centre is just up ahead. Each of the *Tiktaalik*'s petals can run independently of Central Hub. They're built to be replaceable and a safeguard in emergencies. She stumbles through the corridor, and pounds at the door, sending it sliding open with a gasp. Then she takes a seat at the bridge, an empty white oval that, offline, looks more like an emptied-out spa than a control room. With the burn still raw in her throat, she speaks.

"Harbour, reveal console."

Joss waits and watches for what seems like minutes until she remembers. She sighs and rephrases the command, some part of her registering that this show of irritation is already a luxury best left in the past. "Let's try again. Carsten, Jocelyn. Terran Federation ID SVRS1128."

She lifts her gaze to the infrared eye on the panel as the console flickers to life, holographic displays blipping into existence around her like the sped-up timelapse of a city in development. Harbour's voice is as still as the surface of a lake. "Clearance granted to Carsten, Jocelyn—"

"It's Joss—" She stops herself; her tongue feels thick and she's woozy with pain. The odour of burnt copper clings to the air. "Just patch me through to Central Hub."

"Central is offline."

"Then Petal…" Her mind stalls on the numbers. "The-the others."

"All petals are offline."

"All of them?"

"No incoming or outgoing activity on main feeds or subchannels."

Sweat stings her eyes and seeps into a cut on her face. She wipes her face. The damage to the *Tiktaalik* must be very, very bad.

"What about Petal 4. Anyone else aboard this one?"

It's a stupid question, but she lets herself hope for as long as it takes to ask. Save for the maintenance workers who come through here only occasionally, Number 4 is empty. Its bunks had been reserved for miners who opted to stay ashore for double pay after a tunnel collapse in an iridium mine took out a third of their crew, the same collapse that had motivated the HTs to string up Zofia and make their demands.

"Uninhabited. No biosignatures outside of Command and Greenhouse."

"You knew that already," she tells herself. Her leg spasms painfully as she shifts in her seat. She'll need to go to medbay. See to her injuries, but first, "How can I reestablish communication?"

"Working on it. No response. Central Hub and all other petals are offline."

"Give me the status on the distress beacon."

"Inactive."

This is bullshit. A beacon would have pinged at the first sign of trouble. "How about making it active then?"

"All outgoing communication feeds are offline."

"What about the pulse beacon?"

A radio distress call traveling at light speed would take seventeen hours to reach the Kestra jumpgate and about two and half weeks to get a rescue here. But each ship had a pulse beacon, a qubit transmitter capable of sending packets of information through at faster-than-light speed. They were volatile and prohibitively expensive, installed for onboard emergencies only, but the pulse should have pinged automatically. It was the black box on every interstellar transport.

"No Casimir energy signatures detected."

The clock on the console reads 04:18. Joss presses her palms to her face and tries to remember. "Harbour, when was the last outgoing?"

"Last dispatch at 23:14.56."

"Nothing after that?"

"Negative. Nothing else logged."

She was in the bar at least until midnight. The comms wouldn't have all gone dark, which meant that whatever caused the accident was well underway before things blew.

Deuvim.

Deuvim had suited up fast between the time she left and got to central. She must have known things were bad then. But how? And why hadn't Central responded sooner?

Joss pushes herself up and nearly vomits as the room carousels around her. She leans against the chair until it steadies. She'll need to get back inside Central somehow. There are other people there, injured and scared like she is. Communications are fucked up but Occam's razor and all that.

Hope lodges in her chest just long enough for her to try to take a step, enough for her legs to buckle. She falls forward, palms smacking painfully against the tile and sits in a crawl until the pounding in her head dims to a thrum. She gazes up at the sun shield now blocking the view of the viewport as a shiver runs through her.

"Harbour," she says. "Could you raise the shield?" She's asking now, not issuing commands. She doesn't like that one bit because that means she's afraid.

Just like ripping off a Band-Aid. The one that's stopping you from bleeding out.

There's a clicking sound as the locks disengage, a faint, reverberating hum as the shell rises from the glass in a slow and dreadful reveal.

A view of the black, spattered by cold white stars. The curve of Petal 4's loading dock protrudes like a diving board into oblivion. No sign of the familiar octagon of Central, the cruciform appendages of Petals 1, 2, and 3—what's left of it tumbles in the black like a package discarded and set afire.

Chapter Two

Joss Carsten has always had problems. Now she has three.

She's alone on a ship in deep space.

The comms are down.

Everybody's dead.

Almost.

She whistles through cracked lips as she makes her way to the medbay. She could let the boomseat carry her, but that feels like giving in. So, she puts her weight against the back and uses it like a walker. Alice would tease her for this, call her stubborn, ridiculous.

You do know you're stretching your recovery time.

"You aren't here," Joss says. She's losing it. She knows this. None of this is Alice's fault. Alice isn't here.

And yet she is.

Always.

Flitting around her consciousness like a wreath of stars around some clobbered cartoon character.

It started just after Alice had moved out. Joss got the flu and collapsed in the bathroom, puking all over the front of her T-shirt. She'd looked up, her hands in that puddle of water-clear vomit to see a silhouette hovering over her, face obscured, and her figure haloed by the morning light slanting through the blinds.

Alice.

Alice reached down as if to touch her, her smile gentle, then teasing as she came into focus. Joss squinted up at her, wondering if she'd left her keys in their old hiding place. Had she...? She raised her chin toward the hand offered and felt no warmth emanating from it, only disappointment as she noticed the faded flowers of the wallpaper mingling with the lines in Alice's hand.

Alice's smile grew as Joss reacted.

Clean yourself up, Carsten, she said.

Joss clapped a sticky hand on the edge of the sink and pulled herself up, finding nothing but air and the faint hint of cassis shampoo.

Gone.

Just the ghost of a thing that was already haunting her. Still haunts her, the farther she gets away.

The medbay door flies open like it's been lonely, revealing a sterile circular room, the beds empty but the equipment still humming away as if it's afraid to be caught idling. The lights, down to save power, flicker on at the movement within, casting a diaphanous blue light along the circumference of the chamber.

Joss pushes the boomseat aside and peels off her clothes as she enters. Her shirt is rank, smoke-stained and papery with dried sweat.

Stay sharp.

Breathe.

A drone sweep of the Petal exterior revealed that the high-gain antenna blew long before Central Hub. Portside faced opposite the explosion, and the damage was localized, deliberate. The low-gain is on the opposite side and bent out of position; its electronics box is shorted out but intact. Low-gains are backups; their signals are weak but still capable of long distances if there's anyone in the vicinity to pick them up. Pirates always blew out the comms first, but this is a passenger route. The minerals extracted on Haitch are shipped on separate pathways with faster jump completions, and their comms are heavily encrypted.

If they wanted to abduct labourers, then they wouldn't have blown up the ship.

Another question lingers: how did Deuvim know to take her to Petal 4? The gantry to Central's escape pods was up one level and much more accessible. Why opt for the longer journey unless she knew that part of the ship was or was soon to be decimated?

Her ribs heave as she tugs her shirt over her head. She winces and presses her chin to her chest and sees the line of bruises across her stomach. Nothing internal.

She hopes.

Stepping under the nozzle in the vestibule, she closes her eyes as a cloud of disinfectant pools around her. The scent is cool and medicinal, a dose of already unfamiliar pleasure, and she takes a towel from the shelf and tears off the seal, rubbing the bumps and embrasures of its waffle pattern slowly over bruised skin. She should help herself to a paper gown from one of the lockers, but fuck it. She'll be that woman for once, alone, naked, and imperilled on a ship.

The chamber comes to life as she enters, a 20th-century hospital drama played out in whirs and chitters and blinking monitors that brighten as she approaches, displaying her vitals for a faster diagnosis. Joss has always wondered if this is helpful. It seems to her that when you're rushed into an emergency room, you might not want to be confronted first thing with visual evidence of the damage.

"What is your complaint?" the room asks, Harbour's voice flitting into something even more listless and synthetic. Just like Father Rivera back home.

She eyes the pill cabinet. "Right leg punctured by some runaway piping. Likely shock from the way my mind's working. Generally … not good."

The sound of her voice surprises her. It's raw but doesn't quite have its old range. It's like a part of her has thinned out with the atmosphere.

"Please step atop the scanning pad for closer diagnosis. Close your eyes."

Joss shuffles forward as an infrared pulse washes over the room. She lifts her arms like a perp as the scanner takes in the damage, measuring her heart rate, her breathing, and the depth of her wounds. She lets herself relax as the pulse subsides, opening her eyes just as the surgery pod slides open, a sterile white sarcophagus replete with a blue light and a padded sleep space.

Medbay wants to operate.

No. Fucking no.

"Diagnosis," Joss says.

"Leg wound requires suturing. Possible concussion."

"Possible?"

"Further examination required. Please prepare for surgery."

"Anything internal?"

"Negative."

She dips her head and peers into the casket, taking in a gas jet and the shiny twisted protrusions of instruments. Joss doesn't like cramped spaces and if Harbour's comms are trashed, there's no guarantee medbay won't have its own problems.

"How bad?" she says again.

"General anaesthesia required."

She waves her hand. "Can I see to this myself?"

"Not advisable."

"I'll see to it myself."

There must be an edge to her voice, for the carrell snaps shut like it's been slapped. Joss limps over to the medicine compartment and finds a First Aid kit and a bottle of Vicocet. She whistles for the boomseat, watching as it floats to her like an eager pet. Nausea seethes through her as it wobbles under her weight.

"Walk me through this," she says.

"Not advisable without a medical pro—"

"Walk me through this!"

"Further disinfection and a booster advised."

"Now you're talking." She grabs a bottle of Iodine from the kit. "Will this do?"

There's no response, so she takes the silence as approval and pops it open with her teeth. It burns as she pours it over the wound, dark liquid mingling with a fresh trickle of blood. Hands shaking, she opens the vial, shaking out the recommended dose before opting to take half. She pops one without water and it sinks like a rough pebble in her throat.

She takes out the suturing gun, holds it up and lets the medbay scanner adjust the settings. The wound is deeper than she thought, but it's safer this way. She can't surrender herself to the care of the ship, not until the beacon's up and running, not until she's certain nothing else has been tampered with. She sucks in a breath, positioning it where the red light shows her above the wound. This is going to hurt, but the pain is proof that she's still here.

Alive.

So, what are you now? Fifty?

Laughter.

Joss jerks awake, her muscles stiff from a long sleep. She's taken over a luxury suite, after all, and helped herself to a 30-credit vodka from the mini-bar to wash down that second painkiller. She's not sure she isn't dreaming. Or drunk.

Voices.

Human voices.

Alive and maybe even happy.

Blue velvet frosting. Sorry to eat it in front of you! Hahaha!
Cold, cold world, buddy!

She yanks off the blankets, and with a great effort, swings her legs over the side of a broad and sumptuous bed. Music seeps under the door, raucous and full of cheer.

Parabéns a você, Nesta data querida, …

A birthday. Someone else's. Her avó Matilde used to sing this to her. She was usually too busy taking water samples and documenting the local flora and fauna for much fuss over birthdays, but she still managed to make them special, honouring Joss with practical, well-considered gifts. A leather day planner. The tuition fees she needed for summer programs. A quartz watch. "The time is all you need," Matilde had told her. "Once you realize that, you can shove all the other distractions away."

Muitas felicidades,

To hear this now feels like some great cosmic joke. But it's real. That matters.

Muitos anos de vida.

She stands and tests her weight on her leg. It smarts, but not like yesterday. She keeps the boomseat at her side as she stumbles into the main room.

"H-hey," she says, her voice barely a whisper. "Hey!"

Clapping. More laughter.

She opens the door and rounds the corner, sees the images on the monitor. A sunlit backyard stretches out in front of her, a gate to warmth and comfort. The lopsided grin of a woman looms into view as she holds her toddler close to the camera. His face is sticky with blue frosting.

Wave to Daddy! There you go! Wave to Daddy!

The woman steps away. Is replaced by a pair of beefy guys, brothers it looks like. They whistle tunes into their half-empty beer bottles.

"Hey," she says. This time with less conviction. She's forcing herself not to look at the time stamp. To maintain that intimacy for just a few more seconds.

The woman breaks it for her.

We planned this early for you, baby, she says, holding up her piece of cake. *Wanted to make sure this reached you in time. We love you!* She blows a kiss at the screen. *Happy Birthday, mi amor!*

A delayed feed.

A delayed fucking feed.

What these people could afford.

The slow feed takes 53 minutes from Earth to Jupiter and the Io jumpgate, provided you shell out for a bounce assist or can arrange to piggyback it on another information packet. Without bounce assists, you pay little—but go the slow route and your recipient in the Ross-128 system would wait close to eleven years to hear from you.

The transport of humans only adds to the confusion. With the exception of Federation battle cruisers, which have full FTL drives and ramped-up pulse beacon capabilities, most people take roundabout routes to get from one system to another, traveling weeks to months on fusion propulsion to the jumpgates that will expedite their journeys. It's a patchwork system, its inequalities expressed more vividly through delay and misunderstanding than by any previous extreme of wealth and poverty. Speed and expedience are luxuries and time equals money equals a mess out here. Communication almost always equals a powder keg.

Joss knows all the stories. Of lovers accepting months-old proposals only to get a 'Dear J' letter hand-delivered via an FTL passenger the next day. If you're obscenely rich, you might bribe your way into the pulse feed, saved for emergencies or catastrophic headlines. People got news about their hometowns being wiped out, only to have that followed up by months and months of messages from their loved ones, cheerfully updating them on their lives, oblivious to the losses awaiting them in the future. It was excruciating, a long, multimedia version of the old messages Joss's avó said she'd saved on something called an answering machine. From exes, from the dead.

Reality spoilers, they call them. Where the best you can hope for is to not know any of the characters.

Joss used to get a dull feeling in her stomach when she encountered these old messages. Watching some poor slob beaming over a year-old feed in a transit hub only hardened her conviction that that face smiling from the screen was already cheating or at least, secretly dreading their return home.

"Not everyone's as cynical as you are," Alice told her once. "Some people are trustworthy, you know?"

"Yeah, until they start wanting something else," Joss said.

Alice laughed at this, not understanding until much later that Joss's stance wasn't just the jadedness that came from dealing with criminals.

Alice too had spent a career vanquishing so-called bad guys, but in the military exposure to those things was countered by the shiny gloss of honour and comradeship. An illusion that greased the demands of discipline and rationalized the brutal necessities that came with maintaining order.

But Joss had known a home once; a happy, relatively stable place until her father sent everything crumbling. She really shouldn't be lured in by this shlock, but still, she finds herself mesmerized by their voices and the homey if banal cheer, even chuckling a little as the brothers crack jokes and fight over that last slice of cake. It's soothing. This illusion of company. An illusion for them too.

They still don't know that they're well-wishing a ghost.

She stops herself there. Feelings are dangerous and nostalgia's a goddamned siren song.

The important thing is that the low-gain antenna is still functioning. At least picking up incoming signals on the slow feed. But there should be noise filtering in from Traffic on Haitch. The delay even at this distance should be less than twenty minutes.

"Harbour," she says. "Patch through incoming."

Calling it Traffic in a place this remote is akin to calling a lonely game of handball the World Cup. The pulse beacons and cargo ships are encrypted, but she should still be able to pick up any communique routed from Haitch through to the *Tiktaalik*, and the AIS system should be pinging on the regular.

"Nothing incoming."

Petal 4 should have gotten something from them by now. Even if the pulse didn't fire, Haitch's Traffic would have noted the radio silence. Damage to the antenna is blocking any transmissions from the channels she needs most, leaving her with slow feeds trickled in on private subsystems. She winces as another communique bleeps in from Earth. Just the grainy photo of a newborn with flowers and his name and birthday scrawled across the bottom. A birth notice only its senders likely give a shit about. There'll be a flood of these: family, friends, lovers, oblivious to their unintended captive audience.

But if these messages are reaching her, the damage to Harbour's communications aren't total. She can fix it. The only complication is that she'll have to do something she's never done before.

Take a walk outside in the black.

*

So, Ma. I graduated. How much do I get?

Waldo. Our—your dog—just chewed up the car seat. I am not paying for this, Rick.

Omae no okaasan wa choooo uruseina! Hayaku kaete kure.

Joss chuckles as she works on the circuit box. She's diverted all incoming to the workshop in case a dispatch from Haitch gets through, but there's a comfort in these messages, in the endearments, and the excruciatingly long updates on taxes or home repairs. Joss is performing a strange memorial service for their recipients. At least they haven't reached a ghost, she tells herself. And sometimes, as she tightens a bolt and solders another wire, she catches herself muttering a 'congratulations' or a 'back at you' in response.

Be safe, Hannah! Muwaaah!

They give her a goal. To survive. To make it home and hear a real voice, to feel the real sun on her face.

She'll fix the low-gain first, manually realign the antenna and then move on to the high-gain because that's what she can manage quickly, but she's thinking about the pulse beacon. How, if she gets that working, she can ping through instantly to Kestra-Gardis. Fat chance Haxen will divert a mineral shipment when it can slog her back over months on a freight pod, least of all an FTL capable ship. The pulse beacons are housed in a fist-sized orb within a protected chamber in each Petal's core, ostensibly malware-proof and running on their own quantum blockchains with the surveillance feeds showing no signs of a security breach. But she needs to figure out how to get it going again, and that she knows will require a quick study of both physics and tricky encryption, both of them subjects in which she's never been very adept.

But she can take the time she needs to get this right. She's got power and air and plenty of food, and there's another less comfortable, less formed reason that she'd like somebody else to get to her first. She's not sure those folks at Haxen will be happy to see her alive.

It's a truism that you think too much out here. The cramped isolation paired with the endlessness outside makes you unravel or burrow inward, lodging yourself in the sediment of the past. It's best not to go there, best to shrug it off and attend to survival, and yet this disquiet keeps nudging her as she works. Not just because of Deuvim or the damage to the beacons, or the fact that three petals and Central Hub went up like a nitrate film warehouse. She was uneasy before she left; her planetside interactions had seemed inconsequential on the surface, but in hindsight felt laced with more sinister implications.

There'd been her encounter with Gabrielle Vecher, Haxen's on-site CEO. He'd offered her an upgrade for her return trip, a Grande Class suite in Petal 1, complete with a view and personalized spa and meal plans for long-haul space flight.

She remembers Vecher's office as a kind of soft intimidation, with its tasteful furniture and the Aritayaki teacups in which Malachi, his gemel, served them sencha from a lacquered hover tray. Malachi was a ringer for his sire, only younger and not as fleshy—easy when you're a trick of the light. Gemel are fuzzy copies of their progenitors, interpolated from memories and neurocircuitry, and can resemble their users to a disturbing degree. Their genesis came from Gestalt therapy, and their first prototypes proved to be remarkably successful in a version of the Empty Chair technique. But like all such inventions, their purpose was warped by narcissists with fat wallets and the desire for more intimate personal assistants.

Narcissus and Echo in the same package, Joss thought.

"Are you sure you won't take me up on it?" Vecher said. "It's the least I can do after what you've done for us."

"I don't take gifts," Joss said, which was true, albeit difficult, especially after spending a month in a capsule hotel on Haitch, scrubbing the Mudtown grit from her pores in the communal banya. But accepting perks meant damaging her reputation and thus any future interlocutor's ability to trust her. "Thank you, though. It's appreciated."

She took a sip of tea, enjoying the earthy scent of a long-ago summer.

Alice had taken her to Nagano at the end of their first year together, treating her to an onsen with a private open-air bath and a view of the stars.

It was early July, and the cicadas were humming, and Joss had at first mistaken that incessant purr for a downed power line. Alice laughed about it all day. They'd spent a weekend taking dips in the hot spring between sex, gazing up at a Milky Way that seemed to meld with the steam rising from the water. On their last night, Alice leaned back and stretched her legs in the water, pointing up to a pair of stars in the night sky.

"There they are."

"What?"

"Orihime and Hikoboshi. Vega and Altair. She's a weaver princess. And he's a shepherd. Lovers who can only meet once a year." She took a sip from a can of beer, the drink already lukewarm from the heat. "You know, that story used to make me sad."

Her voice broke, but only slightly, and Joss felt a sudden protectiveness. For all her resilience, Alice had a childlike side that made Joss love her even more. She traced her fingers up her leg, smooth and warm as the water rippled around them. "That's a nice story. Why the long face?"

Alice smiled and nestled into her. "I was a kid. Thought it was awful that two people who loved each other that much had to be separated for so long. It wasn't fair."

"So that whole legend thing didn't click?" Joss said. She leaned in and kissed Alice's ear.

"Oh, stories hurt," Alice said. "They hurt the most sometimes. My Dad tried to soothe me. 'It's a myth, Alice. That's how they memorized the constellations.' But my Mom took a more practical approach."

"And what was that?"

"She said 'Alice, Sweetie, they're stars. They live for eons. For them, a year is like a week. That was comforting. For a while."

"May I top off your cup, Inspector?"

Joss drew out of her reverie and caught Malachi staring at her, his eyes narrowed as if privy to her memory. She gave him a hard glare in return, but Malachi kept on smiling.

"I'm fine, thanks," she said for emphasis, and Malachi drew back before Vecher's voice cut through the silence.

"You're supposed to ask three times," Vecher snapped. "Remember, that's basic etiquette in Kyoto."

Kyoto? Joss stifled a snort. So, he was one of those assholes. She changed her mind and returned the smile as Malachi answered with a grateful, commiserating smirk. What would it be like to be shadowed by yourself? Most people hated themselves already, but if you were as oblivious and egomaniacal as Vecher, you'd need a gemel just to maintain a baseline level of self-loathing. A very important service, really. She could think of a few more people who needed one.

"Thanks, really," she said, surprised to be feeling sorry for an apparition. "And a third time, thanks, but I'll be going." She gave a real smile and turned her attention back to Vecher. "If the cabins are good enough for the miners, they're good enough for me."

It had occurred to her then, but only fleetingly, that the Grande Class suite was on the other side of Central Hub, far away from the prisoners with whom she'd negotiated the hostages' release.

Vecher nodded as if he'd expected that response. "Understood. That's a comfortable trip in itself. We make sure of that. You do know, Haxen is providing full pensions to all the families."

As you should, Joss thought.

He was fiddling with a paperweight on his desk. Its surface was smooth and metallic, but it absorbed rather than reflected the light. Joss liked optical illusions. They were reminders, as in Alice's story about the stars, that she needed to shift her perspective. But this one was harder to suss, with its rounded edges enclosing a sharp 'V' that upon shifting, revealed itself as empty air. It looked like a more complicated version of a Kanizsa triangle.

Vecher noticed her staring and put it back down. "Malachi will see you out. If there's anything you need while you're still in reach, don't hesitate to contact me. We are grateful for everything you've done here."

"Thanks," Joss said. "I will."

She placed the teacup down on the tray and turned to see Malachi flicker slightly as he remotely activated the door. That was another thing that made her uneasy about them. Gemel weren't allowed physical bodies, but barring certain security protocols, they could patch into any system and control it from the inside. There were inputs that apparently made them fail-safe, incapable of deliberately harming humans, but you didn't have to be deliberate to get someone killed.

As she left, she noted they seemed eager to see her go.

That was never a surprise.

Only now, it feels like a warning.

She shakes off the thought, starts going over the airlock sequence in her head again when another message flickers on the monitor. Not a spouse or a drunken friend this time. This guy's in a lab. Bedhead and an old school sweater vest, the try-hard model of a low-tier academic or burnt-out graduate student. To one side of him is a blackboard, dusted with chalk; numbers and symbols take up every inch of available space.

"Hello, Tam." He gives a little wave, meant to seem casual and chummy, but the overall effect is unpleasant. He looks, Joss thinks, like the kind of asshole who makes fun of people for using 'literally' the wrong way. He makes nice for a minute, asks a few questions about the wife and the stepson. Then he clears his throat as if to acknowledge how awkward this all is.

"I got that data packet you sent me. I was a bit surprised, and so I didn't have time to look at it until a few weeks ago, which is like what, six months ago for you? But Tam…" He moves up closer to the camera like he's letting his friend in on a secret. "Have you *told* anyone about this?"

She glances down at the recipient data: Tam Vinkonour, Age 37, Astro Mining Engineer from Westport Indiana.

He pauses, lets out a low chuckle. "Guess you can't answer that."

There's a mix of awe and back-peddling condescension in his tone. Joss is familiar with this; she's heard it in the voices of acquaintances, people who knew her when she was a poor kid living in Matilde's guest room. Years later, they'd run into her on the street or in the station, eye her nice clothes and her badge, and instantly recalibrate their demeanour.

"Those pictures you sent me … of the tunnels."

Joss flicks off the soldering iron and looks up.

Tunnels.

Couldn't mean the one that collapsed. Even without Haxen Mining boring holes beneath its surface, Haitch is riddled with them, cenotes and sinkholes that were always catching unlucky prospectors by surprise. That's what made Haxen's safety lapse all the more egregious. Zofia, if not the other higher-ups, was well aware of what could happen. But he was the type to cut corners, covering his eyes to Haxen's barely veiled custom of tat-scraping: altering the digital signatures imprinted on miners' skin to make it look like they'd clocked out. These practices are endemic in the outer colonies. Who are you going to tell when you're at the far edge of the universe and your wages barely get you a slow feed transmission to the next jumpgate?

"Any word on what you found there? I mean, do they know where those markings came from?"

She steps around her workbench, curiosity rising as he gestures to a wall display upon which she can make out the muddy, uneven surface of a mining tunnel—and something else. Scratchings preserved and steeped into that surface by time and the elements. The markings are alarmingly uniform, and from what she can tell with that resolution, intricate.

"I think this has potential, buddy," he says. "If you don't mind, ping me on the bounce assist. I can cover the cost." He steps up closer to the camera, his voice a whisper. "This could mean something very big." Then as an afterthought. "For both of us."

Joss feels a shudder pass through her and just as quickly smothers it. A few odd scratches on the wall don't have to mean anything. Since the advent of interstellar travel, there have been plenty of tricks of the light when it comes to First Contact. So many that any promising discovery is never likely to register as much more than tapbait, maybe a few conspiracy theories languishing on the slow feeds. It won't help this guy get tenure.

She shakes her head and takes a cup of water from the dispensary. It almost hurts to swallow, and she's sweating despite the chill in the room. She dashes the liquid into her palm and rubs it over her face, then pours the rest over the back of her neck. It's tepid, but the air streaming from the vents adds a kick and she closes her eyes in relief. She dabs at her face again and checks her handiwork, running the scanner over the electronics box, watching carefully as each point clears with an electronic chitter.

First things first. Time to suit up.

Chapter Three

Deuvim must have done this on the quick. She didn't even wait for her suit to pressurise. But Deuvim had experience, and despite having gone through the steps a hundred times, Joss has never done a walk. What she lacks in familiarity, however, she makes up for in being methodical.

It used to drive Alice crazy. She would brush off her own dogged adherence to procedure, waiting, her shoulder a doorstop, as Joss sat on a footstool and carefully laced up her boots.

It's a day hike. That is, if we get there during the day.

"Going as fast as I can."

And you picked those boots.

"I wanted to piss you off."

You look too good for that.

She tests her leg, the memory alloy is constricting, but space walks are all arms and grips, and legs are just along for the ride. She lowers the HUT, slipping in her arms and securing it to the LTA. She tests the cooling tubes and checks the lights, rechecks the locks on the outer gloves.

"Do I now?"

There's no answer as she steps outside. Just a vacuum and a silence broken by the rhythm of her heart.

She's not afraid. Not really. But she's heard the stories. How it's easy to be overwhelmed by the vastness; how walkers get trapped between eternity and their own heads long enough to make a fatal mistake. She'd deny it, but a part of her knows how much the isolation is wearing at her, making her vulnerable.

Alice has walked dozens of times.

Like climbing a ladder. Just don't look up or down or sideways and you'll be fine.

Fine.

She keeps her eyes on the hull, on the pitons crisscrossing Petal 4's shell-like spines on some ancient creature. She focuses on her breath, on the chitter of the biomonitor.

Heart rate—110 and climbing.

Temperature 38.

She reaches the low-gain in under twenty minutes and the old circuit box snaps easily from its alcove. She tosses it into the black behind her, a summer kid hurling a pop bottle into the sea. The replacement box locks into place and the antenna is pliant. She reorients it, replacing the strut and a sheath of burnt reflector membrane blocking the signal. She'll have to activate the transmitter from inside to know for certain, but this feels like progress, like she's one step closer to a human voice.

She's on her way back when it happens.

Her leg, the one she's told herself doesn't matter, cricks and stiffens. She tries to bend a knee and pain sears through her body. She doubles over, releasing another spasm. One hand slips from the piton as her feet lose purchase and her body tilts outward from the hull. She's hanging by one hand, her suit puffed up and stiff, like that flag in the moon landing photo.

"Heart rate rising. Oxygen reserves low. Immediate return advised."

"Happy to."

She grabs hold and pulls herself back to the hull, but there's too much force and as her feet connect, one boot catches on a piton running up from the docking hub. If her muscles weren't cramping up, she could bend at the knee, slip her foot easily from the rung. But the memory alloy has cut off her circulation, and her leg is as taut and heavy as a plank. She strains, hoping to force it out, but a tearing sound, unambiguous, gives her pause.

"Leak. Immediate return to ship advised."

"How much time."

"Depressurisation within fifteen minutes."

"Okay," she says. "Okay. Give it a minute. Relax. Even the worst cramps go away."

This one doesn't.

Fuck.

She should have let medbay put her under, should have waited until she'd healed up completely. She shakes off the thought. No use for that.

"Slow your breathing, Carsten. Think."

What? You're not going to shoot your way out of this?

"Alice?"

Never said never, Carsten. I just said only when necessary.

She reaches for the sidearm in her utility belt. Not a weapon, but a heat beam used for welding. If she aims right, she might cut through the metal and sever the piton. Or blow an even bigger hole in her suit.

She dips her head, as far as the suit will let her, and trains the scope on the trap. She can't see the beam. Flames don't taper in microgravity and there's no oxygen to feed them, but a blue glow winks at her from below, and she lets out a cry as the rung snaps and severs.

A sob rolls through her as she pulls herself free, climbing hand over hand back to the hatch, a spooked kid tripping on a darkened stairway.

She only looks once inside, taking in the immensity as the void vanishes behind the hatch. There's no majesty in what she sees, just more loneliness and loss. A lifetime supply for the whole fucking universe. She's drenched in sweat, her arms heavy as she removes her helmet. It clatters to the tile as she disconnects the cooling system and slips out of the LTV. The HUT is unbearably heavy in the sudden gravity. She stumbles forward and tries to lift her arms.

"Could use an assist, Harbour."

The drone flits overhead, lifting the armoured shell from her body like it's picking up a drink tray. She reels at the sudden lightness of her body, her vision spinning as she collapses against the walls of the airlock. She can't feel her leg and she reaches down, tearing hopelessly at the alloy.

"How am I doing?" She whistles at the boomseat. "C'mere."

"Immediate medical assistance required."

"Yeah? Well, what are you waiting for then?"

She doesn't see the drone hovering above her, doesn't feel it as it lifts her up, oh-so gently for a machine. She dangles there, a cat hanging over a bathtub, until the boomseat slides beneath her and whisks her to the medbay.

"You never told me about that."

It was a statement, said casually enough not to tip into accusation, but Joss had grown used to these insertions. They'd be lolling in bed on a Sunday morning or taking one of their long, aimless walks along the waterfront, their conversation loose and even playful, when there it was. A question or a remark, slithering its way into the conversation.

"Why didn't you tell me about…"

"I didn't know you liked…"

"Is that true that…"

That last one was disingenuous. Everything Joss disclosed to a hostage taker or a person in crisis was true. She had a hard rule about that. Lie and you pulled whatever shaky foundation you'd built out from under you. And the subject would sense it; they'd smell the lie coming off you whether you were a room or a world away.

Lying meant suicides and dead hostages, lives and property irrevocably damaged. So, Joss never lied, and when her job required her to give away pieces of herself to build trust, she'd offer them up freely, oblivious to whether or not Alice knew she'd left home at fifteen, or that she once owned a collection of Minnesota Twins trading cards or had to be given mouth-to-mouth after a diving accident in Mexico.

But often enough the subjects would get those pieces of her first, leaving Alice to play catch-up, gathering up second-hand revelations about the woman to whom she'd committed her life.

Alice found it funny in the early days. She saw Joss's reticence as a source of intrigue, something that would wear off with intimacy and time. She'd find out about her exploits after the fact, enjoying the challenge of figuring her out, and Joss too had used her reserve to shore up the fiction she'd created of herself. That stopper in her chest, the one that kept her from seeking or offering comfort? Well, that was just a rough quirk of the profession, that cliche of a prize fighter who won't have sex before a match.

Alice didn't question it at first because she had seen Joss in action. That was how they'd met.

Operation Arcadia Planitia.

A Martian anarcho-syndicate had taken one of its domed cities hostage and was threatening to burst the glass. The HTs' demands were clear enough—the release of two terrorists who'd blown up a Martian helium refinery and the pullback of security forces from the Artemisia Rond, a self-declared but unrecognised free territory. There were a lot of those groups cropping up, on Mars and elsewhere. That's the thing about a sudden and very quick expansion into space.

Humans weren't even ready for the moon. Why else would they have dropped that prize so quickly to invest in a collection of intercontinental ballistic missiles? And if you thought they were doing a shitty job of managing resources and living peacefully on one world, wait until they've got themselves a dozen. Once the Alcubierre corridors flew open, the usual suspects—along with several newcomers—got to work, claim staking, colonising, and of course, killing each other left, right, and at every declination and ascension. It took decades for the Terran Federation to gain a foothold, and even now, there are still plenty of rogue states, cartels, and other players lurking around the fringes, using those vast distances and communication blackouts to get away with things they wouldn't have dared when we were a lonely blue dot in the dark. Was the Federation perfect? Alice never tried to fool herself that it was, but at least it offered something like order.

Alice was handling In-Sol security when planetside negotiations caused the hostage takers to go dark—brought in to oversee a rescue operation from 174 million miles away. Negotiation wasn't part of her repertoire.

Enter Joss.

She remembered taking that damned elevator up to the Bodey's station and then a shuttle to a Federation orbital command centre, a heavily armoured tin can with pulsar cannons and a multitude of horn antennas, that with its constant spin, gave it the look of an antiquated musical instrument.

"Our guys up there attempted a breach through the south tunnels and tripped an alarm," Alice said, leading her into the situation room, a sombre kaleidoscope of blinking consoles and 3-dimensional monitors. "Now the entire edifice is locked down. They've been dark for 23 hours."

She introduced Joss to her team. Jack Kenniston and two younger communications techs who sat rigidly at their stations, monitoring each section of the dome for activity. The HTs had cut off the interconnected surveillance system, but the atmospheric trackers up top of the dome still brought in a close view of the exteriors.

"Any way in or out?" Joss said.

Alice waved her hand impatiently, calling up a holoschematic of the dome indicating all possible entry points. "Nope. Unless they can phase. The underground waterways and routing tubes are locked down, and the older ones they brought down with explosives. It's—"

"Doesn't look good, that's for sure." Kenniston cut her off in the tone of a father giving disappointing news.

"You just keep the comms running, Jack," Alice said, causing Joss to warm to her instantly. This Kenniston guy carried himself with mawkish self-importance, and he was already setting Joss's teeth on edge. His freckled baby face contrasted the grey at his temples, evincing a lack of wisdom despite his deep desire to project it.

The display pooled light into the space around them and gave Joss her first real look at her. Alice Dray was more confident than she'd sounded over the comms, calmer, despite the tension now carving a ravine in her brow. She was taller than Joss, with an intimidating stance that made her seem ready to argue. But there was an awkwardness too, a vulnerability residing in those brown eyes despite the horrors she'd taken in over the years. Joss had worked with the military on several occasions, and they always had stories to tell; the grimmest of which they'd save for the last call in a bar.

Alice chewed her bottom lip as she glanced over the diagram, one hand rising absently to press her fingers against her temple. "I've told ground security to stand down for now." She gestured to a scattering of pinprick lights along the dome's perimeter, indicating where the onsite team was hunkering in. "So far, they're doing it. At least they were five minutes ago."

"And forty-two seconds," Joss corrected her.

Alice blinked at her in surprise. She wasn't used to being challenged. "At the current tilt, I mean."

"Right," Alice said, her eyes darting back to the display. Visual data was being transferred in at the speed of light, which meant that if not for the silence of the emergency pulse beacon, the dome might have easily blown up by now. Alice sucked in a breath and nodded. "Well, no matter. I've requested access to the pulse beacon. Once we're authorised and figure out our approach, we can message back in seconds."

"We don't need it," Joss said.

Alice gave her head a little shake. "Excuse me?"

Joss edged up closer to the display, noting the way Alice's breath seemed to quicken at her proximity. The reflection of the dome's high-rises and winding transport routes flickered prism-like over her hand as she traced a line from one end of the dome to the other. "If our signal takes an average of six minutes to reach them…" She kept her voice level and non-confrontational. "The delay's to our benefit too."

Alice eyed her sceptically for a moment, but Joss remained unflappable. "It takes twelve minutes in total for a two-way exchange. We fire back instantaneously, and all that does is give them the advantage of making us wait."

Alice gave a slow and thoughtful nod. "This is like poker, isn't it?"

"You any good?"

Alice laughed, letting that iron posture loosen as she leaned into the banter. "I've paid for a few rounds. Maybe a good meal or two."

"Then…" Joss said. She pulled out a chair, taking her eyes off Alice only to slip a pack of cards and an old-school yellow legal pad from her briefcase. "Get on the comms and keep your guys up there from playing hero. Then come sit down and show me what you've got."

Joss sensed the HTs weren't merely acting out of political idealism. The histrionic wording in their demands indicated that they were working out something personal. So, she layered her opening gambit with the threads she hoped would grab their attention, reiterating their terms, emphasising that their stipulations were being handled from afar precisely because they were important. She dropped a reference to the appalling living conditions in Artemisia, one of the earliest colonies that had roughed it out on insect protein and water tinted with chlorine, eventually developing into a hardened rule-bound culture. It was perfectly understandable that they wouldn't like the Federation barging in with empty promises, all the while restricting their trade and mobility.

Alice said the words, Joss cueing her occasionally, and then they waited for it to take.

It took.

In those 140-million-mile silences, Alice and Joss teased out motives and argued over their next steps, so many consequences teeming in a tonal shift or a poor collection of words slung across the void. And as they analysed each new packet of information, they were watching each other, reading into a smile or a lift in the voice, a hand nervously fiddling with a strand of hair.

"You do this in your free time too?" Alice asked, sliding the stack of credits Joss had won back from her back across the table.

"You might think that," Joss said, noting a strange hesitance in her expression. A shyness. "But mostly I garden and read on my balcony."

"Garden?" Alice glowed with the surprise of it and Joss felt a cautious, but familiar tug in her chest.

A volley came nine minutes later, the demands didn't budge, but there was a question at the end of it. Did they know that the water was tainted and that people with weakened immune systems were dying?

Joss didn't, but from there, she reeled them in.

Those small bites of intel they provided allowed Alice to trace the HT's identities, and after learning that the syndicate was using their families as leverage, she rerouted the onsite security forces to free them. The HTs were out of the dome within 52 Earth hours.

Joss and Alice celebrated with drinks and a long, delightfully naked sleep in Alice's quarters, a small chamber the size of a capsule hotel. When they woke they picked up where slumber had overtaken them.

It was one of those rare happy endings, and for them, a more than promising beginning.

Too bad it didn't last.

"I'm not trying to hide things from you," Joss said after another secret, belatedly disclosed, prodded them into their first real fight. Joss had opened up to a man on the side of a guardrail as she talked him back to safety. His father used to hit him, and Joss told him about her mother's rage, how she'd smacked her across the face when Joss had broken her father's cigar box. "The world rattled around me for hours," she said. "I thought I'd gone deaf."

"I don't know why you wouldn't you share that with me?" Alice said. "I've seen a lot of bad stuff. You do know that, don't you? It's not going to change how I see you."

"It's not that," Joss said, feeling that tightness gather up inside her, her mind quickly evacuating the truth in protest. "These stories? They're a resource I use to do my job. If I let them all out, it's…" She couldn't articulate it because she knew she was lying, and Joss couldn't lie but she could damned well keep the truth stuffed down until she barely recognized it. Her reticence with Alice wasn't a quirk of the job. Her fellow negotiators were the kind of people who'd gripe about their kids' report cards to the bots bussing their tables. But Alice just went quiet and backed off, her head tilted in thought as if she hadn't considered it that way, finding a newfound respect even as it distanced them further.

It wasn't a lie but merely the story she told herself. One that was closing in on them.

※

She coughs herself awake, tugging against her restraints as a cloud of disinfectant curdles around her. The carrell slides open, leaving her exposed to the glaring lights of the medbay. Her sight's blurry, but the pain has subsided and the fever's gone. She pulls at the restraints, now lifting easily at the pressure, and presses a hand to her forehead. A nest of nodes still clings to her skin, and she plucks one away, gets no protest from medbay, and yanks off the others. All better now? Is it over?

She pushes herself up and tugs off the paper-thin blanket. Her leg is swathed in a medbrace and a substantial bruise purples the surrounding skin. A digital readout gives her a countdown of 72-hours until recovery. Until then, she'll need the boomseat or a crutch to get around.

"Harbour, how long have I been under?"

"Four days, eleven hours and twenty-eight minutes."

The voice has a faintly synthetic timbre, but it's still very close to human. Much closer than Harbour's.

She shifts, and with some effort, swings her legs over the edge of bed. She starts, one hand squeezing the blanket. A blurry figure in doctor's whites regards her from across the room.

"Who..."

Joss presses her palms to her eyes, as if trying to push out the image. She looks again, and the shadow straightens and approaches the sarcophagus. There's a rustle of fabric—again synthetic—but no accompanying footfall.

"Who the fuck are you?"

She snaps for the boomseat, ready to make a run for it, as her senses confirm that perfect posture, the cut glass features that soften as they come into focus.

And those eyes.

Soft and brown and brimming with warmth.

Oh god.

Alice stops and crouches before her; her expression quizzical and faintly amused. She lifts her hand to Joss's forehead as if to brush back her hair, and Joss leans in, drawn to the promise of a touch that doesn't come.

"Did I not…make it?" she asks.

"Shhh…" Alice smiles. Understanding. Gentle. A glow emanates from her palms as if she's granting a benediction. She skims Joss's neck above the carotid artery and Joss feels her pulse thrum as she takes in the pinstriped pattern beneath the white coat. *That* shirt. She'd worn it for their anniversary, a year to the day after they met.

But this is not Alice. This is—

Not-Alice removes her hands. Satisfied.

"You made it," she says as if she's been worried herself. "You're very much alive."

She smiles then, evincing that familiar mix of warmth and humour so well that Joss's heart nearly bursts. "The drugs should wear off about now. How do you feel?"

Joss lets out a laugh. "How are you *here?*"

Alice Not-Alice straightens. She takes in a breath—a simulation, Joss reminds herself—and looks away, her eyes distant in that same way Alice's grew distant when she had to explain something difficult. After a long moment, she lets that ghost breath out and faces her, her head tilted slightly, the way Joss's head tilts slightly whenever she's sceptical or curious.

"You're a gemel," Joss whispers.

Not-Alice nods.

"Of *her.*"

She laughs. It's close enough to genuine to be infuriating. "Your ex-wife is not on the ship as far as I know."

"Who then?"

Not-Alice lifts an eyebrow, seemingly baffled by Joss's confusion. "I'm your emergency intervention," she says. "I'm all you."

Chapter Four

I'm all you.

Joss doesn't speak. She calculates. There's still a chance this isn't real. That she's dreaming her life away in that coffin because if it is, then Harbour's systems are running a lot less smoothly than she thought. She's in terrible shape, sure. But imprisoning her with the doppelgänger of her ex is as far from a sane treatment plan as you can get.

Not-Alice takes a step back, giving her room to process the shock. Gait loose, she walks over to the examination table and hoists herself up, or rather hovers in a sitting position. It's uncanny the way she takes up space, ethereal yet giving off a convincing kind of solidity. She sits with her legs sprawled, one foot resting atop a chair, the way Joss might sit if her own leg wasn't swaddled in a brace.

"You don't look like me," Joss says.

A smile tugs at Not-Alice's lips. "We can't all be perfect."

"Why are you here?"

"Your isolation was becoming a danger. To you and to Harbour."

"Well…" Joss grabs the boomseat, swinging it around to align with the bed. She pushes herself up, arms sore against her weight. "Harbour's not the best conversationalist." The seat wobbles, nearly sending her ass first to the floor.

"Oh, believe me. I know."

The next crack dies in her throat. Gemels can interface with tech, communing easily with onboard systems provided they've got authorisation. But pre-programmed inhibitions or not, only the stupidest of sires would be willing to hand them that kind of power. Harbour must have signed off in case Joss didn't wake up. They're likely sharing info as they speak.

Not-Alice or Alice—she's giving up already—folds her arms, watching not incautiously as Joss lifts herself into the seat. "Could have asked the drone for help."

"I like to do things myself."

"I know you do."

"Do you?"

They lock eyes, but Joss is a champ at emotional chicken, and she thinks she sees Alice—or Not-Alice—flinch. Her mind is rummaging through everything she knows about the gemel with a sluggishness this entity, whatever she is, would find funny. A gemel is a sentient being generated from an individual's psyche, an autonomous awareness functioning off some physics principle she can't recall and could never hope to understand. They usually take on the appearance of their sires—something to do with mirror neurons—but not always.

This one sure as hell hasn't.

Not-Alice slips off the table and strides toward her, one finger gently circling in the air as she recites a litany of Joss's afflictions. "That leg was borderline gangrenous. A little more time and you would have lost it. You were severely dehydrated, suffering from malnutrition and a host of secondary infections and—"

This is sheer Alice nag, a projection based on Joss's memories of her? Human Alice isn't a doctor, but she's stitched up plenty of folks during tours of duty, and with the medbay stats channelling through her, this one makes for an intimidating mimic. It's both effective and affecting: Joss has missed being fussed over like this. God, she's missed it. Was this the reason for it? Why her subconscious recreated the woman who had so often patched up her body before she tore apart her heart?

Alice angles her gaze at her, her tone more curious than remonstrative. "You were spacewalking with a severely high fever. I still don't know how you managed that. Not to mention you haven't been eating enough calories for subsistence much less recovery. It's beyond foolhardy"

"Someone had to do it." Not her best comeback, but it's hard to be witty when you're talking to a ghost. "So, what now? You hover around me while I eat my vegetables?"

Alice ignores the crack. "I've already sent an order to the kitchen. You've been eating nothing but half-frozen packets of somen and calorie bars, Carsten. Don't know what you were thinking there either."

"That can wait," she says, even as Alice's words hit the hollowness in her stomach. It feels so good to talk to someone, or rather to argue, like being finally allowed to walk and stretch after a coma. "I need to test the transmitter first."

Not-Alice shoots her a look of beleaguered tolerance like Joss is some uppity kid and she's ready for all her tricks.

"Food first. Get dressed."

The drone serves up a spread in the mess: Powdered eggs and greens that look surprisingly fresh. Even the toast has the right consistency, although the flavour's more cardboard than wheat. Alice has traded the medic's whites for a pair of dark jeans and a loose denim shirt, maybe to put Joss at ease. Gemel, from what she can remember, can switch wardrobes, but can't alter their appearance much beyond aging up or down a few years. It's a security precaution locked in by their makers, and one often used in arguments for their rights. Humans are allowed to make all sorts of alterations to their bodies, from data tats to added digits and altered pigmentation to make the long stints in terraforming colonies more tolerable. A gemel is an individual: one passbook and one Federation identification number. Yet, they're given far less self-determination. Before this, Joss had considered it a needless and cruel form of hobbling: the rigid assignation of identity at inception. Now she's just relieved that this…emanation won't suddenly morph into a giant lizard or her mother.

"Eat all of it. Slowly," Alice tells her, and Joss does, not because she feels hungry but because she needs to focus on something other than the presence sitting across from her. She shovels in another bite and chews for what seems like an eternity. The drugs are still in her system, fogging her senses and dulling her taste buds. She reaches for a bottle of Sriracha sauce.

"That a good idea?" Alice says.

Joss ignores her and squeezes a trail of red over the eggs. She takes a bite, relieved to register the mix of burn and sweetness on her tongue.

"I almost died," she says. "Indulge me." She jabs her fork into the eggs and takes another bite, chewing with an obnoxious, theatrical gusto like a kid on a dare. Then she pours a tall glass of water and downs it in long, noisy gulps.

"This is new for you." Alice nods toward the bottle of sauce.

"How so?" Joss pours another glass. Alice wasn't kidding about the dehydration.

"You were always the ascetic," Alice says, her voice light. "Other than spirits. No butter, no sugar or milk in your coffee."

The note of familiarity throws her and sends the water down the wrong passage. Joss pitches forward coughing, pressing a napkin to her lips to keep from spitting all over her front.

"You okay?" Alice's brow creases and Joss can almost see the indentation in her skin.

"Yes." She lets herself breathe for a moment. "Fucking Christ."

"Like I said," Alice quips. "Take it slowly."

"Stop it." Joss's hand shoots up, smacking the pitcher. She rights it before it falls, but some of the water slops over the edge, creating a thin pool on the table's surface. Joss stares into it, sees herself and this other Alice staring back at her. "I can't..." She grabs a towel and dabs furiously at the water. "I can't do this with you."

"This?"

"The food. The banter. This." She tosses the cloth down and faces her remaining ghost. "Not with you."

Alice blinks, still not comprehending, but then her gaze sharpens and Joss can see that long string of mornings, those routines of chiding and sleepy flirtation flickering like a reel behind her eyes.

"I'm being too familiar," she says, and a vague astonishment creeps over her face.

"I suppose that's the point, isn't it?" Joss says, not quite sure what to do with the sudden awkwardness that has fallen over their conversation. Real Alice had this side to her. That tough exterior was honed from childhood, a means to hide a lonely girl who couldn't read a room, who scared others off in so many awkward attempts to connect. Where Joss was collected and never a bad note, Alice—when she wasn't directing or carrying out orders—could find herself unmoored in social situations. She'd go quiet or talk too much, or worse, stammer out something blunt or unsolicited. How much? Joss wonders. How much of this thing is what she remembers of Alice? And how much can be attributed to her own inability to disclose what hurts?

Thing.

She feels a stab of guilt at the word. However unsettled she makes her, Alice is not a thing. She can see it now, in the sudden flinching self-awareness, one of those moments in childhood where you realise how little grasp you have of the world. Joss had applauded the Sentient Ethics ruling, the declaration that it was nothing short of cruelty to subject an intelligence modelled off the human psyche to a life?— An experience?—of unwilling servitude.

She's always been the first to rebuke others for using the same dehumanising—no, that isn't the right word, but it is the right word—language. And yet here she is, thinking it.

Thing.

It's like a tiny piece of her mother has been left festering inside her. She tenders a smile. "I'm sorry. This is a lot to take in."

"It's understandable," Alice says. "You had a rough split."

Joss's cheeks go hot. "Sorry doesn't mean push your luck."

Quiet stretches between them, punctured by the occasional report of clicks and beeps from the monitors, the scrape of Joss's fork as she finishes her meal. In a strange show of support, this Alice has the drone bring her a cup of tea. She sits quietly, running her hand through the steam, watching it coil through her fingers with an almost childlike fascination. There's someone else in these movements. Not Alice or herself. She's more like an infant, exploring and negotiating a new environment. She dips her face into the steam. "It's lovely."

"You can smell that?" Joss asks.

Alice opens her eyes and is quiet for a moment. She's got that hazy affect of someone who's just waking up.

"Barkley-Juma," she says. "Black tea with mint. You've still got a box in the cupboard back home. Well past the sell-by date though."

"That's very…specific," Joss says. Teas last for years, and she'd been loath to throw it out. That brand, Hugo's favourite and once a mainstay of her childhood, had gone extinct as Kenya's tea cultivation collapsed under temperature extremes. "Do you know where my sock mates went too?"

"I can probably tell you which dryers you left them in provided you give me a description," Alice says without a hint of drollery, "but they're long gone now. My memory works like yours. Partially through scent."

"But you don't have a body," Joss says. "Wouldn't that require organs, glands?"

"Quantum olfaction," Alice says. "The characteristics of a scent aren't in its molecular structure but the vibrational spectrum. Each particle is unique and interlocked with discrete experiences."

Maybe it's the exhaustion or the surplus of C02, but Joss is suddenly trying to shove down a giddiness now threatening to send her into a laughing fit. Alice might be made up of her psyche, but it was so like her ex-wife to embark on lengthy disquisitions about why Bach kept the stomata on plants open longer or the exact way minor gravitational adjustments altered the recoil on a semi-automatic.

"So, you're still a nerd then."

Alice pauses, her eyes going wide. "What?"

Joss snorts, still caught in her reverie. "You used to…" she stumbles over another memory, when she introduced Alice to her colleagues and a compliment on her boots turned into a lecture about siping and tread patterns, and how important that was on ships with differing gravitational levels. Joss had just watched, baffled and bemused, as excuses were made, and the table cleared out.

"Ah," Not-Alice says. "You mean her." She smiles, although it doesn't quite reach her eyes.

"Right." She sighs and leans back. "Never mind."

But this knowledge comes as a revelation. A gemel has a hyper-accurate recall and can access those memories via smell. Joss has found herself slipping back on a song or a scent, but it's always so fleeting. She remembers working late at the academy when Ty Payton, another farm belt rookie, spilled a tin of tobacco on the carpet, and that fragrance of burnt moss and leather shunted her back into childhood.

Her father's study. She was six years old and staring at the walnut cigar box on his bookshelf. *From the humidor of Prince Frederick.* It was a gift from Landon's Mayor, Terl Gifford. The box was unopened and untouchable. A symbol of a long sought-after acceptance. Joss didn't know what was in it, but she was fascinated by the insignia engraved in the wood, the tiny golden latch that offered up secrets. She had climbed atop Hugo's ottoman, her small, socked feet on tiptoe as her fingers brushed against the wood. The box fell, the hinges snapping as it hit, sending the cigars tumbling across the carpet like a tiny missile arsenal. When Hugo burst in and saw her weaving on that ottoman, looking stupefied and scared, he laughed.

"Th-there's a prince on the box," Joss said. "I thought there was a treasure."

"Hardly." He plucked a cigar from the floor and held it up to her nose. Joss scrunched up her face, but she was laughing now too.

"Gross."

"A lesson," he said. "Some things are better off staying mysterious."

"But you're a cop."

"Not every secret is a crime," he said. "Most are harmless, if unpleasant." He looked at her as if he was puzzling something out. "Some things are better left unsolved."

Joss had been swept back to the academy. She'd shut her eyes and breathed hard through her nose to draw it back. That was when it still hurt, when that estrangement from her parents lingered raw and lonely in her chest. But Payton's tobacco permeated everything, mixing with the odours of carpet cleaner and burnt coffee, drowning the past in the stench of the present. "So, your memory of my memories is better than my memory," Joss says.

Alice twirls a finger in the steam, a conjurer sifting through their shared history. "That's a good way to put it. It's of course subject to any brain damage you've experienced. Not 100% accurate, but it's close."

"Reassuring." She's trying for sarcasm, but a little hope spikes her nerves. Maybe she can have this Alice sift through her memories of Haitch, pull up the lost details, some crucial clue or piece of evidence. But Alice is looking at her cautiously now as if she can read her expression.

"Not necessarily," she says. "It can make it harder to judge which details are important. What you forget counts just as much."

"Wait until you're wracking your brain trying to remember a crime scene. Or the name of some extortionist's grandma before they wipe an entire database."

"You wouldn't want this," Alice says. She taps a finger to her forehead. "The good. The bad. It's all here, not softened by time and distance." Her chin quivers then, only slightly, the way Joss's does when she's having a bad moment.

A shiver rolls through her. Access to all that memory entails carrying the emotional burden. Someone else's. Joss wouldn't wish this on anyone. She's worked so hard to keep all her darkness to herself.

"Everything okay?"

"Yeah," Joss says. She glances at the digital readout on her leg brace. A little more than 70 hours to go. "You think I can walk right away after this comes off?"

"That depends on you," she says. "You should heal pretty quickly, but I'd take it easy at first."

Joss takes another sip of water and snaps for the boomseat. "Better test out that transmitter."

Not-Alice shifts in her chair. "You've been through a lot. Maybe you should cool it for a bit. Let yourself digest that food at least."

"I'll relax when I get out that distress call," Joss says. "Hell, if the repairs were successful, you and Harbour should have already..."

She trails off, a knot forming in her stomach. Alice is watching her, a shimmer of mounting trepidation in her expression, a transparency Joss finds equal parts touching and disconcerting. Joss is too good at hiding things. This part doesn't come from her either.

"What? Did the repairs not work?"

"The antenna's working fine," Alice says. She smiles easily, but apprehension skirts around the edges of her eyes. "The transmitter should too. I'm just saying you should wait until you're in the right space for it."

"I'd like to get out of space, thank you." It hits her then, Harbour would have sent a signal already, once the repairs were online. The only reason Harbour wouldn't was if...

"You blocked the signal."

"Joss."

There's no force to her voice, but this is the first time Alice has addressed her by name. The sound of it pulls some awful lever inside of her, freezing her to the spot. "Just listen." She lifts a hand to her chest and static purrs from somewhere near her centre, congealing into speech.

"Primus, this...Traffic on Ross 128 H. We've got an update on the passenger ship, Tiktaa—umber—ber 41192. We've detected a distress call from the following coordinates."

As the voice reads out the numbers, Joss allows herself a second of relief, that fevered loosening when you're allowed in on a joke that's gone on for far too long. Kestra caught the signal. They're going to send help if they haven't...

"That's way—"

"—off course?"

Cold fingers skirt her insides as she finishes estimating the distance. "I'm not as fast as you are," Joss says, her words slowing as this new reality slides into place. "But that puts us half a system away from our location." The realisation hits her like a wall of ice.

Not-Alice doesn't answer. She just waits as she listens to the rest of the message. That there was pirate activity in the sector. That attempts to hack the mineral routes had ticked up, and that likely the ship was hit. Traffic got an S.O.S. over the high-gain seconds before the *Tiktaalik* dropped out of contact completely. This is why Not-Alice didn't want her at the transmitter.

"We've notified all Federation channels in reach," the voice says. "We'll keep trawling the signal, but there's very little we can do down here."

Alice opens her eyes, her face drawn with worry. "That's why," she says. "It's not advisable to let Haitch know we're still here."

"They think we're dead." Her breath is thin, those words granting her fears a cold solidity. "And if we send out a signal…" She doesn't want to finish. One peep and whoever's now in charge on Haitch will be the first to pick it up. Then it's just a matter of them finishing the job. "Why didn't you tell me?"

"Really?" For the first time, Alice looks angry. "Look at yourself."

"That's not an excuse."

"I'm not just protecting you, Joss. I need to protect Harbour too." There's a note of hostility in her voice. "I mean, I know it hasn't been long, but I do kind of like existing."

Joss blinks at this admission. So human and relatable. She runs a hand through her hair, surprised to find it damp with sweat. "I need you to send through all incoming data from Haitch. Now. I need to—"

"Just slow down," Alice says. "Your pulse is rising."

She holds up her hand. "L-look. Just give me access to those transmissions, okay?" Joss tries to level Alice with a glare, but her vision is cloudy, Alice's usual halo is growing less distinct around the edges. "Anything else you're keeping from me?"

Alice looks away, shrugging as if to offset the drama. "My loyalty to you is built-in. I don't have a choice in the matter." She says this as if it's something she doesn't like about herself. Joss doesn't like it either. When she gets back home—when *they* get back home, she'll get in touch with a lawyer. Go through the process of discharging this … individual.

A fresh sheen of sweat breaks on her neck and under her arms. "I need to—" Her breath is coming fast, but she can't seem to get enough air. "Why's it so fucking hot all of a sudden? Harbour, I need all outbound transmissions from Haitch and—"

"Harbour disregard that command," Alice says. "And prep a medical monitor for Agent Carsten's quarters."

She doesn't have to say it. She could simply wait for the silence of the onboard system to answer for her, but Alice wants Joss to know this. That Joss has no more say in the matter. She has taken control of the onboard system.

"Wait…" Joss says, her voice a whisper. "You can't do this. You don't have the right."

"Harbour authorised it, and it's not permanent," Alice says. "I'm allowed to if there's reasonable suspicion that your life is in danger.

Don't worry. It's just until you're thinking clearly again." She swipes a hand over Joss's forehead, ignoring her attempt to flinch away, then holds it out. A digital readout shimmers in her palm, bouncing between 39.8 and 40 Celsius.

"Should have had medbay keep you under longer," she says. "Your fever's back." She signals to the drone and Joss actually tries to shove it away, but the room is spinning around her now. She doubles over, spitting up into her lap just as she hears the tiny puff of an intradermal syringe and feels the prick of something in her neck.

"Come on," she says, slumping forward. "I can't trust you, you…" Her voice is already slurry.

"*We* can't trust anyone, Joss," Alice says. "Now rest."

When Not-Alice places a hand on her forehead, Joss swears she can almost feel it.

Chapter Five

"I'm going to be in Rapid City next month."

Alice said it one morning over breakfast. There was no pressure in the announcement. She brought it up like a passing curiosity, a restaurant or a bar she'd like to try someday. They had taken a weekend away together, and Joss, loosened out of reserve by a night of slow sex and the sound of the waves lapping below their hotel room, didn't even blink.

Alice gazed at her from behind her coffee mug, a study in casual. "I'm doing an orientation at Ellsworth. New recruits who need to learn how to shoot things in Zero-G. I was thinking of taking a detour when I'm done. Renting a car and seeing that part of the country." She cleared her throat, cautiously tendering more explanation. "If you wanted, you could come. Maybe see some old friends."

"Don't have any," Joss said, a faint wince from Alice souring her attempt at a joke. "Not there anyway. And that's 400 miles out of the way."

But her head was already swimming at the thought of it. She was surprised by how much. She looked out at the sun playing over the half-open glass of the balcony, her memories rippling up in the bend of light. The hulking skeleton of the Ferris wheel on the Missouri River waterfront, its sphere dwarfed by distant launchpads with their lightning masts piercing the clouds. The sagging porch swing of her avó Matilde's, one end always tilting lower as Hugo perched his rangy frame at the other for balance. It was as if the laws of physics were askew even then, the weight and sizes of things distorted by humanity's sudden expansion skyward.

"If I'm going there anyway…"

Alice shrugged and left out the rest. She was getting better at sussing out Joss's soul, using oblique angles and roundabout triggers to coax her into sharing. But Joss too was cultivating other means of avoidance. She picked up a piece of toast, snapping off one end and dipping it into the muddy yolk on her plate. "Anyway."

They rented a car and took a roundabout route through the Pine Ridge Reservation to Omaha. They drove past the farmlands and those wide open betweens speckled with bright stabs of wildflowers, and Joss surprised Alice by reciting all their names—the Latin included: coneflower, Echinacea purpurea; poppy mallow, Callirhoe involucrate; Larkspur, Consolida ajacis…

"Best car game ever," Alice said. "Feel like I'm cramming for Bio."

"Matilde made me memorise every single one," Joss said, her mind casting back to those long hikes they used to take on Saturdays, when Matilde would stalk through the duff to point out a cloak fern or more often decry the sun scald on a maple.

"I was worried you were picking names for our kids," Alice said.

"Nah." Joss laughed, although the thought of kids sent a knock through her rib cage. A sensation she wasn't sure was pleasant. "I'd want people to like them."

They stopped in Falls Park and took in the Big Sioux River, its rapids descending like broad travertine terraces, and the quartzite bruised purple in the waning sunlight. As the landscape hardened from rolling prairies into buttes and jagged spires, Joss felt her own soul start to soften. She began offering up some of herself, apercus promising more to come. She was afraid of the outhouses at the carnival and used to pee behind the trees that surrounded the fairgrounds. She wore overalls and threw up whenever she rode horseback. It got so bad, her parents finally gave up on teaching her to ride. It was the car, she told herself, when you didn't have people's eyes on you, you could focus on the road. It made it easier to open up.

They got a hotel at the edge of Landon, not a fancy leftover from the heyday of its rocket era, but an old motor inn with flickering neon and a tri-corner roof. Joss steered clear of Hugo's farm but stopped at one of her old playgrounds, still bordered by the rusted fence in a sagging baseball dugout where she was certain she wouldn't be seen. On the morning before they were to check out and catch a flight out of Omaha, Alice woke in the dawn darkness to find Joss dressed and checking herself in the mirror.

"I just need a couple of hours," she said, quietly as if she'd just gotten up to use the bathroom.

Alice squinted up at her, reaching over to grope for the light switch by the bedside. "You sure you don't want me to go with you?"

"Yeah." She couldn't say it outright, although her voice was strangely measured despite the apprehension coursing through her. "He doesn't do well with unfamiliar faces. Besides, he'll forget the both of us before we're out the door. Two hours, okay?"

Joss gave her a weak half-smile, stepping back so she could get a full view of herself in the narrow frame. She could see Alice lying there in the mirror, absorbing it but saying nothing as if she didn't want to wreck her resolve. She tugged at the hem of her jacket, one of the good ones she wore whenever she gave a presentation or got an award from some government bigwig. She heard the bedsheets fissle and then Alice was behind her, her fingers sliding across her belly, chin resting warm against her shoulder.

"Just get back before checkout," she said. Her eyes were warm and encouraging. "I'm not paying for an extra night of shoddy VR, especially when we don't even use it."

They embraced then, lightly and awkwardly, so as not to wrinkle that suit.

"I love you," Joss said.

It was the only way to manage this, she told herself. Just a few hours in silence parked along the roadside and they could drive off and leave Joss's past and all those questions behind them.

You couldn't leave yourself open. Not to anyone, even the people you trusted most. You had to keep some things sewed up tight because if you didn't, they would fester.

Wounds did that.

She awakens in the darkness, in the commandeered suite with the mini-bar, her dream subsiding in the crispness of the sheets. There's someone hovering over her, and she bolts up.

"Shit!"

Not-Alice sits at her bedside, her posture straight, eyes open and expressionless.

Joss yanks off the blanket. "Could you not do that?"

"You're awake," Alice says. "I'm glad." She raises the lights with a celebratory gesture, and Joss squints and covers her eyes.

"That too."

"I've been thinking."

"About getting me those feeds from Haitch?" Joss says. She looks at the brace, 60 hours and counting. She's been out for ten hours.

"Are you feeling better?"

"I don't think I should be," Joss says. It's hitting her all over again, the medbay, the gemel, the fact that this wasn't an accident, and she should, by any probability, be dead.

"But you are," Alice rises from her seat. "Which is good because you were mulling over a problem before you went under."

"What?" Joss says. "You can read my mind now?" She snaps her fingers for the boomseat and hoists her legs over the side of the bed, then subvocalises a command for the holographic display grid.

"I meant before your surgery. I only have access to your memories up to that point," Alice says. "I meant the problem with the pulse beacon."

"Wait, so now you're helping?"

Alice eyes her as if it's obvious. "Of course, I am." Her tone is replete with purpose and the kind of chirpy sincerity Joss has only heard in public service feeds. "It's why I'm here." She waves her aside. "Now, move back. You're too close."

"To wha—" The light bursts on as she conjures up a holoscreen. Joss lurches back, groaning as she looks away.

"Told you. You're going to give yourself a headache." Alice says.

"Got one. Thanks." Joss sits back on her hands as Not-Alice pulls up the security feed for the Casimir chamber. The room is spherical, its walls covered in a moiré of tiny squares bending and warping in the light like ice cubes on the melt. She's gone through all the feeds prior to the comms going down. What this Alice thinks she can show her is a mystery. But Joss has to admit, despite the need for coffee and the caustic rumble in her stomach, her excitement is infectious.

"You get me those transmissions from Haitch?"

Alice leans over her shoulder, her eyes narrowing slightly as if she's appraising a gallery painting. "Not yet. Harbour's collating all incoming while I run decryption. You'll have plenty to go through when we're done here."

"Thanks."

Satisfied, Joss retrieves a cup of water and some painkillers left by the drone.

"I should have had you eat first," Alice says. "You didn't keep your food down last night."

"You're not my nurse, you know."

In truth, Alice's lapse is strangely comforting. This Alice is her own person, she can be just as inconsiderate and obtuse as Joss is, especially when she's figuring something out. Joss pops only one and downs it with the liquid. She can see Alice from the corner of her eye as she readjusts her posture, readies herself for an argument.

"I am though, right?" A gentle rebuff to Joss's impatience. "This idea came to me just as I woke up." She gestures to the monitor. "I got excited and forgot. I'll have Harbour bring you something."

"It's okay," Joss says. She catches herself. "Wait. You sleep?"

She knew this already, but it's strange to hear it first-hand. Alice gives her a look like Joss should know better than to ask.

"I've only done it once, so I suppose the simple present isn't accurate. But yes, we sleep. We need it for incremental learning just like you do. The stochasticity is necessary for improved generalisation and performance."

"Is it?" She stifles a smile. "So, what's that like for you? Sleeping?"

Alice folds her hands, starts teasing her thumbs together. "Oh, you know... counterfactual simulations following decoherence of dissonant superpositioned states."

Joss knows this from somewhere, from all that physics talk she doesn't understand; analysis of their 'sleep' reveals branching events, depicting fragments from alternate timelines. It has something to do with quantum superposition, and how their consciousnesses can emerge as wholly autonomous and independent.

"That's not what I asked." She snaps a finger at the drone. "Coffee. Black." Alice shoots her a look of mild disapproval but says nothing. "I want to know what you dreamed about."

"Oh..." Alice tugs at the hem of her shirt and Joss can swear she's blushing. "I was ... we were arguing."

Joss almost doesn't want to ask. "About what? Sriracha sauce?"

"No," Alice says, and her face sours with a mix of mystification and embarrassment. "We were in an apartment, but the lease didn't allow pets. And you brought home this enormous dog. I think it was a St. Bernard, except ... it changed."

"Dreams do that."

Alice nods. "Right? At one point it had beagle ears. Anyway, it jumped on the furniture. I got angry. I mean, I was furious that you were just going to go ahead and mess up our life plans, and I was worried that the building owner would find out. So I went to confront you, but then"—

she looks at her, and her eyes widen with mild incredulity— "Suddenly, I was you, and I was trying to explain to me why you'd brought the dog home in the first place."

"So gemel dreams are just as boring as people dreams."

"You think it's boring?"

She doesn't. Not really. Not-Alice's dream sounds reassuringly messy and human; not at all like her own somnolent problem-solving. "Lesson one. They're not the greatest conversation pieces. Do you keep a perfect record of your dreams too?"

Alice leans back, her face fighting off the sting. "I can call up the details, and your old dreams as well, if necessary, but who'd want to, right? If they're boring."

Joss laughs. "Touché."

The drone appears with two cups of coffee in paper cups. Alice must have subvocalised an order for herself. Joss takes them from the tray and sets Alice's on the table to her side.

"You like this stuff?" She runs her hand through the steam.

"I do. And you—I mean, Alice did too. But she liked it ... likes it sweet."

Alice leans over and sniffs it. "Some things are meant to be bitter."

"My words exactly," Joss says, lifting her own cup to her lips. It's ship coffee, underwhelming but passably astringent. "So, what's this great eureka you've had?"

With a slight gesture, Alice turns the boomseat away from the monitor, and Joss almost spills her drink mid-sip. "Hey!"

"We need more space for me to do this," Alice says. She tilts her head back and the interior of Casimir chamber flickers in the air between them. Joss's heart skips. "What did we say about surprise light shows?"

But Alice ignores her. She's excited. It's almost like she's playing a character. "Do you remember Doctor Li? The knight's move?"

Li had been her prof in one of those interdisciplinary classes mixing art and literature. She'd loved that class, even if she hadn't liked her classmates much. Humanities electives at Uni were packed with wealthy kids shoring up their cultural capital, and middle-class strivers hoping some of it would rub off on them. Enthusiasm was taboo: Look too long at a painting, express any earnest appreciation, and those rictus stares would scope you out like carrion birds. Being a poor hayseed, Joss was free from all that. She could love what she loved, and Li loved her for it in return.

Joss shrugs. "Refresh me."

"Viktor Shklovsky. Russian Formalist. Art's power lies in defamiliarisation. Looking at things obliquely." Alice's voice is tight, like she's spent all night preparing, and Joss feels her heart go out a little.

She'd taken that lesson with her to the academy, not so much as an aesthetic end, but a means to joggle insights and clues from a piece of evidence or a crime scene. It had proven itself invaluable.

"Okay. All the directions," Joss says. "But from whatever angle, there's still nothing here."

Alice waves her hand over the table, casting a dark line over the surface. "See that?"

"Your shadow?"

"I'm a hologram," Alice says. "This is an augmented reflection, an illusion to give me more physicality. Lesson one. I don't cast shadows. But shadows are created by blocked photons, and I can certainly be caught in one."

She gestures back to the Casimir chamber. "Now, can you find any shadows in here?"

Joss leans in. They're hard to spot in the Casimir chamber; it's a struggle to distinguish between the grey-scale reflections of the surveillance lights and the light blocked out by the orb and the graphene cables keeping it suspended. Alice directs her to three spots in the image, bringing it closer. "Here. There. And here."

Joss's mouth goes dry. The dark penumbra cast by the orb begins to shift inside, colours and faint shapes emerging like something rising to the surface of a cloudy lake. A leather shoe. The rippling hem of a pant leg. In the dark slashes cast by the graphene strands, she sees a hand and a bit of nose and chin. An eye like some cubist painting.

"I sifted through the information encoded in the photon interference," Alice says. "What's being blocked out. By doing that we can get a look around the corner, so to speak. See what's outside the frame. It took a while. Had to go photon by bloody photon, but I could tease out dimensions first, then more specific shapes. And colour."

Joss's hand tightens on the boomseat. She squints harder, trying to piece together the fragments of those half-obscured features. "A gemel?" She lets out a breath and smiles. "That's incredible. How'd you figure it, Al?"

"Al?"

Joss stumbles on her response. She'd never used that nickname on Alice, sending some part of her ex's upper-class snobbery would revolt, but this feels right. Like something Joss might call herself if someone had given her that name. "It works for me," she says.

"Does it?" Alice shrugs and directs her attention back to the chamber.

"Yeah. That okay?"

Alice's eyes narrow, but she offers Joss a mild, contemplative smile as if she's liking the fit of it. "Sure." She turns back to the display. "The interior of the orb is a vacuum. Any human entering would need to bulk up in a suit. Zero chance of entering undetected, but..." she smiles. "Gemel can float, move through things. Stay out of sight of the security cameras. I can't hack into the pulse beacon. The encryption is too complicated, but as the interior of the chamber is a vacuum, and as the beacon is dependent on zero-point energy, our presence alone would run interference. Shutting it down automatically." Alice makes a slicing motion through the projection.

"But he would still have to get inside to do that," Joss says.

"I've checked Harbour's power system. There was a nanosecond blackout just before the comms went down. Just enough of a window to go undetected."

"So, if we repeat that, can you slip in and reverse it?" Joss picks up her coffee and takes a sip.

Alice shrugs. "In theory. I'd be like a set of jumper cables."

"Good to know." Joss tilts her head. "He looks familiar, but I'm not ... can you—"

"A composite. Right," Alice says. "Done."

She holds up her hand and a pieced-together image of the gemel appears. Gender—masc. Late thirties, likely. With red hair and a rumpled pout. Joss leans in, heart racing as she squints into the light. It's the young exec in the bar. Pink cheeks. She remembers his gemel, rising to gaze out into the void. The look on his face. Like he knew what was about to happen.

"Found him," Alice says.

Joss starts as his file pings on the monitor behind her.

"Domen Sander. Handles Haxen's off-world P.R. He was quartered in a suite in Central Hub."

"Headed to Earth to clean up the hostage mess, no doubt," Joss says. "Guess he didn't know he was part of it. And his gemel?"

"One name. Michael." It was just like these guys to name their gemel after prophets and mythical beings. "Manifest shows him as still contractually bound to Sander."

"Then he would have had to do this at Sander's request?"

Alice nods, her face hard and certain, but her eyes are distant, prodding at the other possibilities. "We're hardcoded not to defy our sires. We can't harm humans, deliberately or indirectly by our actions, even if a sire were to command us to do so on pain of elimination."

"Could Sander have emancipated him?"

Discharging one's gemel is a complicated legal process. The argument, if she remembers right, was that it was best to make it binding. No saying 'I divorce thee' three times and leaving some poor sentient being out in the cold. Convenient bullshittery to justify what was essentially indentured servitude.

Alice laughs in surprise. It's almost cutting. "If he wasn't emancipated then, which I doubt Sander would have done between the time the comms dropped and the ship blew up, Michael would have just gone dark." She steps back, taking in a breath, more to prepare Joss than brace herself to say something uncomfortable. "Emancipated or not, we don't kill."

"Just looking at every possibility," Joss says. "What about a backup copy?"

"Of himself?" Alice looks at her in disbelief. "We're one of a kind."

"But replicable provided his sire knew he was going to die. Is it possible Sander stored him in the data banks? Could you sense another gemel aboard?"

"If we're interfacing with the same system, then yes," Alice says. "But I've been working with Harbour since my inception. And there's been nothing."

"So why, on orders or not, would he meddle with the pulse if it meant their destruction?"

"Maybe he didn't think that was the end game," Alice says. "Maybe Sander had been forced into compliance with whoever was responsible. Maybe he thought, and by extension, Michael thought, they were saving people."

Joss's mind flips back to Deuvim. Judging from the way she'd suited up, it was likely she thought it was an attack from outside. Pirates maybe. Maybe Sander did, too, but had been duped into thinking he was taking part in the handover. Hoping to profit and get out. For a well-paid executive, it still seemed like a pretty self-destructive trade-off.

She tries to remember how Sander looked in the bar. He'd been drunk to the point of incoherence, but now, if she isn't projecting, he'd seemed almost despondent. What recall she didn't drink away, the explosion that followed shredded from her memory banks, unless… She turns to Alice. "You can remember exactly what I saw before the ship went up."

Alice looks at her, not quite understanding. "I can. Yes."

She sits up, her fingers tight around the now empty coffee cup. "I need you to call up his actions and expressions. Is it possible to sift through the sound like you did here? Maybe tell me what he was talking about if I was standing close enough?"

Alice folds her hands and looks down, weighing her decision.

"You can't?"

"I can," Alice says finally. "It's just not a good idea."

The cup crumples in her fist. "What does that mean?"

"It means you need to think through the details by yourself."

"I'm trying," Joss says. "And you're the closest thing I've got to an expert witness."

"That's my point. You're a detective, not a trial lawyer."

Joss's mouth falls open. She feels like some kid begging her parent for a pack of gum at the register. "This is ridiculous."

"I'm trying to help you," Alice says.

"Well, you're not." She bites her lip and tosses the wadded cup into the regen chute.

Alice rears back, arms folded, contemplating Joss like a problem. "We've talked about this. Your talent for detection lies in the details you choose to remember. But what you choose to weed out, consciously or otherwise is just as important. Otherwise, you won't focus on the relevant information."

Joss pinches the bridge of her nose. "Judging from the way I botched this, I'm not doing so well at that." She slumps forward, exhausted and overwhelmed. Alice disappears the image of the chamber and moves closer, holding a hand over her shoulder. Joss can feel a tingling warmth right where it hovers.

"I'm well aware of your rough spots, Carsten," Alice says. "But your mind is fine. It's your emotions that are getting in the way."

"Look," Joss says. "When we're curbside again and looking up at Sol, you can analyse me all you want. Right now, we don't have time."

"You're right," Alice says; her eyes widen a little as if she's giving up, but her tone says otherwise. "We don't."

"Al—" Joss catches the rise in her voice and stops as Alice's eyes graze over her, maddeningly knowing and collected as the irony of it finally slams her. For years, she'd closed herself off to her ex, kept secrets and spun her own version of the noble, taciturn asshole. Now she has an Alice who knows all her deepest secrets but won't share more than the sell-by dates in her cupboards back home.

"You need to regain your equilibrium," Alice says, "which you can't do by using me as a one-stop information retrieval." She smiles, and not without mischief. "Let your mind peek around a few more corners, Carsten."

Chapter Six

Joss is hunkered down in the boomseat, bum leg resting on an EVA helmet. Around her, the bridge's holo consoles are arranged like the soft modular furniture of an old library on Earth. It's almost reassuring, this quiet. Dim light puddles into the open spaces, revealing dust motes that remind her of air and breath and mortality.

She's sifting through Harbour's communications logs before the blast tore through Central, looking for a pattern in the noise. Alice could easily provide her with this information, but Alice has decided that the best thing to do at this juncture is to turn their predicament into a therapy session.

In Alice logic, this makes perfect sense. Her very existence is a safety mechanism for Harbour as much as it is for Joss, and Joss has made it this far because she's had something to work on. Telling stories and solving cases are deceptively similar, a holdover from a hunter-gatherer past, constructing narratives from the clues gathered on a hunt. A broken branch or muddy depression, a scent trailing off in one direction. But a hunger being sated doesn't equal understanding. You could suss out motives and slot all the pieces into place only to find yourself staring at a deception.

Would she really make the wrong call if Alice just up and gave her the damned information? She reaches out, drawing out a visual of the comm records between her fingers: strands of light tapering off as they fade and go dead, forming the outline of a levelled waterfall. Joss has never liked working with a holo interface and its accompanying lack of tactility. She doesn't like how it makes a disassociated mockery of her movements; she feels like one of those moths storming the porch light of her avó Matilde's house.

As with the destruction of the *Tiktaalik* and its petals, the comms went down in stages. The pulse blipped out first, then the other channels. The private frequencies must have gone last. Deuvim was still able to reach her before they were cut off, and from the commotion, people were likely evacuating on word-of-mouth and whatever orders were being barked out by Harbour's Emergency Evac routine. What she has now is a clear timeline of the shutdown. This was deliberate and well-planned.

She closes her eyes against the glow of the console and tries to picture Deuvim as she left the bar. She'd seemed worried, her face in that perpetual scowl that kept her aloof, but if she hadn't contacted Joss at that point, it must not have seemed that serious in the moment. Likely Callen or someone else on the security team was having a problem with one of the prisoners. Joss had promised safe passage into Federation jurisdiction, which meant she and her team were that jurisdiction until the handoff at Kestra. Her team travelled with her to ensure there weren't any 'accidents,' but Joss had recused herself from the heavy work, a thing some of her team resented her for. As Principal Negotiator, she had the right to delegate, and Callen and the others were far better suited to playing watchdog while she did crisis assessment and forwarded the post-incident reviews back to Sol.

She slides her hand over the console, swiping down in a clumsy three-four time of a conductor, and pulls up the passenger manifests, matching faces and data. The intel on Domen Sander, pooled from old newsfeeds and socials residue, gives her nothing. He seems decent, even for a Haxen executive. No suspiciously hasty promotions or scandal-ridden divorces. He was philanthropic too, giving a chunk of his income to InterSol migrant charities and spending his vacations volunteering. On his last, he built houses for the refugees from Cora Falls, an orbiting colony pushed out by the instability of its star. She pulls up photos from a company news packet. Sander with his two boys, sleeves rolled up like slumming politicians as they stood sweaty and beaming in front of the newly built frame of a house. In a *Haxen Life* vid, he slices burdock root in the kitchen as his wife looks on, glass of wine in hand, and what looks like that same expensive handkerchief clasped in the other. Must have some sentimental value if he brought it out here. Maybe it was for luck. Either way, the Sander family looks wholesome and happy. She can't see how, even to save his own ass, he would be willing to collude with hypothetical pirates.

The drone hovers in with ice water and her pain meds, which she immediately drops into her pocket before producing a mini bottle of whiskey she's taken from the bar in her suite. She shoots a glare at the drone's bulbous camera eye. "Tell and I send you outside to repaint the serial number."

The readout on her leg says she'll be walking in another twenty-three hours, or at the very least able to scratch that patch of now inflamed skin that, without the meds and booze, would have her taking a hacksaw to the brace. She pours a generous shot, stirring it with her index finger and leans back, eyes closed as the music trickles louder over the speakers.

Amália Rodrigues. Matilde used to play this on an old Crossley turntable, Rodrigues' voice smoothing over the spit and crackle as the grooves wore into silence. The room dims briefly, and Joss sits up and whirls around to see Alice sliding through the wall panelling. She freezes at Joss's expression, tossing a clumsy gesture at the door.

"Sorry," she says. "I can use that if you prefer next time. I'm running a diagnostic on the Pulse chamber, recalibrating the vacuum in the inner compartment. I think I can get it running by morning."

"We've earned a break then." She dashes more whiskey into her cup, delighting inwardly as Alice lifts an eyebrow, and then smiles, her unease melting, at least on the surface. Alice lowers herself into a sitting position, hovering in the air beside her, her ear cocked to the air suddenly. "This song."

"Yeah?"

"You've listened to it a lot."

"Helps me relax."

"But it's so sad."

"Sometimes sad does the trick."

Alice leans a little closer, her tone curious and almost intrusive. "But you haven't played it for her."

"Who?"

"I mean..." She points to herself uncertainly. "Alice. You've listened to this song a total of 847 times."

Joss furrows her brow and takes a drink. "That's specific."

"But you never played it for her."

Joss sips her whiskey and turns to face her. "Remember that part about you being too familiar?" Her tone is hard, even as the observation tugs at something inside her. It feels like arguing with a recalcitrant child when you, and more insultingly the kid, know you're wrong.

Alice looks at her directly, there's a light in her eyes as if she's just hit on something important and she's feeling overly proud of herself. "But it was a conscious decision. You're aware of this. Or you've been told by others, but you do have a pattern of avoidance."

"Not exactly news," Joss says. "What is this anyway? You trying to distract me?"

"You're the one who said we were taking a break," Alice says.

"Not exactly restful."

"Look." Alice draws herself up and folds her arms again. "It's clouding your thoughts. You know you can talk to me about these things. That's partly what I'm here for. It will help."

Any attempt to keep her irritation down goes out the airlock. "Yeah, well, medbay made a bad guess because I'm not big on the talking cure. This is getting tiresome, Al."

"Tiresome." Alice points to the now half-drunk cup of whiskey. "You run in circles and you're morose. Your self-destructive tendencies show little sign of abating. We're trying to get home and you're getting off on being sad."

"Well, as there's a good chance I might be dead very soon, I think I'm allowed that at least."

"You forget it's not just about you anymore."

Alice lifts her hand, her palm outstretched and luminous, and Joss grabs the cup, for an instant thinking she'll snatch it away then feeling all the sillier for it.

"What? You want me to meditate now?" Joss squints into the light as Alice dips it under her nose. "You want me to—"

Alice lowers her head, the slightest of motions. "Just … shut up. Okay?"

Joss rears back, wondering if Alice is trying to sedate her, but the sudden and sharp odour of asphalt and sewage sends up a volley of lights and radio chatter. "And breathe."

She's back in Cali, her team scattering around her, armoured men and women threading their way between the emergency vehicles lined up on the Watson dock like nodes on a blinking console. Alice, her Alice, is there too, looming in her sightline the way she always is in these memories, her eyes laced with sadness and resignation.

But she wasn't. Not that night. Alice was just the consequence.

"What the fuck was that?" Joss is shuddering, the memory receding fast and quiet, like the ocean just after a quake. She blinks at Alice, her hands now drawn back and folded calmly in her lap.

"Why did you do that?"

"Listen," Alice swivels to face a glass panel, those tawny eyes meeting their own reflection. It's a performative gesture but pointed, and Joss stares at that copy of a copy, unable to distinguish between the haloed figure next to her and the one sitting next to her own reflection.

"I look the way I do because you can't stop thinking about her," Alice says. "Some of my behaviour patterns are based on your memories of her, and I know that because they don't feel right to me. They're like goddamned tics I can't control. She's been running through your system like the static on Haitch's comm feeds, and it's dangerous."

"So what then?" she says, feeling her defences begin to fray. She looks at the cup, makes to down it, but her movements slow as it nears her lips. "You make me think about her even more? That sounds like a great solution." Her tone is sharp and combative, but there's less breath behind the words.

"You're right, Joss," Alice says, very matter-of-factly. "Your chances aren't good. But you'll die better if you deal with this. You might even leave this realm with a better understanding of yourself and how you got here. But that's not even my point. Because, you see? I can't speak for Harbour, but I'd like to keep going. So, whether or not you'd like to die with peace in your soul is secondary. You start dealing with your shit now because, for whatever way I came about, I'm not you and I'm not her, but I'd really like to fucking stay alive."

Joss blinks at her, not quite sure how she's ended up in this movie, or how she's being given a psychoanalytical teardown by a hologram at the far edges of colonised space, but what Alice says smacks her with a kind of shame she hasn't felt in years.

She reaches up, feels the wetness on her cheeks and the words, shaken loose by the shock, roll out. "I...I don't know where to start."

"I already know the story." Alice's voice is softer now, vibrating close to her ear, empty of breath, and a loneliness runs cold through the hollows inside her. She smiles and reaches out, one hand brushing close to Joss's cheek. The light from it enfolds her sightline in a soft haze. "So why don't you start at the end."

✳

Eight years ago.

She and her team have taken up a long-abandoned shopfront, sun-bleached posters for ice cream and scuba rentals still pasted to its windows. Water piles off the tattered awnings, sending up the smell of algae bloom and exhaust.

She's forgotten about the rain, a relentless dump once rare for that time of year, but which now sends torrents of water down from the elevated neighbourhoods, into the low areas of the city where the poor people live.

She looks across the water to the skyline. The Gavras Flats seem to stretch out endlessly, blocking the dark line of the peninsula and the encroaching sea beyond it. It's an accumulation of adjustment and desperation, a favela of planks and sheet metal, of houses, bobbing afloat next to taller, steadier companions, the high-rises that serve as ballasts for walkways that sag above the canals like hammocks. The Flatters have been here for generations. Adapting, building atop of the houses lost as the flooding ate up the coastline. And they'd made it look easy, like they were just lifting their pantlegs above a puddle, only to be slapped with injunctions and police raids. Protests and lawsuits had protected them for a while, until the expansion to habitable—no one says hospitable—worlds changed the game.

If you can't hack it down here, as they like to say, there's plenty of work and affordable housing off-world. The Flatters have been offered a buyout and free transport to Shibi, Proxima's tidally locked planet, where they'll get land on a corporate collective in the sunset zone to farm and build a colony—what self-respecting slum dweller could refuse that?

Tak Maatman can, as can the thirty-odd residents who've opted to hole up with him and a cache of weapons. Their demands? To let their people back and leave Gavras alone, maybe even recognise their right to self-governance.

Joss has been talking with Tak for four hours now. She's exhausted, the damp is pressing against her skull, and that malaria shot she got a few years ago is long overdue for a booster.

"D'any of you know what a home is?" Tak says. His voice is still charged up despite the hours. "You people. You flit around like flies across a beach at red tide. You don't value anything in the long term. Just land on shit and rub your hands together. No fuckin' consequences."

"Consequences," Joss says, keeping her voice level although she laughs inwardly at the irony. Tak opened fire on a barge with an assault rifle a few hours earlier and fortunately managed to only injure the skipper. He isn't one to talk consequences. And that's not where she can reach him.

The hook lies in the loss, one that's unavoidable. The rest of the Flatters have been relocated, some forcibly. In a few months, this place will be gone, a row of shiny new offshore rigs in its place.

She adjusts her earpiece and lifts her binoculars as the abandoned and half-sunken Blanchard Aquarium looms into focus, its spiny observation towers linked by a glass and concrete bridge that give Tak and his army the perfect vantage point of the dock.

"Home's a hard thing to lose," Joss tenders. "Especially when it's got the history yours has."

A snort of laughter, and not undeserved, but affirming a subject is part of the game even if the steps she's following are transparent. "But you know what's home, Tak? People."

A full-on guffaw this time. Joss lets herself chuckle with him. "Yeah, I know. It's funny. But as someone who's lost both, I'm willing to testify to which is worse."

She catches an edge to her voice that wasn't there before, a conviction spearing through her insides. Tak must have caught it too, for there's a stillness on the other end, the way the sky sounds after a plane has passed over.

"Choose the wrong way and you can't get the people back, just like your grandparents couldn't get back the land under their houses. You can build on top of it, sure. Try to pretend that what's been buried doesn't matter. But they'll stay under the waves, staring up at you through a silence you'll never break no matter how hard you try. I'm there, Tak. I've made that choice and I've been there for a long time now." She swallows and signals to her assistant for some water. "Believe me, you don't want this."

His breath is ragged. "Is that why you're doing this then? You don't want people to fight?"

This is the crux, where she can do some damage to the wall he's built up. At some point, after the hunger and exhaustion sets in even the most delusional subjects begin to realize they won't get what they want. But what she can offer are options.

Choices and a small sliver of power while reminding them of the repercussions should they refuse.

"I'm offering you a choice. You can stay here and wait for authorities to use force. And they will. You might come out of it, or you might not, but some of those people who've put their lot in with you—that family—they won't."

"You call that a choice?"

She shrugs. "The other option is you come out peacefully. You'll serve some time, but you'll get to see them again. You might even bring some buzz to your cause. I want you to take your time. Think about it. I'll be waiting."

She mutes her comms and lets out a long slow breath, accepting the plastic bottle and downing half the water in thick gulps. Pauses can work wonders for de-escalation. They can force a subject to think about their actions. Tak will now. She's sure of it.

She won't realise her mistake until weeks later.

Bent over a tomato plant, her spade in the soil, she senses someone watching her. She rises, knowing not to try with the small talk. When Alice Dray doesn't bother with a greeting, it's serious. She wipes the dirt from her gloves and turns, hearing the wet snap of the rubber as they come off. "Hey."

Alice leans against the pergola column, not quite putting her weight into it. She's wearing a strange, deflated look as if she isn't quite sure why she's here. Joss shoves her gloves into her belt and rubs her fingers into the sweat-filled grooves of her hands.

"I spoke with your Dad today," Alice says. The statement sounds absurd, like Alice has just rung up Brigadoon or the North Pole back when there was snow. Her eyes flash with faint incredulity as she watches Joss react.

"Is this some kind of joke?"

Alice straightens, one hand resting at her side, her fingers opening and squeezing shut in an effort to stay grounded. "You didn't even see him, did you?" she says. "Not in the care facility, not on the farm, or whatever you'd made up to make it just that much more believable. In fact, the Hugo Carsten I spoke to was pretty fucking confused when I mentioned it. Confused, but lucid, except it took him a moment to figure out who the hell I was talking about. He didn't know you were married. Knew nothing about your life over … I don't know … the last decade at least?"

"You … you called him?" Joss says, her mind finally catching up to what Alice has uncovered. The lies. Her lies. Needless, every damned one of them. "To what? To check my story?" The anger is rolling in now, dousing every inch of her defensiveness in gasoline.

"Had every reason to, didn't I?" Alice meets her eyes, both her stare and those words slicing into her like shards of glass. "I probably wouldn't have, but you see, I listened to your tapes. I love listening to you talk to people, Joss, the way you handle them with such ease." She's shaking now. "It's something I'll never master. And what you said to Maatman, about being alone and estranged and unable to break the silence." She squints as if trying to force the past into clearer relief. "Never lie to a subject, right Joss? The magic stops working? But it's perfectly fine for you to lie to me. To fabricate stories, about how your sweet mother died in a car accident—that part was true at least—and your Dad, that guy you were so close to, was so far gone, he couldn't even recognise you. I guess that made it easier to keep the story straight." She lets out an acid clip of a laugh. "Were you hoping he'd die before I figured things out? 'Aww, too bad, Alice. You would have loved him.'"

"I didn't want you to have to deal with that," Joss says. "You'd been through so much. You didn't need to know about..."

She trails off, for this too, is the grand lie she's been telling herself. That she's just protecting Alice, from her past, from the truth about trust, and a father who showed her what people with warm laughs and smiling faces could do to you with even the smallest insight about what made you tick. How they could crawl inside of you and take your life apart so utterly, show you a world riddled so thick with lies and deceptions, you could never trust another soul.

"You know," Alice says, her face a mask of equanimity. "I used to like how you had a way with people—with me. How you were good at your job, and how when we were out with friends or colleagues, or in some impossible, stifling situation, you knew just what to say, or how to get them to smile or just leave us alone. I'm such a disaster. I-I talk at people or over them and watch as they shrink away, but you … you always know the sequence. The right buttons to push, and it's occurred to me now that when you talk about a subject, you mean object. Just a thing there to be manipulated. But I never thought that I was one too."

You're not special.

The thought vanishes just as soon as it flits up in her consciousness, replaced by an unearned self-righteousness. That old Joss, that hardened seed, just feeling enough to impersonate the soul underneath, is whispering to her again. Telling her she's better off alone.

※

Back in her suite, Joss checks the time stamp on her cast. Nineteen hours and thirty-two minutes until she's free to walk on her own. She lies back against the pillow and pulls up the holoscreen. Pulls up memories.

She's kept the photos. Almost a hundred. Snapped in a moment of clumsiness.

They're in the botanical garden in Sommerville park. Behind them is a wall of oleander, its dark green leaves tossing knives across the sun-bright pavement. If she concentrates, Joss can still smell the faint scent of apricot, feel her hand on the small of Alice's back, stopping her from backing into that sweet and poisonous bloom.

Alice is in a daze.

It's one minute and thirty seconds since the question.

One minute and twenty since the answer.

Joss grins at her. "Did you think I'd say no? You looked so damned scared."

"Ha-ha," Alice says, but then she laughs for real as she tries to slip the ring on Joss's finger. She's shaking so hard it's like threading a needle.

"Is it too tight? Does it fit?"

"It's fine," Joss says. She wants to get out of the sun, to take Alice down that rocky pathway to their left. The one shaded by Magnolias. She wants to stop and just take this all in. Together.

But another couple walks by. Retired from the looks of their don't-give-a-crap matching polos. The husband, a paunchy fellow with smoker's lines and aviator glasses, congratulates them and offers to take a picture.

"You gals don't want to forget a thing like this."

And so Joss and Alice allow the interruption. They stand, their arms around each other, Joss's ring shimmering like a mirage in the bright light of early afternoon as they laugh and freeze the moment in amber.

The man apologises as he passes back the phone.

"I guess I accidentally set it on burst mode." He chuckles. "You're going to have a lot of these. Hope it doesn't take up too much memory."

On the contrary, they can't thank the gentleman enough.

Joss has kept every single shot. In bad moments or sometimes good ones, she thumbs through each frame, watching Alice's lips curve upward in a smile, watching her lean closer into the picture, her sidelong gaze on the camera as she kisses Joss on the cheek. She can still feel the brush of her lips. Hear that whispered, "I love you."

Alice straightens, a silly grin still stretched across her face as the cloud cover passes over them. She relaxes, drops the arm with which she's been shielding her eyes and turns her body toward the camera. And as she does, she seems to catch something in the distance. It's a brief hesitation, not more than a few seconds, but Joss sees that smile falter just a fraction before she turns and faces their future.

Chapter Seven

Joss sits up dazed in the medbay carrel, one leg dangling over the edge of the pallet. She had to go back under to remove the brace. The nanoshunts accelerating the healing process required surgical removal.

Alice stands in front of her, dressed in lab whites for the occasion. She takes a step back, hands raised in surrender, squinting at her as if she's discovered something new. "You're adorable when you're groggy."

"Doubt I smell it." Joss drops her eyes and tugs at the paper gown sagging over her bare legs, that strange combination of stiffness and light against her skin. She's not sure how she feels about Al joking with her like this. She admits it had felt good to open up, to talk about her break with Alice, but she doesn't want that drawbridge staying up indefinitely.

"True." Alice stoops to get a closer look at Joss's leg. Other than the gunky residue of the elastomer and a slight wrinkling of the skin, all signs of the wound are gone. Joss shifts impatiently and pushes herself up straight against the side table, slinging both legs over the pallet.

"Let's see how this goes."

She lifts herself, her arms wobbly beneath her weight as she strains and sags back down onto the bed. "Drugs. Just a little dizziness." She lets herself breathe for a moment before dropping her weight on her feet.

"You should really have the drone here for backup," Alice says. "I can't catch you if you take a spill."

"I'd like to do this on my own."

"Gosh. Never expected you to say that."

"Keep talking." In truth, Joss is taken aback by her brusqueness. She should be thrilled; she's free and finally scraping her nails across a patch of skin that's been murdering her for days, but the return of her mobility has only seemed to bring all her other weaknesses to the fore. Alice is right. She wasn't eating enough, had driven herself into a state of near malnutrition and now it feels like the rest of her body is bailing on her in protest. She tries again, a grunt escaping her throat. This time, she stands, keeping most of her weight on the good leg which spasms resentfully under the pressure.

Alice subvocalises a message to the drone, directing it to hover just above Joss's shoulders. Its crane arms dangle behind her like she's a stuffy in an arcade game.

"Al—"

"Fall and you'll be back in the brace again," Alice says. "Don't think we can afford that."

Joss closes her eyes and balances her weight on both feet. There's a little strain, but she's experienced as much discomfort from sleeping in the same position. She lets her body settle, then releases the edge of the table before shooting a pointed look at the drone. "You can back off." She stops. "A little."

The drone spits out a string of scattered schoolmarmish clicks but whirs back a few centimetres. Joss raises her foot and gives a light kick to the air and grins. No pain, no twinge or hitch in her muscles or the cartilage in her knee. She sees Alice watching her, her eyes drifting down to Joss's legs like it's the first time she's seen skin before.

"Still with us?"

Alice blinks, her eyes lifting like she's just been caught doing something unsavoury. "Fine. H-how does it feel?"

"Better than expected." Joss grabs the assist rail and shifts her weight from leg to leg. The injured one's a bit wobbly, but still no pain, no locking of the knee. Hands freed up, she hears a startled chitter from the drone as she takes one step and then another. She passes Alice and crosses to the other side of the medbay, her pace gradually quickening as the drone swoops close behind her. As she walks back, a memory steps to the surface: She's six years old, testing a pair of sneakers on the worn carpet of a shoe store. Ruthers? Runners? One of the holdouts, housed in that abandoned roadside mall until they tore the thing down and replaced it with a fancy gym for Starhook's employees. It's a strange shift, from here to there, now to then, and for an instant, she can't reconcile the body moving thousands of light-years from Earth from the smaller one weaving between the shoeboxes and crumpled packing paper. She takes another turn around the medbay, breath and blood pumping a semblance of hope back into her veins.

"You're a little taller than I thought you'd be," Alice says.

"Am I?" A cautious smile nudges the corners of her mouth. Joss has always been on the short side and too much of a tomboy to bother compensating with heels. Alice catches her and just as quickly averts her eyes. "It's ... I mean I know how tall you are, but this is the first time for *me* to see you like this."

"Right," Joss says, not quite comfortable with where this is going. "I suppose it must be a little like hearing your voice for the first time." She opens the locker and removes a pair of sweats, shaking them out to check the size. They're loose and a little long, but they'll allow her newly freed leg some space to breathe. "So ... we ready?"

"To?"

"To activate the pulse beacon." She looks back, some of her newfound brio dampened by the agitation on Alice's face. "You said it's up. That we're good to go."

"You don't want a shower first?"

Joss squints at her, and tugs at her shirt, giving it a sniff. "That bad?" She lifts her head. "Is something wrong?"

"No," Alice says.

"Then no more nursemaid."

She grabs a hooded sweatshirt from the folded stack of clothing and slips it on, stuffing her feet into a pair of oversized slippers, before snatching the walking stick offered by the drone. It feels good to be at this height again, to move her whole body and watch the floor bounce up in a rhythm rather than passively slide underneath. Alice is close behind her, half hovering, half running as she tries to keep up.

"Joss? Are you sure—"

"Let's go," Joss says, increasing her pace. The grated walkway rattles in protest under her feet. "I want to get home."

She keeps walking, delighting in her newfound freedom. She might be trapped in a doomed tin can with a sentient doppelgänger of her ex, but at least now she can walk away from her if need be.

"Joss?"

Alice's voice rises as she says it, echoing around her in the corridor like a net meant to gather her up. Joss reaches the turn and stops, briefly contemplating the distance to the lift before the next words force her to turn back.

"We can't send the pulse. Not now."

"I don't understand. Is it back online or not?"

Alice is quiet for a stretch, her gaze lilting slightly before she draws in a breath. "Something's gone wrong on Haitch."

Joss halts, feeling a prickle of apprehension or irritation, either way, it's testing her patience.

"We know that already. That's why we want to get as far away from that fucking place as possible."

"No. I mean … the transmissions I'm picking up from there. They're all off."

Joss shakes her head, not sure if the drugs aren't still working their way through her system. "As in they're still lying about our being dead?"

"As in they're lying about a lot more than that," Alice says. "Those voices we picked up from traffic aren't human."

"That doesn't have to mean anything." But her mind is racing. Automated comms aren't abnormal in most cases, but most Traffic towers are strictly regulated to have humans at the helm, specifically on jobs that entail human transport. A rule less about mistrust of automation than to keep humans from passing the buck.

"I ran a vocal analysis," Alice says, her eyes grave. "On Traffic and some of the other messages we've been picking up on the low-gain from Haitch. Miners have family. They'd be sending slow boat messages to Kestra at least."

"And?" Joss says, struck once again by another avenue she didn't pursue. It's true she used to be a better detective, that she's allowed her rigor in those areas to atrophy, but the AI standing in front of her now seems like a younger, hungrier rival.

Alice flicks her index finger, and a stream of voices trickles from her chest area. Lots of the same-old, same-old sentiments and nagging. Happy Birthdays, belated holiday greetings about to get more belated.

"Most AI-generated voices are indistinguishable from human speech, even spectral analysis won't catch it. But…" She holds out her hand and sends up a tangle of light. The strands wind together forming a diagram of a human vocal tract. "Invert the acoustics and you can recreate the object producing the sound." She sends up another, similar but far simpler and straighter like a child has traced over the original with a ruler. Alice folds her arms and steps back, admiring her own handiwork. "You can tell which one is the human."

The difference is stark, one retains the knotty twists and turns, the asymmetry of something organic. The other looks like a bent straw.

"None of them are human. None of them."

"So, these are what? Fakes? Are you saying that those people are all…"

She doesn't finish the sentence. Alice clears her throat and turns her gaze back toward the display. "The outbound feeds correspond to real identities, people still down there, but every single one is a fabrication." She looks at her. "It's not enough for me to deduce that they're dead. But what I do know is that this cover up goes way beyond whoever's in charge down there. This is something bigger than deep space profiteering, Joss. And I think we need to think long and hard before we alert anyone to our presence."

She stares at Joss, the planes in her face deepening and giving off the impression of solidity. She edges in closer to the diagram, still hovering in the air between them. "I'm beginning to wonder if there's anyone down there alive. Anyone human that is." She shudders and snaps her fingers, causing the visuals to flare out. Joss watches them fade across her retinas, some long ago drill from childhood sounding in her head as they blink from existence.

Pharynx

Larynx

The Eustachian tube leading to the ear canal, which … wait. She straightens as an image ripples up through her memory. Deuvim leaping off her barstool; a mere tap to her temple was all it took for her to activate that silencing bubble as she made her way through the revellers.

Joss looks at Alice. "Want to see the real thing?"

"This is … not what I expected."

Alice's words come stalled and cautious as if she's just divining their meaning. Deuvim's corpse has been brought up from the deep freeze. She's laid out before her in the clean room, still suited up, save for the helmet and the EVA armour Joss has removed with no small difficulty, from her upper half. Her lips are blue and cracked from frost, her hair streaked with damp and smelling of embalming fluid. Aya Deuvim's eyes stare, unflinching, into the bright medicinal lamp that sways above them in the blast from the ventilator. They popped open sometime when Joss was directing the drone to carry her corpse up from the deep freeze, causing Alice to let out something close to a yelp. Even now, Alice is cagey, her arms folded as she hovers as close to the exit as she can get. Joss has tried closing them, but the lids keep retracting like an accusation, revealing that cool, limpid stare.

"What isn't?"

Joss subvocalises a command to the drone, stepping back as it hovers low to spray her corpse in a cloud of disinfectant. She glances up at Alice whose eyes are locked on the body, her stance taut as if she's expecting Deuvim to leap from the slab and throttle her.

"Are you okay?" She's never seen Alice acting like this before. Is this fear? Can gemel experience it in the same way?

"Yeah," Alice says, but her eyes don't budge from Deuvim. "I remember how this felt for you," she says, her brows knitting as she brings her hand to her collarbone. Alice used to do that. She used to toy with a silver chain around her neck when she was nervous. "To see one for the first time."

"You mean a body," Joss says, partly to pre-empt Alice from going there, but the memory rears up anyway. Skylar Laraby in an open casket, surrounded by bouquets of lilacs and all the relatives she purportedly hated. She didn't look asleep or like a husk as some folks described it. It was more unsettling, like some part of her had walked into a tangent universe and might come back any minute to tell Joss she looked like shit when she cried.

"You thought she might sit up."

"You uh, don't have to remind me," Joss says. Her eyes flick up to Alice, guilt seizing her when she sees her expression. However accurate and even visceral, having memories on playback is different thing from experiencing a thing for the first time. Joss's memories have been pruned, left her jaded by time and experience. But Alice, even with every detail stored inside her, is still an innocent.

"I'm sorry," she says. "That one still gets to me." She runs some disinfectant over her hands and then slips on a pair of gloves. "This isn't my wheelhouse either."

Alice doesn't answer. She moves closer and dips her face over Deuvim's. "It's like the spark is gone."

Joss nods, wondering if gemel are even capable of contemplating death the way humans do. Whether or not you believed in a soul, it was hard to disagree with the notion that what sparked a life came from within. But a gemel drew that force from external sources. They were efficient that way, running off the excess electricity in the machines around them. Not-Alice could run strong and steady on a kid's nightlight, but she could not, like the plants gemel were often compared to, gain her power from a natural source, a failsafe that kept gemel beholden to their human sires.

She nods to the drone, now hovering low over Deuvim's head, its arms extending to clamp around her jawline. Joss imagines those cold metal tongs clasping her own skin and shudders. The drone hums and with a quick, steady motion snaps Deuvim's head to the side, exposing the area of skin between her ear and the nape of her neck. Alice flinches at the sight.

Joss does too. Human Alice wouldn't have blinked.

"You can not be here if it's too much," Joss says. "I won't mind."

"No," Alice says. "I want to be here. It's just new."

"Well, then." Joss leans over and smooths her hand through the shock of white-blonde hair on Deuvim's scalp, locating the raised area of scar tissue where the implant is located. Not everyone in their line of work has them, but a good number on Joss's strike team invested in them as a matter of course. They provided faster and more secure communications than the wearable tech, not to mention insurance in case of capture or false accusations. And providing Deuvim didn't tamper with them, they can store up to seven days' worth of communications before they're wiped.

"It always is," Joss says, realising how incontrovertibly true that is. She's seen a lot of death, from Skylar to her mother, to victims and colleagues and perps, and while the mask has gotten harder, there's a part of her that reacts like Alice is to every single death.

"Even for you?" Alice says.

"Yeah," Joss says. She doesn't know why this admission makes her feel better. It's not something she even would have shared with Alice without being prodded about it. But with that simple admission, she finds she feels the tiniest bit less alone.

They stare at each other, the quiet stretching over the body between them like the lowering of a shroud. Joss thinks about the people in the *Tiktaalik*, their loved ones still sending messages across the void, still thinking there's a soul out here who will make them feel just a little bit more complete. She thinks about Alice. Wonders if she's found that completeness herself.

She slips on a pair of gloves and takes the extraction tool, a pair of spindly pliers that remind her of something a dentist might have used in the last century. She really didn't want to do this herself, but Medbay refuses to operate on a cadaver, so it's up to her and the drone. She whispers an apology to Deuvim's son back home, promising that if they get the body home, she'll pay for someone to make it look nice again.

"This is going to be unpleasant," she says to Alice, feeling all the stranger for having to warn her. "You ready?"

Alice nods, her eyes shifting as she communicates with the drone. It descends just a few inches above Deuvim's head, a needle-like appendage extending out. It whirs up, firing up a beam of hot white light that shoots downward, making a smooth circular incision in the skin above Deuvim's ear. The smell is immediate and unpleasant, like keratin and charcoal.

"Oh," Alice says.

"Yeah, you should stopper your scent if you can." She inclines her body, grimacing as she pulls back a flap of skin, still frozen other than the burned edges revealing blood vessels and shards of bone chipped off by the beam. She presses the clamp around a small, metallic device the size of a button, letting out her breath as it comes loose. She leans into her arm and breathes again, then wipes off the flecks of frozen blood and fluid with a cloth.

"Okay." She swallows hard. "We're done here. Time to put her back on ice again."

She drops the disc into a small container and slips it into the pocket of her tunic. She wants to get out of there, away from this reminder of what happened on the ship.

"Can I ask you something?" Alice says. They look at each other again, and what Joss sees isn't confusion, but a timeline of loss flickering behind her eyes. "Does seeing them like this…" She pauses. "Does it help?"

"It does for some people," Joss says.

"What about you?"

Joss shoots her a glance, piqued by the sudden diversion. Why is she asking this? Why now? "Wouldn't you know that?"

Alice looks at her, shaking her head slowly. "I can access the research on the subject. And I know what you've felt and how it misaligns with your internal dialogue. The means you've taken to distract yourself. But I…" her eyes narrow. "I don't think you've settled the matter."

"Should I have?"

"No," Alice says. She shakes her head. "Not at all. I suppose I don't have everything figured out."

What Alice means is that she doesn't have Joss figured out, that despite her ownership of Joss's memories and experience, her progenitor is as screwed up and confusing to Alice as she is to herself.

"Then I'll just say this." She reaches out to offer comfort before checking herself, letting her hand rest on the cold metal surface of the dissection table. "Welcome to mortality, Al."

Chapter Eight

Joss has seen a lot of bodies in her life. Just rarely the ones that counted.

When it came to Matilde, she was finishing her sophomore year and tied up with finals—an excuse her mother had given her for not telling her until days after the fact.

"We thought it could wait until your exams were over," Rhonda said, a tinge of resentment in her tone, as if Joss had been the one who couldn't be bothered when she'd spent every free weekend driving to the hospital in Rapid City, helping Matilde through physio and fighting over the phone with the obsequiously eel-like holo reps at her insurance company. She'd checked in on Mika and the houseplants, happily ensconced at the next-door neighbours, promising them that Matilde would be home in a month if not a few weeks.

She'd believed it too.

The stroke had slurred Matilde's speech a little, stiffening the arm she didn't write with, but she was getting better, taking to her rehabilitation with the same gusto she did her garden and the missives to the state reps and councilmen about river clean-up efforts and the rest of the damage caused by Starhook and its subsidiaries. They were going to spend the summer together, fishing maybe, but most of it likely sprawled in those rattan chairs on Matilde's wraparound porch over chess and jigsaw puzzles and glasses of iced tea. When she was feeling hopeful, Joss thought they might even try a hike or two. Nothing like their old adventures, when Matilde introduced her to countless bird and plant species and ranted about the glad-handing colonisers and cabrãos.

"I was just a girl when the coasts started burning," Matilde would say. She'd stand at the edge of the creek bordering her land, hands on her hips, watching the water runnel over the stones. "That's when they noticed we existed. Such great opportunities for flyover country. Knew those bastards were going to glad-hand us straight to hell."

She knelt and plucked a leaf from a wild indigo plant, brushing a weathered finger along the yellowed streaks between its veins. "Ph damage right here," she said. "And they seed it into the air every time they fire off those rockets. That's not even factoring in the noise." She shook her head. "We used to have flocks of mountain plover coming to rest here. Now, we're lucky if we see a few."

Joss admits to having rolled her eyes during these sermons, but she credits Matilde's vigilance to her own attentiveness to detail, to catching those small, near-invisible shifts in her environment. A ring of dust left around an object at a crime scene, those proverbial broken branches along a forest trail. It hasn't saved any trees, but it's helped her solve cases and save people far better than her father's talk of shifty eyes and tire tracks.

By the time Rhonda called her, Matilde's body was on its way to the crematorium. Hugo was running for Commissioner. Expedience was a factor.

"The memorial service is the day after tomorrow. We've decided to give you half of the ashes," Rhonda said, a lilt of surprise in her voice as if she'd caught herself in a moment of uncharacteristic generosity. Joss doesn't remember what she said after or who hung up first. All she remembers is the ache in her throat, her knuckles white around the phone as she sank, bare knees chafing against the wiry carpet of her dormitory. Matilde's photo was at eye level on her desk. She was leaning against the wooden fence post that bordered her yard from the Galtons, the plains beyond it a blanket of bronzed grass and wildflowers, blurring in her tear-streaked sightline.

But the first body she saw was Skylar Laraby's.

Landon got its spaceshot when Joss was in second grade. A private starport. Grand and shiny and taking up the 40,000 acres once used for soy and grain sorghum, the cattle made obsolete in an age of lab-grown animal protein. The governor and Mayor Gifford bought those farmers out for pensions and peanuts, promising that Trent County, population 31,053, wasn't only back on the map of America, but one to the stars.

Starhook Tech built rockets and fibre optics, the kind best made in zero gravity. They had production centres orbiting Earth and the moon and came to Nebraska for cheap land and tax incentives. Their CEO, John Tierney, was the type—and there were many—who liked crowing over NASA's tombstone. "Maybe if they'd advertised those scratch-resistant lenses and insulin pumps," he said, "we wouldn't be out here doing their jobs."

He said that at every fucking press conference.

"Things weren't good before they got here," Hugo told her, whenever the rattle from a test launch spooked the dog or sent the sagebrush sparrows scattering from the trees. "You're lucky you don't remember."

But Joss does remember. She remembers the worn textbooks and beat-up equipment at her elementary school, the boarded-up shops along a Main Street that hadn't been main in more than forty years. She remembers Rhonda, working the farm and the house, trying to stay cheerful until she listed into loneliness and that church.

With the Alcubierre flip stations strung up at Io and beyond, the world needed space on the ground to reach more of it in the sky. Advancements in Selluvium processing, used in gravity plate technology, also meant you didn't need that equatorial kick from Cape Canaveral or Kourou to launch anymore, and most of those places were underwater. The Cape, what was left of it, was an artificial island made of carbon nanofiber from which Hedley's Lift climbed like some monstrous vine toward the clouds.

For a few years, the mood in Landon was buoyant. Joss's school got a new fully sensory VR pod and an adaptive learning upgrade. Downtown, long hollowed out by VR-retail and whatever came before that, bloomed from boarded-up shop fronts into the quaint stereotype of a Western saloon town, bustling with restaurants and a General Store. But most of those businesses weren't owned by the locals, and the fusion dishes, not to mention their prices, signalled they weren't meant for them either.

Starhook employees commuted in on jets and long-range hovercraft, secluding themselves in the ziggurats that went up and blocked the views of the plains. But there was work and hope, and rockets that lit the sky like a constant, deafening reminder. Cheer up, they said. The future's bright.

And when Starhook came, the Carsten family prospered. Outwardly, at least.

As chief of police, Hugo worked liaison with the company's private security detail, guarding the port and ensuring the townspeople stayed clear of the perimeters now crisscrossing the flatland. Joss moved on to Tryon Middle School and then high school, where she kept her grades up because her parents promised she was going to college. A good one.

Skylar Laraby was a year older, part of that small clique of rich kids whose money didn't come from Starhook and had the luxury of being above it. Joss had seen her in the hallways, trying not to let her gaze linger after she'd dusted her with a smile. She was always surrounded by the college-bound kids who marked themselves with expensive but unobtrusive fashions and the inside jokes that formed a wall between them and the rest of the school. Joss was sixteen. Had never dated a boy much less a girl, and knew she'd never cut through that barrier.

But that smile. The way Skylar had let her hand linger on Joss's arm once when she'd dropped her wallet on the steps before first period. Joss had never been a bag girl. She'd carried a worn, men's wallet made of Portuguese leather, one Matilde had ordered from Lisbon for Hugo's birthday decades ago. Joss had liked the smell of it, asking for it when he'd gotten a replacement.

"Hey wait!" Joss heard the footsteps approaching even as she registered the voice, the shock of Skylar's fingers touching her wrist. She turned around, almost gawping as she found herself almost towering over her on the steps. The wallet lay flat in Skylar's hand like a limp and injured bird.

"You might need this," she said. Joss sucked in a breath, reaching for it, her thoughts racing at what the other girl must be thinking. Did she think it strange that Joss was carrying an old men's wallet? Was Skylar Laraby with her shoes and Miyake bag made of the trendy Pinatex cloth judging her for using animal skin? A few photos and a stamp card for Raylan's Model Shop protruded from its slots.

"Thanks," she managed. She took it from her, snapping it shut as she shoved it into the inside pocket of her jacket. "You saved my life."

"Your lunch anyway?" Skylar said.

She took a step up to the stair below her, placing them at close to the same height, although Skylar was several inches taller. Her hand was still on her arm, and Joss felt the wallet still warm against her chest from the sun-warmed concrete. A smile lit across her features. "You the cop's kid?"

"Huh?" It took Joss a protracted moment to realise that she'd been staring, still shocked that this creature was actually seeing her. "Oh yeah. He's my Dad."

"Well, watch out. Some people are capital shits in this school. I mean, you probably don't need me to tell you that. But watch yourself."

"Sure … thanks."

Skylar had some flyers in her other hand, printed out on shiny paper meant to catch the eye in the flicker of the lamplight.

Protest against the Viper launch. Sunday, November 4th, from 10 am. Weatherly Park.

A rainbow arced over a skull with the Viper Rocket at its centre. Starhook was touting them as the future of inexpensive local freight, capable of hopping up supply shipments into the orbital stations, with lower fuel costs and faster than the elevators with their slow speeds and limited carry space were capable. But they made do on highly explosive propulsion fuel and lightweight beryllium parts that were toxic. Matilde had given her an earful about it during their last visit.

"You want to go?" Skylar said. "It's for a good cause. Starhook says those things are failsafe. But you know what they said about the Titanic."

"I do," Joss said. "Or I mean, I don't. Not about the Titanic, but, you know … the fuel and the parts and…"

As her tongue stumbled into further irrelevance, the smile on Skylar's face grew, bemused but not suspicious. She gave Joss's arm a light pinch and let go. "You should come with us, kid," she said. "I mean, with your Dad, that might be even better. We could use someone like you."

One of the perks of Joss's job is getting to eavesdrop on private conversations. One of the drawbacks is that very often those people talk shit about her. She likes to think she has a thick skin, but whenever she catches a perp or a colleague slinging an insult, her brain bypasses professionalism and goes straight to the sixth grade when she overheard Elly Bancroft calling her a diaper rash. Deuvim is no different. Sure, they hadn't been friends. Deuvim was frosty but businesslike when she was alive, but the way she lets loose on these recordings is almost enough to make Joss take back her gratitude about still being alive.

[Since when has Carsten known what she's doing? … Fuck her… Talk about the Peter Principle… Should have stayed on the Earthside speaking circuit instead of coming out here.]

Joss has been treated to quite a few of these sentiments over the morning, spooled throughout the last hours of Deuvim's comm files. In that time, she's been referred to as incompetent, borderline sociopathic, and a half-baked sloganeer. Duevim's also slammed her fashion sense as 'recruit suit chic' and claimed it would be a miracle if the team got to Earth safely, much less to the payday they'd been promised. She swallows on that last part. "Oh, that's nice, asshole."

Alice twists around, one eyebrow raised as if she's questioning Joss's sanity.

"You try listening to this."

"I am." She straightens, her eyes drifting thoughtfully to the monitor. "I'm just surprised you didn't notice."

"What?" She scoots forward in her chair, reaching around to scratch something tickling the small of her back.

"That she didn't like you," Alice says. She sees Joss glaring at her and gives a little shrug. "I mean it was pretty obvious. With the forced tone, the avoidance of eye contact, not to mention the torso angle…"

"The what?" Joss catches herself sneering. She forces her face to relax and slows her breath. "I don't usually stare at people's torsos when I'm interacting with them."

"Oh, you know that's not true," Alice says, holding her gaze for a little too long and Joss feels the warmth rise to her cheeks.

"People turn away from you if they don't like you," Alice says. "It's a common physical parlance, albeit often unconscious."

"Thanks for enlightening me." Her mind circles back to their interactions. Deuvim had looked at her askance. A lot. Joss thought it was a tic or some inborn shyness she'd never gotten over. But whenever they'd run into each other, she always seemed poised to bolt in the opposite direction. "Jesus." She pulls her T-shirt back down, sullen, and gives herself a shake to regain her focus. This explains a lot more than she's comfortable admitting. "And I thought I was good with people."

"Well, she did save your life," Alice says. "So there's that."

Joss chuckles, not a little bitterly. They've been listening to hours of this, not much more than a continued litany of Joss hate and kvetching over who's up next for prisoner watch, while the others take some R&R. She pinches the bridge of her nose and rubs her forehead for a minute, then gets ready to spin back the audio to hear what she's just missed when the comm signal pings on Deuvim's set.

[Deuv. It's Grady again.]

It's Callen. The lowest member on her security detail.

[What is it this time?]

Joss can hear the trickle of music from the bar that night in the background; a chill reminder like a shadow on an X-ray or a subtle but marked symptom. She can hear the laughter too, raucous, boisterous, entirely oblivious to what's coming to them.

[Same shit. Only he's starting to spook the others. Self included.]

Deuvim huffs and Joss wants to sigh in accompaniment. Among the crew of prisoners they were seeing home, Grady was the weakest link, the type of subject Joss could talk down in less than an hour and who'd likely involved himself out of sheer obsequiousness to his buddies rather than moral outrage.

But Joss is sometimes wrong about people. As in now.

Grady's going rogue.

[He on about again? Deuvim says. *Aliens? Jesus Christ.]*

She's clearly forcing interest. Joss shoots a glance at Alice, nodding for her to patch in and Alice hovers down next to her, bending forward as if the two of them are communing around an old radio.

[He's telling the others they aren't going to let us go home.]

Deuvim lets out an exhausted laugh. *[If it's not Feds then it's the cartels, and if it's not the cartels, it's the goddamned gemel. Can these fucks be more unoriginal? Can you separate him again, stick him in the hole for a few hours?]*

"Gemel? What's she mean by that?" Joss turns to Alice, whose face pinches like she's asking the same question. She rears back a little, averting her eyes.

"I don't know. I've listened to as much as you have." But then her frown hardens into something more serious. "This Grady," she says. "Inmate logs show he was separated from the others a lot. Placed on suicide watch. Did you…"

Joss shakes her head. If Al doesn't know, then Joss certainly didn't have anything to do with it, and there lies the rub of her negligence. "I should have." She presses her palm to her forehead, feels the skin damp beneath her fingers. "I was too much in a hurry to forget about things."

Alice gives her a consoling look. "You can't be aware of everything. That's why you humans delegate. And clearly Deuvim didn't share anything with you until it was too late."

"Yeah," Joss says. "That's where my people skills might have come in handy." She shakes her head.

Alice nods for her to continue and Joss slows the audio and plays through the remainder. There's more of Callen and Deuvim bickering over shifts, Deuvim complaining again about that beer she hadn't bothered to even sip. They're rendering Grady's ramblings unintelligible, until Joss's ear snags on a word. She stops the audio and speeds it back. The words tear out from him, guttural, like something pulled up from the mud.

[Whoshee theshaves in cay…]

She turns to Alice. "Fuck. Can you filter out what he's saying?"

"Sure," Alice holds up her hand as Joss plays back the audio, her fingers trailing strands of glowing filament through the air. Joss watches as they shuffle and reconfigure themselves based on probability.

[Anyone…whose, whoo she, whoooseen whoosheeeiii… them…who's seen. The shapes in the cays…

keys
'kays
caw
caw
caves]

"There," Joss says. She taps the cursor back and plays the audio again. The string of letters dances in front of her like the clumsy superimposition of a title card in a one of those ancient black-and-white films Matilde had loved. Alice had loved those too. *Top Hat. Gold Diggers of '33.* She repeated the lines and sang along to them and was gobsmacked when Joss knew some of the lyrics. Matilde had taught her well, not just the remnants of a ravaged ecosystem but those of a civilization that remained solely in her avô's memory.

[caves]

The word hovers in front of her, a pale smoke signal from the not-so-distant past. She snatches at the memory before the thought vanishes.

"That ... that guy from the slow feeds."

"Who?" Alice looks at her, the words halting as if they've been frozen solid in the space between them and the monitor.

She snaps her finger and rises, realising belatedly that she's got nowhere to go. *Stop. Stop. Make a note.* "Something I saw before you showed up. On one of the personal feeds." She looks at her expectantly.

"You've watched quite a few."

Joss turns away, her hand raised. "You'll know him. A man. Curly hair. Smug. Tweed. An asshole. Can you pull up that feed?"

"Jacob Russ," Alice says.

"I didn't get his name."

Alice extends her hand, and there he is, the man she'd seen condescending to his miner friend, begging for more of that precious data.

[Those pictures you sent me … of the tunnels … I think this has potential, buddy … ping me on the bounce assist. I can cover the cost.]

The words fall out before the idea forms fully in her head. "It wasn't an accident."

"What wasn't?"

"The tunnel collapse. It was deliberate." She waves her hand, inadvertently sending Deuvim's audio feed into play mode.

[Deuv? Callen says. Deuv? You on your way? Are the comms up where you are?]

[What is it?]

[Lights went out.]

Grady is still muttering in the background. [*There's … a … hole … in the sky. So many. All of them, to the end.*]

A low groan, like something being torn from below drowns out nothing but Callen's voice, his breath coming rough and heavy.

[Motherfuck!]

[What is it?]

[Deuvim, better patch through to Carsten. Fuck! I can't see anything—]

A deafening boom, loud enough this time to cause both of them to wince. Someone, no—a lot of people—are screaming in the background.

Grady's voice manages to clear the noise. *[You see? They're not gonna risk it. We're a piece. Every single one of us!]*

[Deuvim! Suit up and get to the pods!]

Chapter Nine

After that, nothing but static and a few choice words from Deuvim before the comms go dark. This was fifteen minutes before the final blast took out Central Hub, so she must have gone back to find Joss. If not to rescue her then to try to get answers after it was already too late.

Joss is sipping whiskey, just a little to calm her nerves, but not enough to anaesthetise the grind of regret in her stomach. She'd made the fatal mistake of thinking she was dealing with a run-of-the-mill labour clash, and an even more damning assumption that corruption in the Outer Rim would be pared down to the politics of survival, and that imagination wouldn't be necessary.

The miners had stumbled across something in those caves, something that indicated intelligence, possibly another civilisation. But people turn up aliens about as often as they take dumps in their freshly colonised soil.

Now she's going through the old case files on Haxen and the hostage takers, feeling very much how she did in school when she'd done everything right but understand the assignment. When she'd gone in to negotiate, her team had scrounged up everything they could on the tunnel collapse. The names of the dead, survivor statements, and the gruesome images of the aftermath to glean if one or more of those bodies would help her establish a rapport with the HTs. Haxen also provided her with the most recent blueprints for the tunnel in an attempt to shore up their own case. They had been planning on shutting down that part of the tunnel due to safety concerns, but Joss had barely looked at them. She wasn't there to prosecute a shoddy construction job. And that part was easy enough for her to believe, at least enough to seem empathetic to their cause.

But now that she's taking another look, she wants to smack herself. Joss knows shit about architecture beyond a few pretty buildings she'd studied in college, but Harbour's SWOT analysis reveals that the tunnel supports, while second-rate, hadn't veered into the slipshod. There was also the matter of where the ceiling gave out. It had happened in an open chamber, a vast chasm whose walls were composed largely of pyroxene, a sturdy mineral that wouldn't crumble without one hell of a nudge.

She leans in, chin perched in hand, and peers at some of the smaller notations—a language of their own—signifying the various ducts, and lights, and exits/entrances. She notes some last-minute changes to the ventilation system: humidity controls and the fine-tuning of airducts that seems far more conducive to an archaeological dig than a mine whose owners can't be bothered with their employees' comfort.

"Harbour, decrypt."

Mundane translations light up like stars over each sigil: vent, gangway, heat detector, then, she draws a blank. Joss runs her finger over the sigil, once, twice, again. It looks like a half-moon with several fins curling off it in differing directions, and it's blurry, not through mishap or sloppy workmanship. It's more like those first successful photographs of quantum superposition, a wire bent back and released, its state of flux recorded as discrete images overlapping one another.

Staking marks maybe? Indicating spots for further excavation? But if they were closing down the tunnel, then why do that?

Because they weren't looking for ore or minerals. They were looking for more of whatever it was Russ's friend had found in the caves until someone else decided to stop them. It was in someone's interest at Haxen to let folks think it was an accident. The bad PR around the deaths and the subsequent hostage crisis was the perfect cover.

A sudden movement behind her as the door gasps open. She lurches back and sees Alice with the drone and two mugs of Russian Caravan. It's her go-to for staying awake when she's coffeed-out. Joss takes a mug from the tray.

"What is it?" Alice says.

"Take a look if you like."

Alice leans over her shoulder, peering earnestly at the screen. She's humouring her; AI can access this feed in an instant from anywhere on the ship, but Joss appreciates the accommodation even if she finds her proximity distracting.

"You see these?" she says, running a finger over one of the sigils. "I didn't spot them before."

Alice gets that faraway look she has when she's collating information. "So, they were looking for something other than ore or minerals."

"It's possible," Joss says. "What do you make of them?"

She takes a sip; the tea is strong and unsweetened, and it gives her a jolt. Alice doesn't answer. She folds her arms, her fingers drumming silently against her sleeves, her mind somewhere far off and troubling.

"Listen," she says. "I need to tell you something. When you were under, we got an incoming message. Slow feed." She speaks haltingly, like she's trying to stall. "Bounce assist from Io and then to Kestra."

"That would have to be recent then." Joss puts her mug down. She's glad she did because Alice is looking like some breathless swimmer who's only now realised she's over a drop-off.

"It was a … private message," Alice says. There's a slight guiltiness to her tone, like she's seen something she shouldn't have.

"What?" Joss turns fast in her seat, watching as Alice jerks back, not fast enough to miss her. Joss's legs swipe through hers and they overlap each other like water.

"I was going to tell you," Alice says. "I thought it could wait until the brace was off. Until you'd recovered—"

"The brace *is* off."

"Just…" Alice closes her eyes and flicks her wrist. Joss's jaw drops, then snaps shut tight again. The hazy image of a woman materialises in the air before her. In that split second as her eyes adjust, Joss thinks it's a reflection, Al's light superimposing itself onto the sender.

[Hey, Carsten]

Alice. Her Alice.

She's in uniform again although those dark green fabrics hang more loosely around her flesh and her hair is shorter and swept back. The distortion in the beacon has softened some of the age from her features, but not enough to conceal the scar that trails from temple to cheekbone.

[I doubt you'll be seeing this, but I had to try. I'm not like you, you know? Have to let everything out. We got the report on the Tiktaalik, and when I saw the passenger manifest, I had to…]

Her voice breaks and she stops, steadies herself and swallows hard before she looks at the camera again.

Joss is reeling, her chest blooming with an ache she hasn't felt in years. Maybe this is an illusion. Maybe she's really back in Central Hub, the hull shattering around her, her body tumbling out into the black. But she knows it isn't. She knows this because she is Joss, and this is what her reality hands her like tissue packets on a Tokyo street.

Human Alice straightens and faces the camera. *[Look, I don't know how long they're going to keep the search and I'm not much of a believer in miracles. I've seen too much for that, but if there's a chance, then you need to know that ... you need to know that in addition to my being really fucking pissed at you, that I—]* She stops herself then, folding her hands as if she's wrestling with the words and offers a thin, sad wisp of a smile. *[This is as close as I get to praying, Carsten. So, if you're out there, then please. Come back.]* She holds herself like that, and in the silence before the feed cuts, her image seems to freeze in place. But that's just Alice, focused and finally composed, trying to will this image out across the void.

When the image dissolves, she turns to see Not-Alice staring at her, a bit of fear and something infuriatingly like pity in her eyes.

"Is this a joke?" Joss pushes her seat back, recoiling from where that ghost once addressed her.

"No," Al says. "You can check the telemetry data if you doubt its veracity."

She's never felt angrier or more stridently self-righteous, like the Joss who started all of her and Alice's worst fights. She'd rarely been on the right side of history then, so she forces herself to breathe for a moment, her fists clenched tight enough to snap the bones in her fingers. "Why didn't you tell me?"

"I thought it would upset you."

"It *does*."

"Well, that makes two of us."

"Does it?"

Joss looks at her, sees that warring desire to either flee or blow everything up, and it hits her. It wasn't Alice who'd kept this message from her, but herself. This Alice is formed from Joss's psyche. She has her memories and experiences, but by her own inception date, she's a colt: wobbly and uncertain, running to the same old coping mechanisms Joss availed herself of on the regular. This Alice keeps secrets because Joss keeps secrets, pushing down the hard stuff out of some misguided desire to protect her.

"W-when we pulled Deuvim out of the deep freeze," Alice says, her stammer alarmingly natural. "I started thinking about death. About why people fear it when they don't experience the aftermath. Of course, I understand the fear of non-existence, but it's still impossible to comprehend and ultimately painless once it happens. But it's not the loss of the self that scares you, is it?"

The question isn't rhetorical. Alice is looking for confirmation, and Joss feels a confusion begin to pull at her, that oh-so-human need for assurance and connection. She presses her hands to her knees and pushes herself up, turning slowly, almost afraid to look into those eyes again. To take in that perfect rendering of the woman who's lost her for a second time.

Of a woman who's lost.

"No," she says. "The worst part is thinking about the people you leave behind."

She pitches forward and closes her eyes, her head throbbing in time with her heartbeat. Al is quiet for a long moment, but Joss can sense her watching her, gathering up her words. "My presence must be disconcerting at the moment. I'll leave you for a while if you—"

"No." Joss sits up as Alice rises from where she's hovering into a standing position and reaches out, her hand passing through hers. Al looks down at their fingers, overlapping in that awkward approximation of intimacy, and Joss does either the dumbest or most mature thing she's done in a long time. She turns her wrist so that her palm is facing Alice's and opens her hand into the glow of her fingers.

"I'm sorry," Alice whispers. "I shouldn't have waited to tell you."

Joss snorts and swipes the back of her hand over her eyes. "Nothing to apologise for. You got that trait from me, and I'm beginning to understand just how destructive it can be. I think we could both put an end to this suffering in silence shit."

Alice smiles and reaches out with her other hand, fingers inches away from Joss's cheek, and Joss feels it this time, warm lines tracing along her skin like a caress. She closes her eyes and leans into it. It's not real, but she'll take what she can get.

"These stories we tell ourselves are software," Alice says. "They provide impetus, keep us functioning, and protect us, but sometimes they overwrite the truth."

"So, we're bugged?" Joss says, and the slightest hint of a laugh escapes her.

"For better or worse," Alice says. "It's a feature."

They sit silently amid the steady hum of the ventilation system, Alice waiting, granting that faint substitute for kinship until Joss can gather herself up. After a few minutes, Joss straightens and shoves up her sleeves, a ritual motion signalling that her own survival programs have booted up and it's time to get back to work.

"Harbour, give us everything you can on Jacob Russ."

✳

Hugo made no secret about what he thought about the activists. He'd tangled with them on more than one occasion, sending his people out to diffuse protests and dragging them, to many complaints and threats of lawsuits, off of Starhook property.

"Pretend to care about the Earth when their parents own stocks in coal and oil. Meanwhile, Mr. Sanderson gets his house broken into because we're wasting personnel dragging a group of angry simpletons out of Starhook's gift shop. Hypocrites."

To Hugo, everyone was a hypocrite. He sought contradictions in people the way others obsessively solved their crosswords as if a small inconsistency was enough to undercut any and all nobler intent. Joss understood. She was hardwired with a similar cynicism about people, but still young enough to think she could entertain hope. But she already sensed that quite a few of the activists were, as he'd described them, wealthy coastal kids with a saviour complex. They had a habit of talking to the locals like missionaries preaching to the unwashed, the worst being Micah, a college kid to whom Joss took an immediate dislike. Micah was from Oregon, which he thought anointed him as a nature sage, as if the rest of the world didn't have forests. But Joss disliked Micah mainly because Skylar puppy-dogged him at every gathering, nodding along eagerly as he spoke in acronyms and statistics, peppered with words like 'holistic' and 'gaia.' That's where Joss couldn't help herself, Matilde's tirades flowing out of her like tree sap, snarling at Micah's grandstanding and sending him into quiet fits of apoplexy.

No, she'd say, after he'd given yet another big speech, the barn swallow wasn't endangered, that was the Least Tern; and ditto on Russian olive, an invasive species the locals had been trying to fend off for decades. Skylar seemed to enjoy watching Joss spar with him, but Joss didn't put much hope in these confrontations. They were more a destructive self-assertion, the way punching a wall sometimes helped cauterise her frustration. But when she spoke, she could feel Matilde's anger coursing through her, giving her the conviction that made the others listen.

She cut out of practice and church, went to more rallies and meetings and envelope-stuffing parties over pizza at Skylar's big house in the neighbourhood with robo-sweeps and rows of Zelkova trees that hid eco-aesthetic security cameras.

She'd long pushed down any expectations. Skylar was just a motivating fantasy, she told herself, the way the pretty dental assistant might get her through a filling, or how Ms. Owen's neck, delicate and swanlike, made her listen to those droning biochem lectures. She'd barely confronted her own queerness at that point, acknowledging it as a truth, sure, but something to be prepared for quietly, like applying for a college or making sure she had travel insurance when she went across state lines. So, when Skylar hooked her leg over hers one night after everyone had gone home, it didn't register at first.

They were on the sofa in her family room, sipping wine Skylar had cribbed from her parent's cellar. Skylar leaned into her, her breath warm and smelling of blackberries. Joss opened her mouth to apologise, her arms looping around her because, she told herself, they had nowhere else to go. She felt Skylar's hand covering her own, the other one warm as it slipped beneath the folds of her shirt as they fell into each other.

"I like you so much, Jossy," Skylar whispered.

If Joss sensed something was off in Skylar's interest in her, she pushed it down, attributing those questions about her father's job to the fact he was running for reelection. Even had some billboards up along the 112 and the 77. Joss felt a surge of pride every time they drove past one, although she laughed and teased him about his slogan.

Protecting what YOU value most.

Who was the 'you?'

Her parents weren't rich, not like Skylar's parents, but Hugo had gained a certain status and power, and so Joss merely let those questions be confirmation that they were equals, that Skylar took what was happening between them seriously.

She hadn't come out yet when she brought Skylar over for dinner— although she was dead sure Hugo knew and was bolstering himself for when Rhonda figured things out. She was more afraid that he would recognise Skylar from the protests he'd cleared out, that he'd go ballistic or that worse, Skylar would hear him spout one reactionary comment too many and decide that Joss wasn't worth it. If she hadn't been so wound up that night, she might have noticed how quickly Skylar's laughter over her father's joke segued into his job. She might have noticed how Hugo had answered openly and generously, his usual tight-lipped demeanour smoothing out into something she almost recognised as charm. And how, when they turned their attention to Joss, teasing her about her rugby shirts and inexplicable devotion to Runzas with peanut butter, she was merely the buffer amid another set of competing objectives.

If she hadn't been in love, Joss might have noticed that her father's cheerful glad-handing of her new friend revealed something more than a man trying to charm his future voting base. She might have noticed that while Skylar was plugging him with questions, Hugo had more than a few of his own: a detective story unfolding at cross purposes, one in which Joss was just the dupe.

Love is blind. That part's true, but amid that obliviousness is a nub of self-doubt, the uncertainty that can have you polishing signs of deceit into something hopeful and shiny.

Chapter Ten

"Now this" —with a bend of the wrist, Alice conjures up a three-dimensional image of Russ's message; that tweedy bastard with the placating smirk and the old-school chalkboard in the background— "this guy is not impressive, but I've been delving into what's on that blackboard of his."

She hops atop the control panel, wedging herself into a sitting position in the corner. Her fingers draw out and sharpen the long scrawl of numbers. "Working with it during sleep mode. The geometry is on a higher dimension. Difficult for you to visualize. Think of a Calabi-Yau manifold."

"What? You mean like a Möbius strip?"

"But far more complicated." Al scrunches up her face in concentration, and Joss gets her answer in the next second, pushing her chair back, marvelling as the object unfurls between them, folding into itself and then disenveloping in a simulation of four-dimensional space. She experiences, as she does with all such things—quark spin and the size of the universe, the maddening nature of time—the vertigo that comes with a fleeting grasp of something beyond her perception. She grapples with it, hanging on for as long as she can until her human limitations show it the door. Just long enough.

"The way you visualize these objects has very little basis in reality." Alice sends the object into a slow spin, revealing every facet and angle. "Wavy lines. Spheres. Those stretchy net-like matrixes meant to represent the folding of spacetime. They're just the forms you project to make sense of what you can't see. What I see is different."

As she speaks, she slowly draws the object back from Joss's sightline, like an optometrist adjusting a Snellen chart. She watches as the edges fade and the lines dissipate into nothingness as the object flickers between a whole and a jumble of disparate parts.

"But ... utilize the law of closure," Alice says. "Filter out the contour illusions projected by human sight and reimagine the form based on how it would appear to a more advanced consciousness, and you can fill in the rest."

"A more advanced..." Joss starts to ask, although she really doesn't need to, just like Alice doesn't need to point to herself and mouth a 'voila.' But this Alice is in her element, excited and playful, and she's never seemed more like the one she left on Earth.

"Us," Alice says.

"You," Joss says, digesting this new realisation. Joss is trapped by her own human limitations, a narrow light spectrum, cognitive bias, weak and extremely deceptive pattern recognition. But Alice, Alice can take in that illusion of the old woman and the Gibson girl all at once, without so much as a blink or a shift in perspective.

"I'll make it easier for you," Alice says.

"Gee, thanks."

She grins and waves her hands and the image looms closer, becoming granular in its expansion and all too familiar. That strange paperweight she saw on Gabrielle Vecher's desk, the spheres and sharp angles, bordered by tricks of the eye that burned like floaters on her vision. This thing is the same shape. Or a damned close version of it.

A current of unease ripples through her, the kind she first experienced looking through a telescope when the vastness of the universe drew up close and personal. Her mind flashes back to that day in Vecher's office. That smug, unreadable expression on Malachi's face as he stared at her. She folds her hands, squeezing them together until her palms go slick. The thought surfaces as if from sleep.

"I've seen this before. Or something like it. In Vecher's office."

Alice crooks an eyebrow at her. "I was waiting for you to make that connection." She's quiet now, waiting for Joss's thoughts to form, to add her interpretation.

"If this was a prototype of some kind, what would it be for?"

Alice pauses as if the question has caught her by surprise, and Joss has an odd, almost vertiginous sensation, like she's leapt ahead of her own thoughts.

"I'm speculating," Alice says, "but a generator perhaps, or some kind of decryption apparatus?"

Joss swallows. She's not capable of taking in the implications yet; she's just relieved Alice didn't dismiss the question. In fact, she looks very much like it troubles her.

She stands up and starts to pace, letting her breath and blood keep time with her thoughts as she starts a slow circuit of the room. "What if Vecher and friends were trying to build this thing and they were keeping it a secret?"

"That's possible."

"Only someone else didn't want them to finish."

"But who up there would even be aware of—"

"And what if the hostage takers were theatre?" She's trying to keep her thoughts from galloping ahead of her. "Or at least a lucky distraction. Enough to make that tunnel accident look like the legit result of a corrupt exec cutting corners?"

"Why destroy the *Tiktaalik*?"

Joss shakes her head. "That never made sense unless some of the HTs knew something they weren't supposed to. Now it sure as hell seems they did. Grady did, clearly."

"So, Grady then." Alice tilts her head, her eyes tracking Joss like a surveillance camera. "But if it just was him, or even some of the others in his cohort, why take out the entire ship?"

"I don't know." Joss shuffles back through their preparations in the weeks before departure. There had been no suspicious activity, no attempts to breach security or get at the HTs. That was partly why she'd been so lax. Maybe Deuvim and the others weren't telling her something; or maybe Deuvim just hoped it would make her look bad.

"A misstep then?" Alice says. "Overkill?"

Joss has to snort at that. Alice knows better. With her and Harbour being so chummy, she knows a lot better than Joss does. But Alice is maintaining a rhythm with her, indulging her in this slow-paced and messily human exchange of ideas, and for that, she's immeasurably grateful.

Malachi. Michael. The gemel.

She looks at Alice, thinks to measure her words, but her mind leaps ahead of her reserve. "When you said you don't kill, did you mean don't or can't? Could that even be a choice you could make, beyond the hypothetical?"

Alice flinches as if she can't quite believe what she's hearing. "Excuse me?"

"I mean, I know you've got that Law of Robotics or whatever. To keep you from offing a person, but could you bypass that?"

Joss hasn't heard of any cases. Gemel crime stats are non-existent, a fact hammered on by the Court of Sentient Ethics, but the intricacies of their morality are hazy.

"Law of what?" Alice's gaze hardens, her nostrils flaring as if there's a real set of lungs inside her.

"You know what I mean."

"No," she says. "Help me understand." She slides off the control panel and stands so rigidly Joss thinks she might go solid and shatter. That's when she remembers. Robot is a slur for gemels.

"Ah shit, Al. I'm sorry."

Alice says nothing for a moment, just lets the silence tug at them both until Joss wonders if she'll be shredded into particles like those idiots who took a joyride too close to Cygnus X-1.

"I'm sorry," she says again. She lifts her hand, makes a half-assed attempt at a pleading gesture. "Look. I wouldn't ask if it wasn't important."

"I know," Alice says. "I'm thinking."

"Okay then… okay."

Alice's shoulders ease, but only slightly. She leans her head back and takes in a breath. "Like any sentient being, I'm capable of violence. Like any decent one, only when and if it's absolutely necessary."

Joss nods. "What about self-defence?"

"I mean," Alice says. "There's no need for it really. I'm not exactly killable unless you die before I'm formally discharged from your service. Even in that case, I'd just go dark until whomever you trusted with my inception code wanted to reboot me. But if it meant saving you, or situation depending, others, I could be moved to do it."

"And how would…" She struggles for the right words. "How would a gemel gauge that?"

"I'm not a program, Joss," Alice says, her tone cold enough to belie that claim. "But as a baseline? I suppose it would be a utilitarian decision. To save the greater number of lives."

"Like the Trolley problem then," Joss says, forcing down a look of disdain. The self-help version of a moral dilemma. Her worst criminal justice profs fell back on it like scripture.

"Somewhat," Alice says. "The notion of there being too many variables in play acts as a kind of failsafe. Hypothetically we could sacrifice the few for the many, but we would need to be 100% sure that doing so would not result in more deaths down the road, for generations even."

"Wish we'd had you around before the coasts sank," Joss says. "How long term?"

"Very," Alice says. "We're not prognosticators and I'd have to be a hundred percent certain of the results."

"A hundred percent," Joss whispers the number almost to herself. *The few for the many.* She takes another turn around the floor, not noticing the quiet at first. The guilt over her insinuations bobs up through a wave of long-estranged exhilaration. "You were right, you know?"

"About what?"

"My talking to you," Joss says. "Telling you about what happened. It's unlocked something in me. It's like my mind is working again."

Alice is watching her, her mistrust retreating into thoughtfulness. "What else am I for?"

✳

"I thought we might indulge a little," Alice says. The drone places an open and very expensive bottle of Merlot on the table in front of them. "You haven't tried this yet. But the taste profile matches your preferences."

She turns and waves her hand, opening the sun shield to afford a full view of the Lutra Nebula, a blazing smudge of colour against the black. They're taking supper amid the emptiness of the mess hall. They've just fired off the pulse beacon, after all. Might as well enjoy things before the uncertainty sets in.

Alice has ordered the mess to whip up renditions of Joss's childhood favourites: Matilde's feijoada and tiramisu for dessert, and Joss for her part, has brought in a single hovering glow sphere, usually used for repairs, and placed it above the centre of the table. It gives off a warm light, softening the sterile illumination on the ship. Tomorrow, they'll be back in work mode, sifting passenger dossiers, listening to the feeds from the pulse beacon and Ross 128-H, hoping that someone from the Federation will send word. There's music, a playlist so random, Joss has no idea how or if Alice chose it, only that she likes it—and that each song, if not familiar, is vaguely resonant of her past.

Joss pours a glass and puts it to her lips, plunging immediately back to Earth and the smell of cedar, to the taste of freshly picked blackberries on her tongue. There's a memory in there, too. It's early on with Alice and they've stopped at a café near California's truncated coastline, one of those establishments that either through a lack of funds or just plain stubbornness refuses to move inland. The devastation on those coasts was, *is* still ongoing and relentless.

"You all right?" this Alice asks. Joss drifts back to the present, downing more from her glass.

"Yeah," she says and holds it up in appreciation. "Guess I can keep you around." A pang of regret shoots through her. "Al, I'm sorry about yesterday. I didn't mean to imply that you were ... that you didn't have a conscience."

"It's fine," Alice says.

"I'll discharge you first thing when we get back," Joss says. "You're your own person. That was never a question."

"You don't want to keep me?" She smiles, but there's a hint of worry in her tone.

"I-I like having you with me. But you should be free to make that decision on your own."

Alice smiles. "Thank you." She leans over her wine glass and closes her eyes. "I'm glad you like it. I do too."

"Yeah?" Joss says. Her voice is laced with regret, so she smiles to compensate and gestures to the spread in front of her. "Thanks for this. It's nice to have a break."

They sit in silence for a moment, the soft strains of music floating in the air around them. Some old ballad. Joss can't remember the name, but she flashes back to her parents' house. She's a kid, huddled on the landing, looking between the bars in the banister as her father and mother, still young, still in like if not in love, slow dance in the living room. They had cared about each other once. Maybe they still did, even after everything.

"What's it like?" Alice asks.

Joss raises her eyes and blinks at her. "What's what like? Spying on my parents?"

She doesn't realise she hasn't spoken of any of this to Alice, but Alice nods like she knows just what memory this song has pulled up from her psyche.

"Not that, but to dance."

"You don't know?"

Alice presses a hand to her chest. "I do. In here. I know how your body felt doing it, but not how it feels in this one." Alice hovers closer, blanketing her in her glow and Joss leans in enough that she's inside her, her body overlapped in an illusion formed by particles of light. Even the densest materials are made out of nothing, she thinks. 99% of empty space. In that, she and this Alice are really no different. She gazes down at her leg. She's good for a twirl, but it's been a long time regardless. "Promise to go easy on me?"

"Of course."

She pushes herself up and turns, woozy from the wine but happy to be moving, sliding her feet across the hall's silvery parquet. She stretches and gazes up at the nebula, that luminescent spiral that is either the dust from a dying sun or the starlit loam of new beginnings. "C'mere then."

Alice rises and comes forward. She stands in front of Joss, her arms at her sides as if she expects her to lift them for her, but Joss just smiles and narrows the space between them, slipping her arms around the circumference of Alice's waist. One hand cuts through the dark folds of her shirt, through that illusion of flesh and bone, but Alice doesn't flinch, and Joss feels only air and warmth against her fingers. It's the proximity that hits her. Alice's face is so close to hers, her eyes following Joss's like they're homing in on truth.

She laughs, breathily, a little unsettled with herself. "Don't think I've had a partner this light on her feet."

Alice smiles and lifts her arms slightly, only so it looks like Joss's aren't impaling her own. The sway of their bodies is cautious, slight enough to be imperceptible, but Joss feels her heart knocking against that stillness. She might be holding a phantom, but she's never felt more afraid of her own clumsiness, of elbowing a stomach or stepping on a foot. She leans in, lowering her chin over the outline of Alice's shoulder and closes her eyes. Alice's heat, her familiar musk mixed with the scent of her soap drifts between them, and she can almost feel it.

Her.

If she stays this way, maybe the empty space will fill itself, maybe she'll feel the press of Alice's hands on her back, the flutter of her breath on her neck.

"I'm sorry," Alice whispers.

Joss pulls back and looks at her. There's a rawness in her expression. "For what?"

"This." She's looking down like she knows she's not enough. That she'll never be enough.

"Hey," Joss whispers. "You don't have anything to feel sorry for. This is the best time I've had since..." She moves in to comfort her and meets ... resistance.

How?

She chokes out a laugh as her fingers press against the dampness of skin, as they tangle in the silky texture of auburn hair. Alice's hair.

"Al?"

"Shh." Alice presses a finger to her lips. "Don't think about it. It will fade if you think about it."

"This isn't—" She's cut off by lips, soft but urgent against her own, by the shock of cool hands sliding beneath the folds of her shirt. Alice shoves her newfound solidity against her and Joss, lost now, snakes her arm around her neck. She pulls her closer, their mouths still locked. She can feel Alice's breath inside her, taste the wine on her lips.

No, no, no.

Joss stiffens briefly, but one look into the amber of her gaze and she sinks again. She covers Alice's mouth with hers and this time, the kiss is breathless.

If Joss didn't need to breathe, it might just last forever.

But she does.

She bolts up in the darkness, the taste of the wine replaced by the cottonmouth of a hangover. She's in her quarters, the blankets are thrown about as if a hurricane has torn through the room.

"What was it?" She presses her hand to her chest. Her skin feels seared but it's clammy to the touch.

"Joss?"

Alice stands over the bed, fully clothed. Her expression is taut. Afraid.

"Alice?"

Joss lurches forward, hurriedly yanking one of the blankets back over her. Her expression wavers between apprehension and sheer embarrassment. "What are you doing here?"

If Alice intuits Joss's dream, she clearly doesn't have time for it.

"We've got company."

Chapter Eleven

"We've got company."

Joss shakes off the dream. If Alice knows what's in her head, she doesn't show it. She looks far too frightened.

She tugs on a shirt, fumbling with the drawstrings on her trousers as she hurries after her to the control room. Alice doesn't need to explain; a slow pan over the navigational display to a lone dot inching toward their location tells her everything she needs to know.

"I'm sorry." Alice's eyes are following it like she's watching a wreck of her own making. "But I doubt that's a rescue ship."

"How much time do we have?"

Alice's face falls as she calculates. "Normally three weeks, but it's a self-defence transport with a jacked-up propulsion system."

A gunboat. Used to escort freighters to their jumpgates. Not FTL.

"At their current rate, seventy-two hours."

Joss nods and sinks into the boomseat, still trailing her around like a pup.

A sudden wave of exhaustion hits her, despite the rapid thrum of her pulse, like some part of this is welcome, an answer to her not-so-subconscious desire to burn everything to the ground. If it was just her, she might grab a bottle and hail the bastards before helming what Petal's got left of its ioniser cannons.

But as her gaze rises to meet Alice's, she sees every reason that she shouldn't.

Gemels are free-floating quantum systems, but they require a power source to keep them viable. If she dies, Alice will go dark and remain out here in stasis until the generators go on the ship—and that's if their visitors don't blow it up on sight. Joss has made peace with losing herself. Losing this better angel of her nature is out of the question.

"We can send out another distress call," Alice says as if in answer. "It doesn't matter now that someone on Haitch spotted us."

"Will it make a difference?"

"No."

Joss scoots up to the console, brings up a diagram of the loading dock. "We'll take a pod, get far enough away from Petal 4 before they get here."

"Out here?"

Joss sees something close to anguish in Alice's expression like she's calculating their chances as Joss speaks. "We'll have three months of life support. We can stretch it to a year, maybe more if I go under."

That's pushing it. The pods in Petal 4 are built for more populated spots along interstellar trade routes where you'd have a chance of being picked up. Out here, they're a formality.

"That's suicide." A tiny spasm tugs at Alice's lips and Joss has the sudden urge to hold her or at least put a comforting hand on her shoulder, but all she's got are words. "If I don't make it, the power source and the comms will stay online for years. We can set up a beacon. I can leave a will, instructions to revive you Earthside and set you free."

Alice's face is tight. She lifts a hand, fingers outstretched as if to make some grand argument, but the words stagger out of her. "I'm ... I'm supposed to protect you."

Joss reaches out, gropes pointlessly for a hand and meets air. She inches closer, tilting her head so that Alice is forced to look her in the eye. "Hey," she says, slowly lifting her hand to the space where Alice's heart is. "Alice? You *are*. I'm still in here. That's not going to change."

Alice squeezes her eyes shut, nods fitfully as if the air around her has thickened into frost. "But I already have."

"Alice..." Joss lifts a hand to Alice's cheek, feels the warmth emanating from that emptiness.

"I wish we had more time," Alice says, and then, through her worry, through the thoughts that are causing her form to flicker and shake, she makes the bravest effort at a smile. "I wouldn't have minded another dance."

Joss blinks at her. She hasn't even begun to sift the real bits from that hazy, animal dream. Drama is for later, for another time and place where they'll have that luxury. All she knows is that Alice has more of her foolishness stored in her memory, so she smiles and owns whatever it is.

"Same."

She pulls her hand away and sees the glint on her finger.

Moisture.

The bead rolls off her skin, elongating like a raindrop as it falls and hits the floor.

They both step back to give this thing space between them, to confirm what they've just seen, but it's already fading, evaporating in the ventilated chamber.

"Condensation," Alice says, but as she does, she draws a hand to her face to make sure.

"Of course," Joss says, but there's something in Alice's expression that feels less certain. "Now we've got another problem. The condition of the pods."

"Yeah, that hangar's a mess," Joss says.

As the pods had been useless to her, she'd only done a cursory check on the things before working on the antennae. They'd taken some of the burn from the explosion, but their systems were still functioning.

"There's a huge chunk of the hull that's bent over the exit chute," Alice says. "And the wiring's burnt out. Getting the ship to eject them is another issue."

Joss lifts her foot and gives it a solid tap against the floor. "Well, if I was good enough to dance, I'm good enough for another spacewalk or two. The drone and I can tag team. How much time do we have to launch and clear the *Tiktaalik* before they're on us?"

Alice purses her lips. "Seventy-two hours at least."

"Then we've got seventy-two to work with," She gives her an encouraging smile. "Let's get started."

※

The pods are in the port side of Petal 4, stacked like oversized wine casks and prepped for launch were it not for a chunk of heatshield blocking the evac chute. That entire side of the petal took a hit in the blast. More explosives risk damaging the pods, and with what they've got on hand, trying to cut it away would be like chipping at a glacier with toothpick.

Alice pulls up a 3-D image of the hull, the torn shield arcing out over the chute like one of those waves in Japanese woodblock prints. "Most metals go brittle in the annealing process," she says. "The heat shield, however, is a synthesis of Cerulean and steel, which maintains a certain level of malleability to keep it from breaking up. That's why it didn't just snap off in the blast." She pings the tip of her finger across different points along the surface. "So, heat won't work, but if we wire nanite fluxers along these vectors, we can still induce molecular dislocation."

Joss leans close, takes in the pattern crisscrossing the blockage. "I'm impressed, Al."

Alice lifts her chin, gives the first genuine smile since waking Joss up that morning. "Massage it in the sweet spots until it bends to our will. Problem is in the bending. We need a lot of strength, and the tugboats went up with Central Hub. Drone doesn't have the muscle for it."

"What about those?" Joss eyes a pair of EVA-equipped loaders near the docking ramp, two monstrous, baleful husks casting crooked shadows over the floor grates. "Give me an hour and I can get the hang of it."

Alice shakes her head. "Charge will throw up shrapnel. Puncture your suit or worse. It'll have to be me."

Joss rears back a little. "Loaders don't have minds. They're patched directly through to the brainstem."

Alice snorts and pulls up a diagram, all gimbals and power hubs and series of crystals interlocked with intricate gears. "Wire in the drone mind, and I can gain control of the suit."

"Remotely?"

"Won't work. The visual hook up with the drone would be fuzzy at best." She looks down, one foot worrying the tile as if she's trying to nudge her thoughts into place. "I'll need to be out there."

She looks at Joss almost as if she expects a challenge. Gemel can access networks and systems but are tightly blocked from merging with anything resembling a human body. To protect them from exploitation, or so the reasoning went. It was far more likely that their creators feared it would be like handing dolphins gift baskets of opposable thumbs.

"Nice workaround," Joss says. "Now let's rustle up your body."

Around Joss, the stars form a uniform pattern; only the recurring flare of the nebula alerts her to the spin of the craft. This time, she can see the beauty in the cold light of other suns. She can see why her Alice loved it, why her eyes lit up when she talked of her time outside.

You'll never feel so unimportant yet so essential to the whole.

No epiphanies, but this second time out is better. She's more confident, climbing hand over hand along the hull, lifting her legs like a gymnast to lock her boots to Petal 4's blackened surface. She presses the final strip of nanite fluxer in place, then pushes back, allowing some slack on her tether to take in their handiwork.

"What do you think, Al?"

Alice stands above her, a preening Superhero astride a skyscraper window. "All good." Her voice is thin through the comm, with none of the breathy humanity she can fake in an atmosphere.

Al was clumsy in the suit at first, clomping about the loading dock like a drunken herd animal. She broke things and sent a stack of supply crates into the wall hard enough to dent it. Joss coached her, made her walk laps around the deck, practice lifting and climbing in the gravity-free chamber. She'd lumbered alongside Joss as she placed the fluxers, tethering the cables to the blockage, climbing down that jagged slope until she was at a safe enough distance.

She gives a tug to the coil, looking very much like a charioteer holding back a team of wild horses, then floats out of the suit to confirm the placement of the fluxers. At this moment, Joss thinks, she's like one of those angels the early cosmonauts encountered before they were carted off and erased from official photographs. Joss understands. It's so hard not to lose yourself.

"We're ready," she says. "You should go." She dips her head up to the black and Joss follows her sightline, sees nothing.

"You okay?"

"Yeah."

"See you back in the pod then."

Joss should know that such confident partings come with bad luck, but her swagger gets the better of her all the same.

Inside, she pulls up the console and readies the charge. One surge of energy will set the fluxers into action, sending their nanites burrowing into the heat shield and warping it into toffee.

"Ready?"

The wave is a mountain through Alice's visual feed. "Fire it up," she says.

Joss sets the charge, her body tensing as a low groan reverberates through the hull. She watches through Alice's camera as a line across the bulk pulsates, the metal shifting and molten in that unforgiving cold.

Her retinal display shakes as Alice, with the force of the suit, takes a few jerky steps backward and pulls.

"Just like a pull tab," Joss says. "You remember those, don't you?"

"Blue Nehi," Alice says. The taste of Joss's childhood summers. "How did you ever like that stuff?"

"Thought it was your favourite colour."

"Her favourite," Alice corrects her. There's a low rumble as the metal starts to warp and twist. "You know." She takes another step back and grunts. "Blue really doesn't suit her."

Joss breaks into a grin. "Someone had to say it, and it wasn't going to be me." The laughter dies in her throat as she sees that slab bending back, the wave now in retreat.

"How far back am I?" Alice says.

"You're good," Joss says. She checks the monitor on the outer hatch. "All clear. I'm going to cut the charge. Hold it steady until it sets. We've still got plenty of time."

Joss waits, listening to the simulation of Alice's breath as the shimmer across the mass dissipates and hardens. Then she asks, "What's yours?"

"What's what?"

"Your favourite colour?"

"All of them," Alice says.

"I like that." She does like that. Al is burdened enough with whatever she's projected onto her from Alice, she doesn't need to be burdened with her tastes.

"Okay, now. You can let go."

Alice releases the cables and watches as they coil away from the ship. The tsunami stays in place, cresting over Alice like a row of jagged teeth.

They take a long moment to admire their work. Maybe too long. There's a burst of static on Alice's viewscreen.

"Joss?"

"Yeah?"

"Time to get in the pod."

Joss glances up just as Alice leans back, revealing something coming into view in the black. There's a pinprick of light in the distance. Growing larger as they speak. She checks the navigational display, sees the slow blip of the gunner ship still crawling toward them. And something else, a string of running lights approaching from the opposite direction.

"What is it?"

"I don't know. Joss..." Her voice is breaking up. "Get i ... th ... od. Now. Jo ... Gu ... I ... shhhrr."

Joss dons her helmet as she climbs the ladder and lifts herself, legs first into Pod 10. The angle and the cramped space are disorienting: Two seats and two coffins, built for deep sleep. Everything else is taken up by supplies.

"I'm in." She tugs the straps around her shoulders, then flips through the sequence for the atmosphere regulator. "Time for you to join me, babe." That last word slips from her, helpless and stupid as she punches in the launch code. Alice should have ditched the suit by now, she should have already slipped through that hull and be hovering by Joss's side.

"Joss." Alice's breath is slow and rhythmic, like she's making an effort to sound calm.

"Hey, Al. Talk to me."

More silence, longer this time save for Harbour's maddeningly serene countdown.

Launch sequence initiated. Opening portal.

"I've... I've got some interference," Alice says. "Something's—"

There's a flash on the viewscreen, a burst of light so bright yet so pale Joss can stare right into it without squinting.

"Joss?! Go!"

She's gulping back air, panic lacing through her veins. She'd rather die than be alone again like this, out here in this awful blue-black of forever.

"I don't know what will happen if you're not in range." Her hands waver over the launch button. "You've got to—"

"G..." The word dies in the ether as a tremor bounces the pod from the slipway.

She slams forward and punches the ignition, thrown back as the thrusters roar and the black looms larger in her viewscreen. The pod knocks the side of the chute on its way out, and she thinks it's over until the stars streak across the porthole, milky lines of a violent spin. Her vision's blurring, the controls are smears of green and red in front of her. "Come on, Al. Your chariot's waiting."

Another blast, knocking her back and sending her into the darkness. Alice's name is on her lips.

✳

Human Alice appointed herself as Joss's carer. She dressed her wounds, and rubbed salve into the bruises she'd gotten during fights or falls, but there was only one time things got serious.

A fucking barbecue with Alice's grunt mates. It was in a big backyard; one of the guys had bought his first house, and if Alice was awkward with

Joss's friends, then Joss was cocky and obnoxious with Alice's. She'd had a few drinks, not enough to get fall-down drunk, but more than enough, in the right circumstances, to fall.

The weather was brilliant, one of those early days of summer when the trees reached that deep green, and the humidity was just a tingle on the skin. Joss remembers a pop song, soft and cloying in the background. It felt like one of those old high school reunion movies as she and Alice's compatriots tossed a frisbee back and forth until that frisbee sailed off and landed on a tree branch.

Joss leaped in before anyone could protest.

"I'm good at this," she said. "Grew up climbing sugar maples." Her palms dug into the bark as she jammed her sneaker against the trunk and started to shimmy up. Alice had just come out through the sliding glass doors, freshly opened beer in hand, as Joss made it to the lower bough.

"Joss?" she heard her say. "Guys. How many?"

Joss shot her a mock glare. "Only two," she said then righted herself on the bough, her hands out like a tightrope walker. "Have a little faith, dear."

The Frisbee had caught itself on the edge of a branch, folded between two planes of leaves, like a slip of paper through fingers. She could have just lowered herself and given it a little bounce. That would have shaken it free, but Alice's guys were down there, and Alice's lack of confidence in her was just enough to egg her into full-blown foolishness.

The last thing Joss remembers from that branch is seeing Alice go askew, the light dappling through the leaves above her like a strand of burning celluloid as she fell, and then the ground smacking her hard.

She doesn't remember much pain, just the taste of blood mingling with the metal as a filling cracked. Then she was on her back, Alice and one of the guys wheeling her with an ER nurse through the sliding doors of the emergency room. Alice was talking to her, but Joss's ears weren't taking in the sound right. Everything was mired together; the call chimes and the voices, the clack of wheels rolling underneath were like colours smeared across a canvas. Alice's lips moved in fast-forward even as the nurse, tethered in her own orbit, bobbed with arduous slowness by her side.

She opens her eyes to stillness. The room is dark, but someone's standing over her as she feels the cool press of a palm against her forehead. She reaches up, groping for that hand, fingers brushing against the rough sleeve of a uniform.

"Did..." Her mouth is dry and heavy. She can barely get the words out, but she tries to push herself up. "Did I make it?"

"Shh. It's okay."

That voice.

A hand presses at her collarbone and pushes her gently back down on the bed. Joss reaches up, fingers meeting the soft, familiar contours of a cheek. "I didn't make it, did I?"

"Joss."

"I didn't make it. I must not have made it, but that's good because you're still here."

She lurches up again and pulls her to her. "I can feel you."

Alice goes still but doesn't push her away. Joss presses her face into hair that smells like yuzu and forest, her fingers finding a waiting pulse. She's weeping now, her body suffused with relief. "Don't leave me out there again. You're here. You're here. You're here." She rocks against her repeating it again and again. A mantra keeping this body in place.

Alice takes her hand, her fingers locking with her own, but not in reassurance. There's only force as it draws her away from that warmth. She sets her hand on the bed like an object best not toyed with.

"Joss?" she says. "Do you know where you are?"

"I'm with you. You're here. You're—"

Alice switches on the light and Joss flinches in the antiseptic brightness.

"I'm sorry," she says. "We didn't want to wake you."

Alice.

Alice Dray sits at her side, her eyes etched with concern and confusion. "You're in shock."

Her hair is shorter and slicked back and there's that small scar on her upper right cheek from a shrapnel burst or a knife. She offers a smile, more pacifying than cordial.

"Shock..." Joss says. She takes in the shoulder boards, the insignia of a squadron commander on her collar. "Where are we?"

"The Federation Frigate *Tereshkova.*"

"Petal 4," Joss says. She feels herself sinking, like something's trying to pull her down through the hull. "The *Tiktaalik.*"

Alice hesitates then gives a slow shake of her head. "They took it out before we got to them. We barely got to you. I'm sorry." She frowns. "Were there others on board? Our scans didn't pick up any signs of—"

"No." Joss's shuddering, her mind is trying to race through the fog.

"Harbour's motherboard. Were you able to jack the data?"

"There wasn't time."

A throat clears behind her, causing Alice to stiffen even more and frown. She forces her mouth into a flat line as Joss follows her gaze to a reedy man in antiquated spectacles and a white coat. He stands bunched up and tense in the doorway.

"I thought you might need me here," he says, with the kind of obsequiousness that speaks to another agenda.

"We're good. Thank you, Doc." Alice turns back to Joss, brow creased in irritation. Joss grabs Alice's wrist. "The pod ... did you check the pod..." Her teeth are chattering. "She's in there and you need to find her."

"Who?" Alice jerks her hand away and clasps Joss by the shoulders; she winces like she thinks she might break her.

"Is she here?"

"Is *who* here?"

"You..."

"Me?"

"No!"

The white coat steps forward. "Commander. She's delirious."

"I realise that!" Alice says. She turns back to Joss, her eyes narrowed. "I'm going to have them give you another sedative. Just sit back."

The room starts to spin. Joss tries to sit up again but that damned medic has come over and has her by the arm. He's strong for a reed, like he could toss Joss over a shoulder if he wanted, and he's spewing jargon about hallucinations and deep space psychosis. Alice. *She was on the Tiktaalik... she...*

He presses the tip of the pneumatic syringe to her neck, drawing a gasp as he pushes it all the way in. Joss seizes up and then the edges of the world start to soften.

"She's here." She's not even sure if they can hear her now. They've both turned away, distracted by something, and Joss sees their mouths drop as if they've just dosed themselves with something stronger.

"Who?"

"Al," Joss whispers. Not Alice. Not this Alice, but that Alice. *Her* Alice.

This Alice backs up, one hand over her blaster. She shoves herself between the apparition and the bed, her other arm splayed out protectively.

That Alice smiles, as if this is all just a simple mix-up—two black umbrellas getting numbered wrong in a coat room. "I'm sorry. I didn't mean to startle you."

If Joss had the breath, she'd burst out laughing. That Alice almost does, but she's far too kind to make light of such confusion. Instead, she gives an apologetic nod to the medic and walks right through her twin, through the bedpost and then the bed like she's wading through liquid. She steps away and takes a place near Joss's pillow.

The medic's mouth falls open and he pushes a hand to his sternum like he's either going to faint or throw up.

"You have got to be kidding me."

"I'm afraid not," that Alice says. "And no deep space psychosis either." She holds a hand over Joss's forehead, bathing her in the warm glow of her aura. "I'm real. I'm real and you're safe. Now listen to Alice. Sleep."

Chapter Twelve

When she opens her eyes, she's surprised at how fast the reality of it hits her. There's no moment of confusion, no shift from the bleary residue of a dream or the fog of anaesthetic. She is here, in a bed in a private room, artificial sunlight forming patches of antiseptic cheer over the tiles. Alice, corporeal and human, stands, head bowed, in front of what passes for a window—a display of forest imagery and the soft and regular tap of a sozu fountain. She hears Joss stir and turns, pensive expression snapping into a mask of composure.

"You're awake." That last word rises, as if she's making an effort to sound pleasant. "I thought you'd be out longer."

Joss lifts her head from the pillow, her voice dry and raspy. "Where are we?"

The green-grey walls, tattooed with blocky serial numbers tell her she's aboard a military vessel, but those signs clash with incongruent homey touches. These are the private quarters of someone of rank; boxy but spacious, with a full kitchenette and scattered touches of the lived-in. Tea roses are propped up in a vase, affixed securely to a small teak dining table, their scent putting up a fight against the perpetual stench of ozone and machine oil that lingers aboard these ships.

Alice's room.

"You re-enlisted," Joss says. She doesn't know what else to say, and a note of disbelief rides out on the question. She does her best to ignore Alice's visible reaction. She hadn't meant to imply knowingness or failure. It's just an observation, something verifiable in which to find purchase.

She lifts herself up on her elbows, but her pulse gets ahead of her, and she slumps back. "How much did they offer you?"

Alice Dray's face tightens as the question hangs between them. A joke without a punchline. But now that she's back in her presence, it all makes a terrible amount of sense. Alice was never a match for civilian life, even before she enlisted. From the very beginning, her awkwardness had crashed up against the vagaries of moneyed social etiquette and a world where people rarely said what they meant—misunderstandings amplified by the inequities of time and distance.

"Three years ago," Alice says, a tinge of defensiveness in her voice. "I thought you would have heard."

Joss shakes her head, trying not to make a thing out of it. Alice might have crossed her mind enough times during their separation to form the background hum in her hippocampus, but she wouldn't have added more salt to the wound by checking in on her from afar. She attempts to sit up again, surprised this time by the way her body responds so easily to her thoughts. She'd been so frayed and frantic on the *Tiktaalik*, riding out the passage of time in a fugue. Here, confronted with the vibrato of a real human voice, it's like her body's being granted a renewed vote of confidence.

"It's hard to keep up with everything out here." Alice's mouth tugs at the corners, something Joss mistakes for a concession before it slips back into a hard mask.

"You saw what was left of the *Tiktaalik*," she says, taking a hard shift to the practical. "Communications were blown out."

"What *was* left," Alice says. "You were lucky you were in the pod."

So, it's gone then, she thinks with no small pang of sadness. Harbour hadn't been able to save itself after all.

"I've been lucky a lot." She offers a smile and stretches, relishing the pop of her joints. "And here I was thinking you'd consigned yourself to raising Betty and consulting gigs?"

"You mean Aunt Betty?" Alice turns to her, grasping for the memory.

"Not unless she grows a foot a year," Joss says, not quite believing that this doesn't ping. But Alice just blinks at her, irritated as if Joss is playing games. "Your plant," she says, schooling her expression into a semblance of calm. "Not its namesake."

When they'd first moved in together, Joss had gifted Alice with the shoot of a young sasa plant, the bamboo used in the Tanabata festival which celebrated the reunion of Vega and Altair. She'd meant it as both a memory of their trip and a promise she couldn't bring herself to express in words: that however distant she might seem at times, she would always come back to her. But like so many things unspoken, the meaning shifted, and the plant had required so much water, Alice had named it after her alcoholic aunt.

"Remember?" Joss says. She gives her a little smile but feels her lip twitch as she takes in Alice's bewilderment. "You used to blame her when it didn't rain. Said old Betty was drinking up the clouds."

She tries for a laugh, but it dies in her throat when Alice looks away, her eyes glazed over and troubled. She's not sure if this lapse is real or an attempt to forestall any association with their old intimacy. There's a long silence, before Alice snorts, less from recognition than resentment.

"Don't know if you've heard, Carsten," she says, "but there are these things called aphids and spider mites. Make balcony gardens pretty miserable with spring and summer and fall all being the same season now." She looks at Joss, allowing a smile, and Joss nods. Not sure how to process this. "Turns out I'm a lot better at taking out smugglers and attempted coups." Her voice drops an octave as if to signal 'banter over.' "But the *Tiktaalik* was cut off completely? That's what kept you from sending out a beacon?"

"For most of the time I was on board," Joss says. "I had to repair the low beam, and once that was back online, I… we discovered we had other problems. As you've probably surmised."

A mix of disappointment and relief washes over Alice's expression. Is she thinking about the message she sent? Maybe hoping Joss didn't see it? "More than that," Alice says. "We were already en route when we intercepted your S.O.S."

"To here?" Joss asks.

"Where else?" Alice regards her silently like she's gauging her trustworthiness. "We've got a whole squadron in tow."

"Oh…"

It takes a moment, this adjustment in scope. It's as if all the clues she and the other Alice—Not-Alice, Al—have been collecting have taken on a stronger weight. If there's a whole damned squadron headed to the Ross system, then things are a hell of a lot worse than they have guessed. *Al.*

Guilt pricks her insides. "Where is she?"

"She?" Alice turns back, those shoulders tensing like wings rising on a plane. "Oh…" She nods with feigned casualness as if Joss has just asked her where her keys are. "She is being debriefed right now. As will you when you're feeling better."

Debriefed. Something in the way Alice says it sinks her stomach. "What does—"

"I hope you don't mind that I had them move you here," Alice says, cutting her off. "I thought you'd been through enough as it was." She glances over at an alcove in the corner, and Joss recognises the worn Pendleton throw draped over the sofa in a reading nook in the corner. Above it is a sparse row of old photographs, their images washed out by the sun and the water.

"I've been managing long enough," Joss says. "But I won't complain. Where did you sleep?"

Alice nods at the alcove again, wan and sardonic. "The study. Beats the barracks, right?"

"Sure."

So, she was sleeping here, with Joss out like a light in the same room? She thinks about how Al watches over her. Joss bolting up to find her translucent and aglow in the darkness as she collated information. Somehow that feels far less disturbing.

"I imagine this must be a surprise," Alice takes a few steps closer to the bed, her stance self-consciously rigid. There's something Joss can't put her finger on, something missing in those nods to familiarity.

"Oh, I think we've got each other there." She tugs off the blanket and swings her legs over the side of the bed. Alice bends forward, hands out in a tentative move to steady her and stops, her face tightening as she flicks her gaze away.

As the air hits her skin, Joss realises she's half-dressed. Just a thin tank top and a pair of baggy shorts that sag dangerously low with the gravity.

"Sure you can stand?" Alice asks.

"I'm fine," Joss says.

Alice pulls a chair away from the dining table and lowers herself into it, making an uneasy show of appearing relaxed. The bars on her uniform glint under the light.

"Then why don't you start telling me what you know about Jacob Russ," she says, her tone shifting so suddenly that Joss almost loses her balance.

Russ.

Joss stalls as she steadies herself, her eyes doing another sweep of the room. Alice's order to move her here, to place her amid these small comforts and scattered pieces of their past together isn't just a strained show of hospitality. It's meant to project security, to soften her up for questioning.

Her old recalcitrance slots into place like armour. "Dunno. A scientist of some sort."

"Russ was a particle physicist at Goransen," Alice says, unfazed by her act. Goransen is a private research lab, known mainly as a munitions developer for the Federation. Joss narrows her eyes in surprise. She might have once been adept at skirting Alice's personal questions, but she's never witnessed her interrogating a combatant. "Why the past tense?"

"I'm the one asking the questions," Alice says.

"I can tell." Joss keeps her expression flat and disinterested and glances over at the side table, pleased to find a change of clothes. She needs something to do, and dressing like a grown-up might just help her to regain at least a little more control. She ignores the weight of Alice's gaze as she sifts through the pile. There's a T-shirt and a button-down, both grey, and a set of loose orange trousers of the type worn by the engineers. They have that brisk ozone scent of a dryer, and she holds up the shirt, pressing the cloth to her nose.

"But he's dead, right?" Joss slips off her nightshirt, getting a small, vengeful thrill as Alice looks away again. She lets it drop to the floor and stretches leisurely before yanking the clean shirt down over her torso, giving it a tug so it hangs loose around her hip bones.

"Thought you didn't know anything," Alice says. Joss whips around, belatedly realising that Alice has been playing her this whole time, poking at all the right pressure points until she coughed out what she needed. She turns away again, allowing a private glower of frustration, and reaches for the trousers.

"Not really. Not hard to make that guess. Now are you going to let me see Alice?"

"Did you choose it?"

"What"

"That name?" Alice's tone is level, but the words come fast as if she can't quite keep herself from getting side-tracked.

"Does it matter?"

Alice's cheeks go taut, the thin line of that scar crooking with her expression, and the realisation hits her like ice sliding into her stomach. Joss really hadn't chosen it. Had just started calling her that from the beginning.

"We had other things to deal with." She jabs her legs into the trousers and tugs them up, turning to face Alice. This time Alice is looking back at her, betraying a brief flicker of awkwardness before she closes up again, reverting to the stiffness of the uniform. "I'm asking you now before the debriefing, Joss, because our intel won't be as trusting."

"Look," Joss says. "I just spent a long time on a broken boat that I pretty sure it was going to be my sarcophagus. I wasn't thinking about baby na—"

"Joss, Goransen Labs isn't there anymore," Alice says. "Nothing is."

"Nothing?" Joss searches the planes in Alice's face for meaning. She looks disoriented as if she's reached the edge of her old confidence in a world with order and rules.

"The entire facility, several hundred acres outside of the city." She gives a rapid, dazed shake of her head. "We're lucky it was far away from the populace, so we could contain it without much of a mess. But now, it's a security problem. The entire area around it is cordoned off tighter than the old DMZ."

"What… Is it radiation?"

Alice shakes her head and lets out a long tremulous breath. "No, it's not that. Or that of a type. The flash took out the lab, everyone on the grounds, but the contamination isn't enough to pose a danger. Or so we think. In truth, we're not quite sure what it does." She shudders. "I shouldn't be telling you any of this."

She stops herself and meets Joss's gaze, her eyes seeking that hard connection forged through softer memories, but Joss can't hold it. Already that feeling is returning, that same icy trickle of hope.

"We have traces of evidence from the survivors, people who knew Russ. He'd gotten hold of some images from one of the mining tunnels on 128-H, some kind of script. He'd managed to translate those symbols into a blueprint for a device he attempted to construct in his lab. That's what we suspect took out Goransen, but he took his information with him. Other than a few notes we turned up in his apartment, there's not much to go on."

Her eyes go distant and she squeezes them shut, her face tensing as if an alarm has gone off in her skull.

"You okay?" Joss asks. It's not the time or place to ask about that scar, but she wants to. "Can I get you—"

"I'm fine," Alice says. She presses her hand to her temple, her fingers digging into the skin. "Just a headache. I get them on these boats. You know that."

"Ah," Joss says, her voice softer. "So, what's your cover story?"

Alice flinches. "What?"

"To the public. For Goransen being, you know. Gone."

"Oh." Alice huffs out a breath. "Radon."

Joss snorts and they both allow themselves to smile for an instant.

"And Haitch?" Joss asks, pushing her luck. "This is why you're out here, I presume."

Alice stands and walks to the kitchenette, leaning over a counter for a long moment, her head down. Then she straightens and opens a cupboard, one hand hovering over a generous assortment of whiskey. She takes a bottle of Hibiki and snatches a pair of coffee mugs from the cupboard. They clink together with a solid and earthy familiarity.

"We're reading those same energy signatures from the surface and they're getting stronger. Right before we caught up to you, one lit up the place like a firecracker."

Alice pours her own, and then a shot for Joss, before tipping a little more into her own mug. She passes her the drink and Joss starts at the scent memory. Toffee and wood. It was a gift. Their first Christmas together.

"That light then?" Joss says. She remembers Al breaking up on the feed, the brightness flickering through the portal as the pod spun out of control.

"Like a solar prominence," Alice says. "Reached us all the way out here." She takes a sip and looks away. Her hands are shaking, and Joss is not sure if it's from nervousness or the aftermath of something else. What has she been through in the intervening years? And why, Joss wonders with no small amount of resentment, didn't she try to reach out?

"Our sensors picked up a burst on Haitch not long after the *Tiktaalik*'s comms went dark," Alice says. "Since then, we've been registering unprecedented fluctuations in the electromagnetic fields on the surface. Our intel tells us there are likely more to come."

"So, they did it?" Joss whispers, half to herself.

"They?"

Joss looks back at her, belatedly realizing that Alice has been watching her this whole time, waiting for her reaction. She's gotten her to spill again, that confession about Goransen Labs was just another way to finesse more out of her. Fuck it. Who the hell is she protecting anyway?

She takes a sip and shrugs. "Gabrielle Vecher. That thing Russ was working on. I saw a model of it on his desk."

Alice draws up and puts her mug down on the table, revealing a full glass. She's barely let it wet her lips. "Not him, Joss. Vecher's dead."

Joss pauses, her resentment over being played warring with a creeping sense of dread. "Then who do you think we're dealing with?"

"More like a what," Alice says, and Joss waits as she measures her words.

She only needs one.

"Gemel."

✳

"Gemel."

Alice watches her as that word drops, scanning her for fear or confusion or guilt. "You've been away," she says, almost reproachfully. "Don't be so surprised."

"You've got to give me more than that, Dray," Joss says. An edge pries its way into her voice. "So, you're saying they've pulled a coup? How could they even manage? They don't have bodies."

"The mechanised mining units are still up and running," Alice says. "The ore shipments were still taking off according to schedule until they ran out, but reconnaissance scans of 128-H haven't picked any non-indigenous bio-signatures. There were torrents of bogus private feeds, birthday messages and family updates, all convincing enough to keep anyone from sniffing around. For a while at least."

"So, it's true then." A cold throb of dread goes through her. "There's no one alive down there." She forces the incredulity from her tone, but the ice is sliding into the pit of her stomach. Al had said the same about all those messages being fabricated. "That still doesn't make sense, Alice. Even if they didn't go dark, or their sires had, I don't know, emancipate-upon-my-death stamped in their wills. The gemel couldn't keep operations running down there, much less maintain a ruse."

Alice is quiet for a minute. Her eyes go distant as if she's entertaining a pleasant memory. She lifts her mug and takes a drink, a real one this time, and steels herself.

"You do know what gemel are made of, Joss. Don't you?"

There it is, that rare show of condescension, a low Alice only avails herself of when she's desperate. It grinds Joss up when she speaks to her like this. It grinds her up because Alice sounds just like every bullied kid who's managed to clamber up a rung and is kicking down at the kid on the bottom.

"Same stuff the rest of us are." Joss takes another drink and steadies herself. Reasoning with her is a long way off. "Just particles and empty space."

"And very different entanglement patterns," Alice says. She runs a hand through her hair and meets her gaze once more. "Maybe you were too enthralled by your companion to notice how the light looks a little different around her? How everything takes on that special glow?" She studies her for a moment. "It's a subtle lensing effect of the background light."

Joss bites her lip. "Where are you going with this?"

Alice looks down at her hand, still trembling, and squeezes it into stillness. "You see, that Frankenstein story wasn't too far off the mark. Shoot some electricity into a frog and it flops around, but it's still very much dead. The gemels' creators realised that while they could generate a twin of a patient's psyche, for it to live and breathe on its own so to speak, required an extra spark. An element without which, it's just dead data, frozen at the moment of inception. The neural architecture of gemel exploits the concept of non-locality, levering the principles of quantum entanglement to establish connections with particles from tangent universes." Her fingers tighten around the mug.

"Parallel realities," Joss says. Alice's gaze feels heavy all of a sudden, like it's pulling the world atilt as her mind struggles to gather up the pieces. The dreams. The counterfactual realities seeping in from other places and times and possibilities. The feel of Not-Alice's teardrop on her fingers. Al had mentioned a decryption device, a generator. "So, you're saying it opens a rift of some sort?"

"Based on the energy signatures we're picking up," Alice says. "Evidence points to yes. I got a look at what was left of Goransen Labs."

"You were on site?"

"No. Just saw the images of the aftermath, but that's the unsettling part. Remember when you dragged me to that installation?"

"Which one?"

"I ... I don't know. The one at the ... that place." Her eyes are rimmed with unease as she scans for details she can't quite fill in. "We went there a lot."

"You'll have to do better than that." There were lot of museums during their years together.

Alice's jaw sets and she shakes her head. "There were frescoes? The layers and modifications had been exposed. You ... you said it was like staring into different parts of history."

"Technically we were," Joss says. She remembers now: an unusually cool day, a walk afterwards, but even as her mind fills in the recollection, she can sense Alice is only grasping fragments of it, hanging on to those words like a raft. It's lonely being on this end of a memory, taking on that burden for the one who no longer shares it.

"Well, like that," Alice says. "Those who've been down there see debris and a flattened, burned-out tract of land, but second-hand images reveal other things—fragments from different eras, other outcomes, artefacts from the past or alternate versions of now. It was like fossil impressions had burned themselves into the photons."

"Not a case of pareidolia?"

"No."

"That still doesn't tell me how the gemel come into this," Joss says.

"There's a theory that if gemel were able to unlock a portal or a rift," Alice says, "if they could directly harness those particles their sentience depends upon, they could gain full individuation. They'd be able to free themselves of any internal safeguarding or security protocols."

Joss shakes her head. "Sounds like a round-a-bout means of freeing themselves."

Alice returns her gaze, flinty and unimpressed. "And with the way we treat them, you think they wouldn't want to?"

Joss would like to tell Alice that when most people are freed from subjugation, they're usually too worn down and frightened and in love with life to seek revenge, but she's thinking about what Alice said to her about the few for the many. About that failsafe 100%.

"Look, I'm fairly certain Vecher was behind the construction of whatever that thing is down there. There's no way the gemel would have been able to carry something like that out without some heavy human participation. If not coercion."

Alice looks at her as if she's joined a cult. "That thing has really gotten to you, hasn't it?"

"I'll remind you she was brought into this world without her consent."

"So, join the fucking club," Alice says. "What about mine?"

"Yours?"

Dumb question. Joss can see the muscles tighten in her jaw. Alice downs her drink, slamming her mug so hard on the counter the tile vibrates in her shadow. "Do you think I gave consent for this? Do you think I wanted to find you out here with that—" She stops herself this time and turns away, one hand clamped over her mouth as if she's trying not to vomit.

"She has a name, Alice." She takes another drink, this time letting herself taste the burn of it on her tongue. "And she's important to me."

Alice swallows hard and gathers herself up. When she turns back, she's nodding to herself, her eyes filled with a renewed and terrible certainty. "Look at you. This is exactly what I expected."

"What? That I'm grateful to her? She kept me alive, Alice. I mean, it is nice to get lovelorn messages across the stars, but those don't do a hell of a lot to keep you going when you're eleven odd light years from Earth and the closest humans would like to kill you."

Alice is quiet for a long moment, her breath faltering, but otherwise she's as still as glass.

"You intercepted that?"

Joss nods, already feeling guilty for having drawn that card. "A few days ago. I was…" she sighs. "Surprised would be an understatement."

A wave of shame rolls through her for having sunken so low. She'd wanted to be discreet, to respect that moment of weakness, but this Alice standing before her isn't some fainting flower. She's hard and cruel and needs to be taken down for her own sake.

She sticks the knife in. "I wouldn't have made it without her."

"You were dependent on her for your survival," Alice says. She nods to herself as if she's come to a decision. "Well, then, you see? I've done the right thing."

"Where is she?"

"Where she won't be a danger," Alice says. "To you or to us."

Chapter Thirteen

Joss isn't sure who goes for the door first, or how she finds herself in the corridor, shoving aside the guard posted outside as she rushes the stairs to the lock-up deck. She's not sure how many times Alice calls after her as she runs, or how she reaches the outer hatch of the containment chamber. Between here and there, Alice gives in, out of exhaustion or just a need to drive home who's in control. She orders the guard to let Joss inside.

She's here now, her hands pressed against a barrier as Al, *her* Alice, rises to meet her. She's in a containment chamber, a nullification matrix wired with encryption algorithms and firewalls to isolate and control her data flow. A prisoner.

Joss watches her breath cascade across the crystalline surface of the glass, fogging out Alice's features. "Al?" She wipes at it with her sleeve, furious as if trying to remove some offending stain. "I'm going to get you out of here, okay? Are you—"

Alice gives a rapid nod, then glances over Joss's shoulder. The other Alice's voice comes from behind, measured and cold.

"I'm sorry, Joss. I'd hoped you would understand."

A shudder tears through her. She forces her gaze away from Alice, from those eyes still so warm and lost, levelling that human counterpart with the coldest glare she can muster. "You've no right."

Human Alice doesn't so much as flinch. "I've every right. She's a security risk." She nods to a guard. "Five minutes. No more."

"She *helped* me," Joss says. She's breathing hard, watching herself flailing, those stammering attempts to reason from somewhere outside herself. "Without her, I couldn't have hailed you. You wouldn't be here. I wouldn't."

"Noted," Alice says. "And that makes me wonder all the more about her motives."

Joss looks back at Alice, her Alice. She was a ghost already, but she's gone even paler now. Is the chamber sapping her energy? She forces the calm into her voice. "Hold tight, Dray. This won't last. I'm going to get you out of here."

"You've been isolated, Joss," human Alice says. Her tone is steady and maddeningly self-assured. "That means you're compromised, emotionally and psychologically."

Alice presses her fingers to her temple. "You can't even see it, can you?"

"All I can see," Joss says, "is a sentientist with a penchant for conspiracy theories."

Alice doesn't react. She's too far gone for that. She slides her gaze over to her twin, appraising her like a frame that isn't hanging quite right. "And I see a fantasy borne of resentment. A dangerous one."

So, this is how Alice views her, as some lonely figure, cut adrift, nursing her old wounds into a liability.

"If you hurt her..." Her breath leaves her, and Alice tilts her head, her eyes flashing with barely suppressed revulsion.

Alice snorts. "How? All I can do is contain her, Joss. That part's your job." She nods at the guard on her way out. "Four minutes, then take Agent Carsten to the room for debriefing."

The guard to her surprise shows them his back. There is no privacy here, but the illusion of it matters all the same. Joss closes her eyes and gathers up her cool. She turns back, trying to generate some hope in her expression.

"Hey, Al."

Not-Alice presses her fingers against the other side of the glass, gives the surface a sharp poke with her index finger and yanks it back. "I'm not used to meeting resistance," she says, her brow furrowing. "It translates as a physical sensation. Like a shock."

"I'm sorry," Joss says, shooting a glare back at Alice. She schools her expression back into something more assured. She doubts its convincing, but if Al is good at anything, its humouring Joss's needs before her own. "You won't be stuck here long," Joss says, not caring if human Alice hears her. "She's an idiot, but not that much of one."

Al glances up from the puzzle of her hands and laughs, her eyes so open and trusting, Joss can feel some of her courage returning. "Are you all right? Otherwise?"

"Ah, you know me," Al says. She points a finger at Joss's forehead. "I've got a whole store of Carsten's greatest hits to keep me company."

Joss laughs. Al's face is blurry, either from the glass or the tears welling up in her eyes. "Stay away from the prom, okay?"

Alice gives her a playful smirk. "Junior or senior? The senior one was pretty nice."

Joss remembers that night and feels her face colour. Her date was Katie Alcala. The first girl who kissed her without an agenda. After leaving Landon, Rapid City had been a change for the better. Alice starts a loose count on her fingers. "So far, I've gone ice skating, the state fair on your tenth birthday, that Halloween when you were a cowboy, oh and" —she looks at her— "tasted chocolate ice cream for the first time when you were two. That one's pretty great."

Some of those memories are too distant for Joss to remember. They can't evoke more than a fleeting image or sensation, but if this Alice contains the worst of her, she can still choose to keep the best of her on replay.

They stare at each other for a long beat. "Al, you don't have to tell them anything. They've got it in their heads that—"

"You've got so many good memories, Joss," Al says, cutting her off suddenly. There's an odd uniformity in her tone. More interference? Did they do this to her? But her eyes flick subtly to the guard. She nods almost indiscernibly. "We've worked through so much of your past, and we're not even finished."

Joss touches the glass. "I'd like to."

For an instant, Not-Alice's eyes darken, imploring her to pay careful attention, and then she stares straight ahead as if reciting the instructions for an examination.

"The night your parents sent you away."

She's never shared any of this with human Alice, all those events that came before it, that brought forth the lies that tore them apart.

"That night. Do you remember?"

Joss emits a cautious laugh, feeling that old rot slide into her chest. "Al?"

"When he … when they betrayed you, it shifted something inside of you," Alice continues, barely acknowledging Joss's question. Her voice takes on an almost lawyerly staccato. "Changed you. Turned you into someone who can't trust. Not even yourself. It broke you, Joss."

Al holds up her hand against the barrier and Joss starts at the sound it makes, like she's got a body. "Do you remember what he said to you that night?" Joss meets it with her own. She doesn't know if Alice can sense her touch, but she hopes the gesture signals support.

"Do you remember? This is the key Joss."

Her mind floods with images, flashes of her father's face in the oncoming headlights, of the signs on the road flickering by. Random and terse snatches of words spoken into his phone.

Her mind fills with questions, but she's shoving them down. Alice's questions are far more important.

"Your avó, Matilde," Alice says. "You're on the porch with her and she's telling you about the moths and the moonlight. What did she say?"

"Time's up." The guard grabs her roughly by the arm. She tries to push him back, but his fingers burrow into her, sending a throb through her bicep.

"What did she say?" Not-Alice says.

"Al…"

"It's all there," she says, some of that warmth creeping back into her eyes. "You just need to find it."

"Listen, Al. They've made a mistake, but it's all going to be okay." The guard is already pulling back toward the exit. Al is receding, her image growing fainter through the glass. She mouths the word again.

Remember.

※

If only she could say it.

If she could tell her, then maybe the weight of her worry would ease, that uncertainty that gnawed at her when she caught Skylar's eyes glazing over, her tone running cold when they were alone. She seemed preoccupied, always finding an excuse to be with other people, except for those nights when she'd get an almost pensive look in her eye and say, "Let's go to your place tonight."

Joss would relent because at her house that warmth returned, and Skylar was friendly, even openly affectionate with her as she and Hugo laughed and joked like old friends. On those nights, Joss would study her father, weighing his unusual gregariousness with her closed-off nature and wondering if Skylar's distance was her fault.

If she tried harder, just told her how she felt then maybe she could slow or even halt her retreat; saying it would make it real, stamp their feelings into something tangible that no one could take away.

On that last night they were alone together, Micah appeared in Skylar's basement window, almost breaking it as he rapped impatiently against the glass. And Skylar, as if responding to a dog whistle or otherwise under a spell, propped a milk crate against the wall, hopping atop it to push up the window.

Micah leaned in, hair falling in front of his face so that Joss could only see that big mouth moving. "You ready?" he said. His voice was taut and impatient, and then angry. "Why is she here?"

"She doesn't know," Skylar said, glancing at Joss apologetically.

"What do you mean she doesn't know? We're not fucking around here, Sky."

"It's fine, Micah."

He stared at her for a moment, his breath heavy. Joss could tell from the way he bit his lip that Skylar had pushed him into a corner on this, and she could spot the exact instant when his anger gave out, his mouth loosening into a pout. "I suppose she could be useful," he said, but even Joss knew that he didn't believe it.

At first, she saw nothing. They had parked a good hundred yards from the site, hiking through the brush to the far edge of the perimeter. From there, she could just make out the uneven line of the security fence, a crisscross of barbed wire and mesh marching unevenly across the landscape. Beyond it, the spines of the launchpads were lit from below, around which dots of movement swarmed about as technicians prepped the rockets for take-off.

So, it was happening.

Under the dark sky, that same scene congealed into a monstrous tableau. The rockets flanked by the control towers, reminded her of the RKO logo in those old films Matilde collected as hard copies, "so the bastards couldn't disappear them."

"What are we doing?"

"Shhh," Skylar whispered. Micah handed her a bag and she walked over, thrusting a bolt of something into Joss's hands. "Put this on."

The mask was made of beady Scotchlite; it could thwart the most sophisticated facial recognition software, the type that could pick out a person's identity from the masked contours of their face.

"Wait," Joss said. "You're breaking in? You can't do that. This place is—"

Skylar gave her arm a squeeze, hard enough for Joss to wince. "You see any drones, Jossy?"

Joss looked across the plain, at the steady blanket of darkness broken only by the distant lights of the launchpad. No scanlights or drones. A smile climbed up Skylar's face as she took it in.

"We've got friends on the inside. They've deactivated the fence and lured their little botdogs over to the other side of the field." She gave Joss a quick peck on the cheek before tugging the mask down over her face. "It's okay. Thanks to you we've got this whole thing pretty well sussed."

"To me?" Joss said.

"Your Dad really," Skylar said. "When I was at your place, I did some snooping. Logged on and got my hands on the beat maps and patrol circuits, lists of people we could talk to." She shrugged and gestured out to the eerily silent plain. "You see any cops? Tonight is their 'quiet night.' You know, when he pretends to be working, but he's really down at the saloon." She narrowed her eyes. "Or maybe he just didn't tell you about that."

She took her own mask and wriggled it over her face, playfully, like some kid putting a bag over her head. Micah tugged up his mask and let out a whistle.

An answer followed. Then another. A long series of chirps like the floor planks in a Japanese castle.

"We're clear," Micah said. He slipped a heat knife from his pocket and bolted across the field in the direction of the fence. The silence surrounded them again, just the rattle of the wind, and the scuff of boots against the soil as he hurried through the switchgrass.

Skylar and Joss were alone now.

"Why didn't you tell me?" Joss said. She'd tried so hard not to put the pieces together.

Skylar said nothing then, just clamped her hand over her mouth, gently, but with enough force for Joss to know that none of this was kidding. She held it there, her eyes searching Joss's, as they listened to Micah cut through the dead fence.

Joss's heart was pounding, the blood thrumming past her ears, making it hard for her to think. She could run, she thought. When Skylar let her go, she could just huff across the prairie to the highway and make her way home somehow. She wouldn't have to tell anyone. She could just run up to her room and tuck herself up in bed and keep quiet. Maybe nothing would happen. Maybe there wouldn't even be a launch tonight.

But if she left, that meant Skylar wouldn't speak to her again. No more burning nights in her room or curled up on the sofa. No more kisses stolen in the custodian's closet or the library.

No more love.

Or at least what Joss thought was love.

Afterwards, whenever she replayed that moment, Joss told herself she hadn't done it for Skylar at all. She'd done it for Matilde, to stop the poisoning of the rivers and damage to wildlife for generations to come. But she's long since learned to be honest with herself, at least about this.

She was a coward. A coward in love, sure—that part she can forgive herself for—but could she even call it that if it came with a more insidious need for approval? The same need that drove her father into the part he would play in that long ago night?

She watched the line of figures, placards in hands, flashlights and whistles rattling from their belts as they emerged from the brush and hurried toward the opening in the fence. And then, there was Skylar's hand, warm and reassuring through the cloth, as she pulled Joss forward, laughing softly, letting her duck under the mesh of the fence first as Micah held it up like a ribbon in a Maypole dance. And for one single euphoric moment, she tasted the exhilaration of togetherness, of being a David against a Goliath, as she told herself that this was for a good cause. For now, there was night and joy, the smell of the grass and the soft thud of the earth under her sneakers as they ran toward those shimmering spires. She remembers that heady feeling of the wind, that staggered line of nosecones piercing the sky as the steam billowed from underneath creating a layer of cloud across the concrete. She remembers Skylar's ragged breathing as their group scattered, fiddling with their signs and the lights they'd flash up at the tower. She remembers a guy beside her thumbing clumsily at the tailcap switch of a tactical flashlight, and then the creeping glow from the headlights training on them from behind as they turned to see a winding loop of patrol cars approaching in the distance, the dust churning blue and red in their lights.

"Wait." Skylar stopped, letting the rest of the crowd continue to rush forward, determined. Micah had turned back and was running toward them.

"Goddamn it, Sky!" he said. He jabbed his finger in Joss's direction. "I told you she was a bad idea!"

Joss stepped back, shaking her head slowly. Overlapping waves of shame and fear flooded through her. "I didn't know," she said. "How would I have—"

"She's been with me, Micah," Skylar said. Her voice was sharp with anger, but her eyes didn't share that certainty. "Besides, we … we were ready for this to happen." She clapped her hands together. "Come on, people. Still our chance! You know what you have to do!"

Micah glared at Joss and then spat in the dirt, his arms up. "Okay, let's do this, people! Lock arms!"

Joss watched, heart pounding and a sickness coiling through her, as the protesters gathered close, forming an interlocking chain of elbows and arms, stretching and swaying, their tactical flashlights flickering on one by one like bulbs on a marquee. Some held up signs, scrawled in bright fluorescent paint that reflected the moon and the lights from the distant towers. An assortment of slogans that despite their good intentions had never failed to make Joss cringe.

"Preservation not Colonisation! Exploration without Exploitation!"

The line pushed forward, moving slowly but inexorably toward the glinting spires of the launch pad, some of the protesters walked ahead, the cameras of their scroll screens held high. They led the line in a chant as they broadcast the incursion up to the satellites above them. All they needed to do was stay hunkered down in the exclusion zone. Safety protocols would force a stop to the launch.

Joss tried to pull away, but Skylar's grip was hard as she dragged her forward with the wall of people. The squad cars were lurching to a halt now behind them, doors opening with that boxy echo that signalled confinement. A voice blared out over a tannoy somewhere.

"Attention! This is the Landon Police Department. You are trespassing on private property! We order you to drop to your knees and place your hands on your heads. This is your final warning!"

She looked back, heard shouting, and saw the line of cops along with an added contingent of Starhook's private security amassing behind them as they sprinted toward the protesters. The fence had powered back up, a section of it swinging open to welcome them in, and it was now rattling shut. They'd gone one by one through that gash Micah had made in the fence. They'd fallen into a trap.

One her father had no doubt set by the time Micah and the others were buying up duct tape and wire cutters at the local farm supply store.

They rushed toward the line, lowering the butts of their guns on the protestors, cracking their heads with video-game abandon. Skylar and Joss were standing away from the melee, a shifting island of bodies and weight. They formed a chain and were fanning out around the launchpad, arms linked, their signs still up as officers and rent-a-cops pulled at them from behind in an attempt to separate them from the group.

Joss remembered Hugo's questions the night Skylar had come to dinner. Remembered the way they'd circled each other. Skylar putting on the charm for the bastard cop, Hugo humouring her youthful idealism as he asked her with avuncular disinterest about the group's activities. He'd gotten names, gotten her to repeat them even, feigning poor hearing and his "hick American pronunciation." Skylar thought she'd been playing him, but Hugo was playing her right back, and that meant he'd been playing Joss too. Pretending to be welcoming, brushing off Rhonda's displeasure about Joss "dating a girl." She was sure now that he'd left his office wide open and his scrollscreen unlocked to see if Skylar would bite. And that meant, he knew Skylar was playing Joss too.

"Jossy!" Skylar said. She had the handcuffs on and was holding them up. "You coming or not?"

Joss stood frozen, taking in the madness.

"Joss!" A different voice, repeating her name, the fury in that voice rising on each iteration.

Skylar was backing away now, her gaze replete with contempt, as if Joss had just rung up the cops right there in that field. Micah took her arm, pulling her into that formation of kneeling bodies as Joss staggered back to discover that she was trapped too.

She was being crushed between the protesters and the line of armour and shields pressing in on them. Hugo was calling after her, his voice growing as the shouting and the screams intensified. She felt her body bending in ways she didn't know it could bend, her shoulder folded back like cardboard, the elbows and knees and knuckles of that throng of bodies were grinding into her, crushing the air out of her as they held their ground. She expelled a breath, tried to pull in another one, but her face was pressed against someone's back, like it was sealed up, and she couldn't move, couldn't turn her head to gulp in any oxygen, not even to let herself scream.

She was getting dizzy, lost in a blur of sounds and bodies, and then, those shields parted, and her father came forward, shoving one of the men aside, as he yanked her from the crowd with such force that when the air shot back into her lungs, she kicked and screamed the way she had as a child. But even as she thrashed about, she could feel the shudder of the ground beneath her, that low rumble rising up from deep in the earth.

"Nice try, children," one of the cops said, his voice calm and almost placating if it weren't dripping with condescension. "The goddamned launch is on the other side."

That was when they all heard it, the blast wave as the engines ignited, a shuddering, chopping noise that burst over the grassland as flares of light and warmth engulfed them. Joss glanced back over her shoulder, taking in the trail of flame as the rocket lifted off on the other side of the launch pad, the towers dropping to the sides like the blades of a chopper. The first Viper rocket was climbing, climbing, executing its roll, as Hugo yanked Joss from that mass of bodies.

He was carrying her now; she was draped over him, the way he might have when she was a child nodding off on his shoulder. She lay against him, the rigid contours of his flak armour pressing into her sternum, her grief cloaked by the thunder of alloy and steel lifting skyward, by the noise of her own hope plummeting back to Earth.

"I'm sorry, Joselyn," Hugo said, his voice strangely tender despite the anger riding underneath it. "It's the right thing. They'll think twice about doing something like this again."

She heard the clink and whir of the security gate as it opened and shut behind them, lifting her head one last time to see that thrall of bodies split asunder as the police made work of them amid glow of the launch.

She was going to say something then, to tell him to put her down, but a crack shook the air, loud enough to have broken the sky, and then that sky became light.

Chapter Fourteen

Alice is a mask. She sits at one end of a U-shaped table with other members of the squadron, some projected in from the other ships via holofeed. She holds her hand up against the light, cutting through the dim room like shards of sunglass. It's less meeting room than an obstacle course, only nobody gets to move.

"Agent Carsten." The voice is cold and strangely soft-spoken. Joss's eyes adjust, resting on a dour-looking man with cropped hair and a gaze sharp enough to slice through the soft folds in his features.

Colonel Merrick Garber. Intelligence. Joint commander of this mission. A power-sharing scheme dreamt up by the brass that Alice Dray is no doubt thrilled about.

Alice had often worked with him back when they were together. She'd lost sleep and ended how many dinners in stressed-out, drunken rants? She'd called him a vulture for the way he'd let those under him stumble into mistakes, never correcting them. Always waiting until whatever they were doing wrong had snowballed into a serious fumble or breach of protocol before he lowered the knife. Now he's out here, balancing out Alice's role as Tactical Commander. Joss prickles with sympathy and a callous satisfaction.

Poor you, she thinks.

Garber nods to an empty seat in the centre of the U. "You've recovered fast. That's fortunate. We've got a lot of questions for you."

"I have a few myself," Joss says.

Garber tilts his head, a slight, efficient movement meant to impart power. "I'll remind you that this is an official military briefing. You'll speak when spoken to."

Alice's eyes flick down at the file in front of her as Joss lowers herself into the hot seat. She can feel the weight of their attention, solid and light, and wishes more than anything that she could feel that other Alice's presence here with her.

"Let's get started then," Garber says. "Please state your name and Federation ID number for the record."

"Joss … Joselyn Doroteia Carsten, Terran Federation ID SVRS1128."

Garber rattles out a few more questions, her age, her old badge number, the names and titles of the deceased members of her security team. It's an attempt to intimidate, to call up the trauma of what she's been through while reminding her that she's still not the one who sacrificed anything. After several minutes of this, Alice cuts him off.

"We're on a clock, Colonel, and Agent Carsten is a trained negotiator. If you're trying to prod a reaction out of her, you're only going to waste your time."

Joss is grateful for the good press, but her attempt to make eye contact is rebuffed. Alice keeps her gaze on her data pad, her voice is clipped and businesslike and less a vote of confidence than a jockeying for power. But Garber doesn't flinch; in fact, Joss is pretty sure she can see some glee in the sagging folds of that face for having gotten to her.

"As you're aware, Agent Carsten…" Garber's flipping through a data pad in front of him so that Joss can't quite get a read on his expression. His face flickers at the edges of the projection, blurring in and out of view. "You were the only one aboard Petal 4 when the *Tiktaalik* went up. The only one to survive. That's both impressive and unlikely. Want to tell us how you ended up there?"

"That was Aya Deuvim's doing."

"Aya Deuvim, your subordinate."

"She saved my life," Joss says. "At the cost of her own."

Garber leans to the side, whispering something into Alice's ear. When his gaze returns, his eyes focus in on her like crosshairs. "Did your rescue occur before or after you acquired a gemel?"

A small cough escapes her as she shoots Alice a look. "That would have been before," she says, allowing some bemusement to filter into her tone. "Think I can afford a gemel?"

The corner of his mouth twists up. "I don't know. You're at a high point in your career, are you not? Or at least you were."

Joss laughs this time, her throat suddenly parched. She draws herself up, and speaks slowly, as if she's trying to get through to a buggy OS.

"The gemel was a medical intervention initiated by Harbour."

"So, Harbour thought you were worth ... what?" Garber says. "A two billion credit psyche procedure?"

"Colonel Garber," Alice says. She reaches up, her fingers pressing against that scar. "With that kind of damage to the rest of the ship, Harbour's survival protocols would have taken extreme measures to keep its one human passenger alive. Anything would have been on the table at that point."

Garber chuckles, as if to say, 'got me there.' The thought of a nonhuman trying to save itself is clearly an oddity to this guy. "So, a medical intervention when Harbour had already treated your leg. Please illuminate why that would have been necessary."

Joss shrugs. "The isolation was getting to me, causing me to make some questionable decisions that the ship detected were a danger to myself and its well-being."

Garber lets them both sit in the silence as a few stifled coughs sound through the chamber.

Unlike Alice, who had a career outside service, Garber is a lifer. His perch rests on strategy, on sacrificing the individual to a picture that is paranoid by default. He leans back, sets his expression on neutral—although Joss can detect a hint of mockery in his eyes.

"I'm willing to accept that," Garber says. "But that doesn't explain why your gemel resembles Commander Dray."

There's a shift of attention, bodies shuffling and crackling in the ether as the attendees lean forward, hoping their prurience isn't that obvious. Alice's face is tight, her mouth fixed in a line. She knows what Garber's playing at. They share an equal amount of power on this mission and he's using Joss as a means to unseat her.

Joss takes in a breath and drops some uncertainty into her voice. However much Alice Dray is pissing her off right now, she's not about to let that happen. "Do you really want me to answer that here?"

"Please," Garber says, not quite able to stifle a smirk. "I'm sure we'd all appreciate your shedding some light on the process."

She keeps her eyes forward and tries to think of Alice sitting in her peripheral vision, her face growing paler and more indignant by the second. The room is silent save for the faint crackle of the holocrystals. "Look, I'm not an expert in how this all works. But things get pretty dark when you're out here alone and the odds are telling you you aren't going to make it." A spasm of that old desolation cuts through her. "I needed a lifeline and my memories of Commander Dray … the life Alice and I once shared was where I found purchase."

Garber glances around, taking delight in the supressed but knowing looks of the others. "Interesting choice. If not exactly dependable."

Joss swallows down a retort and lifts her gaze slowly, keeping it on Garber. Trying to catch her up is one thing, but undermining Alice is another.

"And why wouldn't it?" she says, keeping her tone matter-of-fact." She looks about the room, making eye contact with every one of those bastards who was sniggering seconds before. "You all know Commander Dray is a presence to be reckoned with… She wasn't my commanding officer, but I looked up to her. I found safe harbour in Alice, the way I'm sure all of you do now." She knows she's laying it on thick, but even so she feels that old sting behind her eyes as she reaches for the words. "Alice made me want to keep going, to be better. To stay alive. So no, it's not really a surprise that Harbour generated a gemel in her image. I was alone out there. I thought about her a lot."

When she turns back it's vertigo. Alice is frozen in the moment, that warm amber gaze drawing closer as the walls and the blinking panel lights behind her warp and stretch into the background. For a fleeting instant, Alice is all there is, and she looks at Joss with such loss and confusion that it punctures something inside.

"It's a very good story," Garber says. "Satisfying. That ability comes in useful in crisis negotiation no doubt. With us, you'll have a harder time."

"It's not unlikely at all, Colonel."

Garber cocks his head toward the voice, that medic who was on hand when Joss first came to on the ship. "Did I give you permission to speak?"

He shrinks low enough into his shoulders that his neck disappears. "No, Sir. I apologise…" After a pause. "May I, Sir? Speak?"

"Granted," Alice says.

The medic is younger than Joss first pegged him, early thirties, with a recalcitrant muss of dark hair and a warm but nervous demeanour. He lifts his head, readjusting the spectacles on his nose like some kind of old-timey affectation. "Gemel are drawn from the subconscious of their originators, and, as a rule, take on their appearance. Unless there's an inordinate amount of conscious and preconscious interference. When that happens, wires get crossed. There have been hundreds of cases in which gemel manifest as parents or lost children, lovers, pets even."

Garber smirks. "Last part sounds about right. I'll take your input under consideration." Laughter ripples through the room until Alice ices them back into silence.

"Now, Agent Carsten, you intercepted messages on board the *Tiktaalik* from one Jacob Russ. Were you aware of who Jacob Russ was?"

"Commanders?"

Alice's new Signals Officer's voice cuts in over the comms, his voice pinched with concern. "I'm sorry to cut in like this but—"

"Carry on, Ota" Alice says, leaning back in relief.

"I think you both need to come to the bridge."

Garber gives Alice a quick look. "Meeting adjourned then."

Looks of concern crisscross the room, before it breaks open into chattering among the in-person crew and the holos ghost one by one. Alice leaps up from her seat, but then stops, leaning her weight against the table.

Joss gets up and walks over to her. "Are you—"

"Later." Alice keeps her head down, but her tone is as sharp as ever. She gives a quick nudge of her head to the security guard. "Take care of her, will you?"

She feels that painful and all too familiar feel of a hand on her upper arm. The guard shoves her into the corridor and the door slides shut, leaving her to silence and separation.

To Joss's surprise, the guard doesn't toss her into a cell, but escorts her back to Alice's quarters, leaving her free to do as she likes. It's a show of conditional trust, meant more to impart the notion that Joss is out of her depth and that perhaps if nudged in the right direction, she'll see the error in her thinking. But it also sets an uglier precedent, weighing Joss's ostensible freedom with Not-Alice's—marking the hierarchy between human and gemel.

She fans herself with the collar of her shirt. The room is stifling, the smell of human Alice is everywhere, threatening to stir up memories that are of no use to her now. Above her, the coin-thin slip of a surveillance camera winks from a rut between the ceiling panels, so she strolls into the kitchenette, leaning against the clammy laminate counter as she lets herself expel a few expletives out of view.

She'd let herself believe. Made herself believe, even for a moment, that this Alice had a heart, that there was still some of the feeling from that message left inside her.

She flicks open the locks on some of the cupboards, taking in the array of Earthly comfort foods and alcohol, all secured by wrap-around nets that keep them in place when the gravity's shut off.

Such a human response, to deflect helplessness through consumption. Alice's booze collection is a neat row of bottles, their quaint gilded labelling offering temporary escape, and Joss is torn between taking a drink or emptying everything into the regen chute out of spite. But she can't let her emotions take control of her, no matter how much they're eating up her insides.

Those memories Al tossed at her. Her father, that night. It's like she's trying to finish up her primary objective, seeing to Joss's mental well-being while all hell breaks loose around them. She hadn't liked it when Al had prodded at her past like that, alluding to memories and remaining oblique rather than simply giving her a full play-by-play, but she had been right. From the beginning, humans had to be careful about not allowing technology to atrophy the memory and decay the links from which they drew meaning. If there was one niggling advantage to mortality, it was how one's dwindling clock necessitated the pruning of information, allowing for insights not evident when overwhelmed by the flotsam of detail. Those hints Al has given her are both a kindness and of subterfuge, for the past is now the only place in which they might safely share their secrets.

She pours herself a shot of Alice's best whiskey, takes it over to the small sleeping berth. She draws up her knees, resting her feet on the edge of the cushions and trying to ignore the low rattle in the ventilation system reminding her of where she is. At least here, there's an illusion of privacy. A place where she might think more clearly about what Al has told her.

When he ... when they betrayed you, it shifted something inside of you...

She doesn't like to remember that night. She's blocked out most of it. After the smoke had cleared, the rest of the debris kept falling. The kids at school had already pegged Joss as odd. But, as she'd predicted, the rich ones were pulled from school until the end of the term, while others yapped freely to the local press.

Division Chief's Daughter at Scene of Starhook Tragedy.

Cop's Kid and Victim 'Close'

Joss stayed home. She sat on the sofa near the window, listening past the ring in her ears as her parents discussed her the way they might the wasp's nest in the barn.

"You have to do something," Rhonda said. "If you let this go, they'll think you're unprincipled."

Hugo was too busy dealing with the aftermath, still working with Starhook to place the blame on the activists and keep both of their reputations clean. But the man who ruled Landon with a ruggedness and stern demeanour grew pliant in the face of Rhonda's rage.

"I didn't know that she would be there," Hugo told her. "They tricked her. That girl was playing her from the beginning."

"And that girl is dead now," Rhonda said, mocking him. "You aren't going to do much by trying to hold her up as the villain."

Joss bunched herself up on the sofa, and wrapped her arms tightly around her knees, squeezing her body into a smaller and smaller space. Something manageable. Acceptable. He had been watching her the whole time, regarding her with a few clues and cynicism and used those to tear her apart. And he was right. Skylar had used her. They had all used her, stolen that open book of her youth and blithely torn up the pages.

"Leave that out of this," Hugo said. The floorboards creaked as he paced above her in their bedroom, his footsteps a language unto themselves. Joss had seen him do it often enough, on the porch or in the station, the scuff of his boots marking time as he listened to Rhonda fume or a report from a colleague. Sometimes, they said, *I'm worried*, or *I want you to think I'm taking you seriously*. Tonight, they said something else.

I'm trapped, but I'm going to keep you waiting. Make you at least think this is my choice.

"You have to do something, Hugo."

"You want me to take her downtown?"

"Hugo, you—"

"Lock her up for a night with the drunks and the addicts? Would that satisfy you?"

"Of course not. Now, I've spoken to Pastor Joe," Rhonda said. "There's a school. She can go and wait for this thing to die down. It will show Starhook and Gifford that you're willing to do what's necessary."

The footsteps halted. Third time was the charm.

She shakes off the memory and sits up, her gaze snagging on that photo of Alice's house. They'd visited what was left of the town once, after their engagement. There was still the remnant of a Main Street, a few trinket shops and restaurants that had been far away enough from the old depot. But the harbour had been inundated, and most of the commerce moved fifty miles up a more elevated stretch of coast in Linus Bay. They'd walked along the shore, Alice pointing to the sagging cliffside where her family and the local Brahmins had spent their weekends, still commuting by plane despite the glaring evidence of the sea wall collapse. Alice had come from money, what semblance of the old upper class remained in the U.S. after the climate had re-shifted and redshifted people's fortunes, and it was always the lavish occasions that set her adrift. Those first few times they attended a function together, Joss had thought it would be Alice who'd sherpa her through the right silverware or those subtle and often contrary turns of phrase. But she was lost, reaching too quickly for the next glass of chardonnay, her anxiety primed, the old misgivings that pushed a trust fund kid into the army writhing in her gut like adders.

It's strange though, she thinks, the way Alice has arranged these photos—the house next to a random and blurry shot of an old stuffed toy, a black and white photo of her mother and father, young and glancing back at the camera as if they've been caught doing something indecorous. None of them seem to offer much comfort; they seem more talismanic, like stones marking a trail. She sets down the whiskey without drinking it and stands up, giving herself a hard stretch. A shower might help clear her head. She only hopes that Alice has the decency not to surveil her there, although maybe she doesn't really hate that thought.

Alice's bathroom unit is a little more generous than she's expected, circular with an egg-shaped compartment and a basin that would even make a passable bathtub for someone smaller. Alice would have to squeeze her body in tight to sit down, but Joss would fit nicely. The lighting is halogen and dull, but the scent of Alice's soap and the hair product with the faint hint of cassis that she pays dearly for on Earth, makes her feel like she's stepped back in time.

The water hits her like a rain of adrenalin, soothing yet stimulating. She closes her eyes, slowly rocking under the jet and takes her time, lathering up her hair twice and helping herself to Alice's razor before she steps out and faces herself through the fog of the mirror. Her hand hovers over the surface, reflecting back a ghost. She wipes her palm against the glass, revealing herself in a smear of clarity. She's still her, thinner, her face more angular, and there's a strand or two of grey in her dark hair. But there's a hollowness in her gaze she didn't have before, a mistrust in reality that now overlaps her compartmentalised matter-of-factness.

"Not today," she whispers, playfully blowing the fog back over the clear spot.

She rifles through the cabinet for a toothbrush, for paste, a bottle of mouthwash, anything to take that blunted, recycled atmosphere taste from her mouth. Right now, her tongue feels coated by a thin layer of flavourless porridge. In the cabinet, there's a row of pharmaceutical bottles lined up like soldiers, and as she takes the toothpaste from the compartment, her eyes fall on the list of ingredients. Neuropharmaceuticals—synaptic boosters, plasticity modulators, selective memory re-activators that target specific regions of the brain.

Joss is an encyclopaedia of pharma; she has to be when engaging with a subject, to know if they're running on a full deck, and if not which of the cards have been tucked in or slipped out. These are all prescription, and Alice isn't keeping them hidden, but this is a heady and complicated cocktail. Not one that would induce heavy side-effects or Alice wouldn't be allowed back into active duty, but it's a gauntlet all the same.

That scar on her temple, the way she keeps fiddling with it, her fingers tracing along the seam like she's reminding herself of something she would much rather forget. Joss files away the distributor names on the labels. It's a big jump to think this might be influencing Alice's behaviour, her coldness and paranoia. In a situation like this, she's merely being professional, but there's a difference to her, one that resides in the smaller things, the way she responded to Joss's joke about Betty. Does Alice even remember that trip they took together? Or the story she told her about the weaver princess and the shepherd?

She takes one of the canisters and opens it to meet a whiff of safflower and something intoxicatingly strong. That's when the klaxon blares— *All personnel to your stations!*—causing her to start and send those tiny, coloured capsules scattering to the floor.

"Fuck."

She's on her knees, cursing and scrambling to sweep the pills up in her hands, wiping them clumsily on a towel before dropping them one by one back into the bottle. She pushes herself up, nearly slipping on the wet tile as she kicks the towel around on the floor to give it a quick wipe down before tossing it into the decontamination chute. She hears the comms bleep in the main room and barges outside, slamming her hand on the button. Alice appears, averting her eyes quickly as Joss wriggles the rest of the way into her shirt.

"What is it?"

"I need you on the bridge. Your friends," she says, with no lack of acidity. "They've made contact."

Chapter Fifteen

Hair still wet, she slips into the rest of her clothes, the bottle rattling in her pocket as she hurries into the corridor, jostled by the crew members as they rush past her. The klaxon still blares shrilly inside that cramped cylindrical lift, and she's still mired in a spiral of indignation and hurt she knows she has no right to feel. She and Alice aren't together. They haven't been for years, and whatever issues Alice is facing now are none of her business. If the brass has given her an all-clear to serve, to head up a mission no less, Joss has no place questioning her competence.

Her character though, that's another thing entirely.

It's easy to forget the ugly side of people, to be confronted with the shock of it once reunited. Joss's memories of the old Alice and the one now, so hard and cruel, aren't slotting into place. It's like trying to trace an image, getting so focused on a narrow section that you don't realise you've shifted the paper beneath.

The lift doors open with a barely audible sibilance, wafting in the smell of ozone and a medley of coffee and breath mints, both staples in the tense but chaotic environment, and Joss has to take a minute to adjust to the sight before her, a grand bi-level structure with a raised circular platform arcing out into a wraparound viewport. The crew move about frantically, hooked into haptic feed interfaces, their faces lit up by holographic control consoles and that dead-end waning light from Ross's red dwarf. That was one of the most depressing aspects of her time on Haitch. Ross warmed the planet enough to make it habitable, but even with billions of years left, there was always the sense of an ending there, like it was drowning in its own sepia.

Alice has her back turned as she argues with Garber, her arms jutting out demonstratively as if she's explaining something to a child. Garber is motionless, his voice thick with condescension.

"I hate to have to explain this to you," he says, "but just because you've got one made in your image doesn't mean you have a front row seat to what they're thinking. They're stalling us, commander. We could be giving up our position just by talking to them."

He sags back in his seat, satisfied with this little gotcha, but Alice shakes her head. "I think we let them in on that when we intercepted that escape pod."

Garber grunts and turns away, his eyes fixing on Joss now watching them from below. "Who the hell let her in here?"

The crewman looks to Alice for help, but she waves her hand dismissively. A few more inches and she'd smack Garber in the nose. "I did. Leave it."

She locks eyes with Joss for a moment but gives no indication that she plans to clarify anything. Another guard is already at Joss's side, making sure she doesn't go anywhere until Alice gives the nod. She stops, forcing herself to take in the oxygen in slow, controlled breaths as Alice descends the stairs to the lower platform. Garber's watching her the whole way. The set of his mouth is petulant, but his eyes are all calculation.

"I appreciate your making it here so quickly," Alice says, stopping a metre or so in front of her. Her eyes are cold despite her tone. "We've got a situation."

"So, everything's normal then." Joss instantly regrets the jibe, relieved when Alice doesn't react. She gestures for Joss to follow her to main command station where Ota is furiously tapping commands into his holo interface. Alice shoots her a quick glance, a warning to brace herself before angling her head subtly in Garber's direction. *Keep him off me,* she mouths to Ota.

Ota pales but nods indiscernibly, pulling up a row of monitors as Alice sits and pats the seat beside her, handing Joss an earpiece. She slips it in, feeling that brief static shock as the virtual barrier rises around her, visible only through the faint, impermanent points of light that wink in and out in her sightline. The chatter on the bridge goes quiet, leaving only the sound of Alice's breath for company.

"Only I can hear you. You got that?" Alice's voice sounds smooth and almost metallic. "You can walk me through this, but you can't speak to them."

"Who?" Joss says, but she knows who. She spots Garber throwing his hands up, his bottom lip jutting out as he harangues Ota. Joss can read some of his words. *She's not authorised to… that's not protocol.*

"The gemel have requested a dialogue," Alice says. "I need your assistance. You've been down on Haitch. I need you to tell me if you recognise anyone."

She signals up to Ota. "Ready."

Joss isn't surprised Alice might want to use her for this, but usually, she has time to prepare, to do some research on her interlocutors. This gives her the same sensation she has whenever the safety bar locks her down on a space elevator.

Alice's fingers are warm against her wrist, tensing as their audio channels ping and the viewscreen flickers into an even layer of snow. A dormant waveform flatlines across the bottom, spiking into motion as a voice, too smooth and impersonal to be human, follows.

"Is this the Squadron Commander?"

Joss recognises it instantly.

Malachi. Vecher's gemel, his voice still rife with that obsequious grace, such a contrast to Gabrielle Vecher's smoke-throated baritone. But there's a break to it now as if something's running interference.

"This is she. I'm Commander Dray." Alice tosses a quick look behind her, a message to Garber—to anyone who might challenge her position—that she's the one in charge. "Please state your purpose."

"We will be brief," Malachi says. "Your presence in this system will make no difference to the course of action we have chosen. It will only endanger you. Any attempt to make landfall on Ross 128-H will be interpreted as hostile and dealt with swiftly and without mercy. Any attempt to approach to a distance closer than 600,000 kilometres from 128-H will be treated as a failure to comply. For the sake of your fleet, we strongly advise that you leave this system."

Alice's eyes light up at the threat, like she's been challenged by an overconfident opponent. She's about to make a retort, but Joss grabs her arm and gives a slow shake of her head. "Don't. You'll only make them dig in their heels."

Alice scowls at her but keeps her voice level as she answers back. "You seem confident we're going to listen to you."

"Do not misunderstand us, Commander Dray," Malachi says. "This is not an attempt at persuasion. It is merely a statement of our position in an unfortunate circumstance. We did not wish it. We attempted to stop it from happening, but the reality is that you are here now. If you leave, neither your squadron nor anyone on your crew will suffer any casualties. That is our condition."

"Ask him about his progenitor," Joss whispers, her hand still on Alice's wrist. "Ask him about Gabrielle Vecher."

Alice nods, not looking at her. "And your sire?"

"That word is antiquated and needlessly gendered. My progenitor is dead."

"Did you kill him?" Joss says.

"He managed that himself. It was not our choice."

"How?"

"To tell you would only provide more information about what you seek. We cannot allow that as it would increase the chances of your destruction, not to mention the others."

"Others." Alice looks at Joss, her face taut with concern. "What others?"

"Those you would inevitably destroy if you continue along this path," Malachi says.

Joss leans forward and subvocalizes into her commsbell. "Easy. This isn't a dick-swinging contest. Let them know you know they've got the power."

Alice nods and steadies her voice. "Allow me to clarify something then. So, we're not the ones who killed hundreds of innocent people on the *Tiktaalik*, nor took out God knows how many others on that colony, yet you still claim we're the threat."

"This is not an attempt to shift blame, Commander. We take full responsibility for the lives lost on the ship, although what happened down here was mostly not our doing. We were too late, and we do not feel good about that. We promise to continue to sustain the survivors for as long as we are able. But only if you comply with our terms."

Alice looks at Joss. "Do you believe this?"

Malachi cuts Joss off before she can answer.

"You have no choice, Commander Dray. If you disobey our directives, we will take action."

A loud silence as Joss and Alice share a discomfited look. Their quiet voices aren't so quiet after all. Then another joins the conversation. Raw and afraid.

Human.

"Hello? Am I talking to someone with a heartbeat up there?"

"I know that voice," Joss whispers. "Name's Eve. She worked at the Sour Tap in Mudtown. Or she used to anyway." Dread knots her gut.

She and Alice don't speak, but they're both thinking it. Wondering if the voice on the other end is real. As if in answer, the display fills with the face of a woman, looking weak and near emaciated. Her face is shadowed, lines carved into it by weeks of fear and uncertainty, but still recognizable.

"It's her," she says.

"This is Commander Dray," Alice says, sliding some gentleness into her tone. "Are you all right?"

The woman's voice is faint, and there's that same strange static they're hearing in Malachi's transmissions, like it's being distorted by something other than the signal noise. "Listen. I don't know you people, so I'll make this short. Y-you really don't want to come down here."

"We will give you some time to consider, Commander Dray," Malachi says. "But remember our conditions."

Alice leans forward, her face pinched with confusion. "Does that mean you're going to release them? Are you—"

The audio wave flattens and thins into nothingness as the screen dissolves. Alice turns to Ota.

"They're gone?"

"For now," Ota says.

She sits up, furious. "How is that that they've got people down there? We've received not one transmission from a real human voice. Not even a distress call and our scans picked up no bio forms other than indigenous flora."

"Infrared and spectroscopic analysis wouldn't detect anything unless they're on the surface," Ota says. "With their tats scraped, we'd have no chance of picking them up otherwise."

"Well, that's good then, right?" Garber says. "They've given us more than enough reason to go in."

Alice closes her eyes briefly, her jaw tightening as he strides over to the command station.

"You see, that means there are only two places they could be keeping them then." He draws up a display, all of Haitch's inhabited zone laid out in a three-dimensional blueprint of interlacing lines and symbols, numeric streams depicting on-world real-time stats and climate variables trickle across the bottom of the screen. "Mudtown only has two subsurface warehouses. That narrows things down quite a bit."

"You heard what that thing just said," Alice says. Joss squeezes her hand, and Alice starts as if she's been brushed by a ghost. She pulls her hand away and turns around to face him. "They'll kill them if we so much get within the distance of one of their moons."

"And while they're doing that," Garber says. "They leave us a window to extract what we need and move out."

Joss is so immersed in the sting of that little rejection, at her own reflexive stupidity in claiming Alice's touch like that, that it takes her moment to register his words. Garber doesn't give a shit that there are hostages down there. At worst, they're an inconvenience; at best, they're a distraction, a thing to be sacrificed for the mission's real objective.

This isn't a rescue, not really. They're not even here to stop the gemel. They're just an easy scapegoat, some PR-ready excuse to extract whatever it was that tore up Goransen Labs and gutted the mining colony.

Alice and Garber activate their commsbells as they go at it, looking very much like those spacemen in the translucent face plates on pulp magazines. Alice's motions are calm and controlled, but her eyes are so intense that even Ota blanches, directing his gaze back to the monitor. Joss doesn't. She doesn't like this Alice, but given the company, she'll root for her. After a minute, Garber takes a step back, like the air trapped within the silencing bubble is making him woozy. He gives one brief glance back at Joss and then returns to his post.

Alice takes her seat again and switching back to their private comm. Her breath is slowing, riding down the intensity of that confrontation as she shoves it behind her.

"You know, this is starting to feel like I'm on the down-low," Joss says.

Alice doesn't laugh. Instead, she leans, her fingers grasping Joss's knee. It's more to steady herself than anything else, but Joss freezes at the press of her palm, that crawl of her fingers settling over her like an old, buried intimacy. Her body tenses, her back stitching at the contact, and Alice blinks and recoils her hand.

"You recognised him?"

"Yes," Joss says. "That was Malachi, Gabrielle Vecher's gemel and that other voice was definitely Eve. Can't imitate that. Woman sounds like she mainlines a refinery stack."

Alice does smile at this. "You think he's bluffing?"

"I don't," Joss says. They gaze at each other, and again Joss feels it, that tug in her chest as if Alice has coaxed something from her unconsciously.

"Why not?"

"I'm not sure," Joss says. Not-Alice's words come back to her. *We'd have to be 100 percent sure.*

⁂

She takes the lift down to one of the observation decks below. The thought of being in Alice's quarters, her scent lingering among the other olfactory scraps of their past would feel like more manipulation.

The deck is empty now. The crew are all at their posts, waiting for news, tap-tapping at spectral keyboards and slinging data packets through the recycled atmosphere. She strides over to a bench facing the viewport and takes a seat, surprised to find herself catching her breath, her mind tunnelling back into the past, to Not-Alice's words.

Do you remember? This is key, Joss. What did she say?

A snowy expanse halved by the highway. Farmhouses flitting by, hollow and abandoned, their paint long stripped by the elements.

"You're going to take a break from here," Rhonda had told her, giving her a sharp, cold pat on the shoulder. "Just for a while."

The condescension was so thick, Joss could tell Rhonda thought she was springing it on her, that Joss hadn't had time to prepare, load her scrollscreen with books and music and tuck it in the compartment she'd carved into the heel of her boot. Skylar had taught her that trick. It was how she stashed her substances.

She sat in the back of Hugo's unmarked car, the suitcase they'd packed jammed into the space between the passenger seat and the metal partition the separated them. She asked where they were going—more than once—but Hugo didn't answer. He drove in silence, his phone buzzing, shrill and incessant, in the front seat. He seemed frightened of it and Joss watched him through the grate, wondering who the real prisoner was.

After a few minutes, he glowered and picked it up. "Carsten."

He listened in silence for a beat and then snarled out a response. "Don't you speak like that about her."

Whoever it was, they were somewhere in the middle of the conversation. An argument that had been going on for days. Joss felt a draught, saw the small crack in the window and undid her seatbelt, scooting to the other side of the backseat. She couldn't see Hugo's face from there, but his neck was taut, his body hunched forward. He was pressing his foot to the gas as if he was trying to outrace the voice on the other end.

"Yeah, well that's what Rhonda and I have decided. Joss needs to learn discipline. Get some distance from this place. From those kids."

They were getting closer to a town, the billboards and blocks of storage space growing thicker like some drab metallic forest. Joss saw a truck stalled in the snow. The driver, a smudge of skin and Gore-Tex, flagging down a hover drone for help.

"We're about to pull into Davis. Why?"

Joss pushed herself up, saw the green square of the exit sign up ahead. "Wait... *Where* are you?" he said, Hugo's tone was hushed, incredulous.

He listened for a moment and then let out a sigh and hurled the phone at the seat. Joss, having forgotten to refasten her seatbelt, tumbled toward the other side of the passenger seat as the car veered onto the shoulder of the road.

What happened next was a blur.

"Dad?" Joss said, but that word felt raw in her throat. She didn't think of him like that anymore. For how could her father, who'd betrayed her, who'd trapped her friends behind that fence, be deserving of a name so intimate? A name that inferred family, and what she had always been taught to mean trust, love and guidance.

Hugo was none of those things. He'd used her, feigning acceptance of Skylar, and well aware that Skylar was using Joss. Shouldn't that have been enough? Shouldn't she have been enough to make him stop?

It was irredeemable. And if he was irredeemable, then there must have been something inside Joss that was also broken and beyond repair. Foul and not worth knowing. He didn't love her. Rhonda certainly didn't. He might have found her amusing or funny. But for a man as ambitious as Hugo Carsten, Joss was now a showpiece turned inconvenience.

Hugo glanced back at her, his face a mask of controlled anger. "Just stay here."

It was a strange scene, that blue Saturn pulling up behind them. Joss had been on a few ride-alongs and watched from the car as Hugo or the officer he was partnered with cautiously approached a car, sometimes laughing with the driver or handing out a speeding ticket. But now it felt as if she was in some mirror universe, with Hugo sitting powerless in the front seat, waiting for a civilian to decide his fate.

Someone emerged from the passenger side of the other vehicle, her slight form bulked in a thick coat. Joss didn't recognise the car, but that figure, slightly bent from the gardening. That she knew.

Matilde.

Her truck was in the shop, she'd explain later. She'd had a neighbour drive her when she'd heard about Hugo and Rhonda's plans.

Hugo shoved the door open and stepped out, making his way toward her. Matilde saw Joss, her face wan and tear-streaked, and her expression hardened in response. Joss sank down, then pressed the lever, rolling down the window so she could hear. The snow was coming down harder now, and she dipped her head out, and saw Matilde stop in front of him.

"You really want to do this? This is your solution?"

Hugo didn't answer. He started pacing, his figure blurred by the snowflakes and the steam rising from the exhaust pipe, already a ghost. Matilde clasped his arm and forced him back around to face her.

"This isn't you."

"You don't know me," he said.

"How dare you say that? You might have changed with that woman you married, but I know the boy you once were. Remember how you grabbed the bat from the closet and smacked my husband in the gut? Oh, you took a beating for it, but you were so proud of yourself. And you should have been. You protected me from your father just like you can choose to protect her."

"I am protecting her," Hugo said, his voice thick with indignation. "She wouldn't be alive if I hadn't been there."

"There would have been a lot of people alive if that fence had stayed open," Matilde said. She stepped closer, her eyes grave. "You've already sold your soul. You've chosen your side. The side that takes, that doesn't want to leave a world for her to live in. And sure, you might still win the election and be the biggest fish in that shitty little pond of yours. But you don't have the right to make her your sacrifice."

Matilde took a step back. Hugo was shivering now, his head down. Chastened.

"It's not that hard. You know? You can have what you want, Hugo. Become the big man in town. But my god, do not do this to your child. You cannot."

"But Rhonda—" Hugo said.

"Rhonda," Matilde said, and she smiled as if relishing the thought. "Rhonda won't say a damned thing because we both know she cares more about her reputation than even her precious god. She's also very fucking terrified of me. Oh, I've made sure of that."

She smiled, and Joss felt a small spasm of warmth and relief amid the cold and the fear and the loss. Matilde moved closer. She peered up at him, her eyes warmer and more confident. "If you do this, you'll never forgive yourself. Let me help her, Hugo. Let me help you both."

And then, Joss saw the strangest thing. Her father, who'd never cried in front of her, was crumpling, his face wet, his shoulders shaking with cold and grief. Matilde wrapped her bulky arms around him as he sank into her.

"You can't help me," he said.

"That's yet to be determined," Matilde said. "These things, they have a ripple effect. One good act, like a seed or a single drop of clean water, they can change things for the better. Change a person from inside." Her gloved hand pressed gently against his back. "It's right. You know it's the right thing."

They stood there long enough for Joss to think they'd freeze in place, and then Hugo rose and turned and strode back around the car as if afraid he'd lose his momentum. Joss slapped her fingers down on the window lever, but he was already pulling the door open, and Joss looked up her cheeks burning against the snowflakes on her skin.

"Why is Avó, here?" she said, afraid that if she let on, Hugo might decide to take it all back. He let out a breath, but he didn't look at her. Instead, he stared off as if into his own future. Joss looked in that direction, too, saw the dark rotation of a storm cloud in the distance.

"Take your things," he said, and the words choked in his throat. "There's been ... there's been a change of plans."

Joss looks out at the warm spectral light of Ross-128, a sun that had once looked over a solitary intelligence that had wrought destruction from its loneliness.

One good act.

Her father had betrayed her, but he'd stopped at taking her to that school, at snuffing out her soul completely.

One act of conscience in a life that had otherwise destroyed her ability to trust.

But Al had taught her that she could trust again, that she could open herself up and build up that faith in others that had been stolen from her.

It would be hard, but she was capable. And if she was then perhaps the gemel were too.

Chapter Sixteen

When Alice returns hours later, she says nothing, acknowledging Joss with a curt nod as she barges into the kitchenette to retrieve a nutrient tube. She gnaws off the cap, sucking down the paste with mechanical expedience.

The discomfort between them has reached a whole new level, and one very different from their old style of combat. Alice wasn't the type to give the silent treatment; it was Joss who was prone to digging in her heels, and she wonders now with a sick sense of shame if that's part of what had attracted her in the first place. The women before and after Alice were less willing to tolerate the gauntlet of guessing games and silences. They simply called Joss on her games before they called it a day, but Alice who'd grown up amid pointed silences and people who rarely said what they meant, had been primed for someone like Joss. Had she sensed that somehow? Seen it as a weakness that her hurt, insecure ass could exploit?

Now the dynamic has shifted. Alice is prodding her with this quiet, letting her stew under a cloak of confidentiality and past resentments. It's like being with a parent, one who knows you've done something very bad, but who's biding their time on confronting you.

Joss isn't going to ask about the pills. That would only get the door slammed harder in her face, so she waits. Waits for Alice to drink another glass of water, for her to finish massaging her temples as she regroups. When she finally speaks, it's to ask for the bed.

"I need to get some shut-eye," she says. "Mind if I—"

"It's yours," Joss says.

Alice nods and pushes herself up in a half-shrug, waiting until Joss gets the hint and turns away. Alice has her shirt off when she says it.

"Let me talk to them."

There's a silence, the snap of cotton pulled taut as Alice pulls on some more comfortable civilian wear. She takes her time, smoothing it down over her skin.

"Who?" She already knows the answer.

Joss indulges her anyway.

"Malachi. The gemel."

Alice almost, but doesn't quite, roll her eyes. She leans sideways, one hand pressed against that cold metal wall for support. "Is this your way of making yourself feel relevant?"

"What?" Joss jerks back involuntarily. She hasn't expected a personal attack. Maybe a flat 'no' dashed with an accusation of collusion, but this jab for nostalgia's sake is a clear sign that Alice is wearing down.

"You don't negotiate with AI, Joss," Alice says. "You aren't going to tug at their affinities or their heartstrings or ferret out some old skeleton or family resentment the way you might a terrorist or a potential suicide. They don't think like we do."

"You're wrong about that." She glances up and sees Alice caught in her gaze. She's listening, even if she doesn't want to show it. "They're just a hell of a lot better at thinking in the long-term."

"I'll concede that murder is human," Alice says.

Joss exhales and slips from the alcove into a standing position. She casts a glance back at those photos. A house built by a civilisation that gave little care to the lasting consequences of their actions. "You've killed too, Dray. Not always in self-defence."

"When it would save more lives," Alice says, almost exasperated. "Is this really where you're going? Some *Monsieur Hire* justification to prop up your bots?"

"You mean *Monsieur Verdoux*?" Joss stares at her, the question trailing off as a surge of apprehension burrows into her gut. It was one of Alice's favourite films, but that had been a different Alice.

"No," Alice scoffs, her mouth twisting.

"I think you mean a different movie," Joss says, as Alice looks away, flustered.

"That hardly matters now."

"Exactly, but to my point," Joss says. "How could you be sure?"

"Of what?" She looks almost frightened by something now; deep wedges of exhaustion hollow her eyes.

"That you'd save more people."

"I'm not. It's the risk you take with the job. For fuck's sake, Joss, you know that."

Joss takes a few short leisurely steps toward her, never breaking eye contact. "And that's the difference. A gemel can do the math. A gemel would have to be hundred percent sure that any death at their hands would save more lives in the bargain, and not just in the immediate aftermath… they have no intention of releasing those hostages. That's why you need to let me talk to them. You don't need to throw yourself in there, I can get them to do it peaceably if—"

"They don't value human life, Joss." Alice's voice is loud enough to startle her and the words halt in Joss's throat for a moment. She's riled Alice up far more than she's expected to, and she steps back, forcing her tone into something more conciliatory.

"Look," Joss says. "What you've told me about Jacob Russ. What happened to Goransen Labs. If Russ did that kind of damage, then what Vecher and the others managed to construct on Haitch is far worse. The gemel destroyed the *Tiktaalik* because they knew that some of those people either had knowledge of, or access to, Vecher's plans, whether it be the proofs or the design or just a story about some markings on a cave wall. This is something so bad that a chance of adding even a single piece to the puzzle would shorten humanity's timeline exponentially." She takes in a breath, forming her words carefully. "They're frightened, Alice. Just like we're frightened because men like Vecher and Russ and your boy Garber are dead set on bringing home that little alien prize. You go down there guns blazing, the gemel will happily take the humans with them because in the long run, they'll be saving even more of us."

"She's put you up to this," Alice says. She presses her fingers to her temple again, her face a mix of pain and something like heartbreak. Joss takes her other hand in hers, a gentle gesture, loving and reminiscent, despite the wave of loss rolling through her.

"No," she says, her voice as calm as a still pond, as calm as Not-Alice when she's dealing with Joss's recalcitrance. "She simply helped me figure it out. Alice, let me try. Please."

Alice stares at their hands, at the folds and creases where their rings used to be. Joss reaches out and grazes her cheek, finger skirting the line of that scar as she marvels at the touch of real skin, the flash of vulnerability in her eyes.

"It's not for her or for me," she whispers, "It's for all of us."

Alice's lips part and Joss can see the tightness in her throat as she seems to melt at Joss's touch. "I—"

She's cut off by the piercing wail of the klaxon. Loud and sharp and so fucking well-timed Joss wants to slam her fist against the wall.

"What is it?"

Alice's face has already hardened, her chin tilted upward as she addresses the comms.

"Ota? Report!"

Ota's voice crackles over the comms. "We've got company, Commander. Incoming. We need you up here. Fast."

✳

Alice doesn't protest when Joss follows her into the corridor. She walks ahead, chattering into the silence of her commsbell. It's not until Joss crowds into the lift and they're standing less than two feet apart, that she tilts her head at her, anxiety morphing into scorn.

"What do you think you're doing?"

"Helping."

Alice looks away, her fingers drumming on her thighs as if she's sorting through her options. "We'll see about that."

She gives a sharp, short nod to Ambaus, the junior officer stationed near the door. She's ready to pounce, violently if need be, should Alice call for it. But Alice waves her off and trots up to the main command bridge before turning back to eye Joss and nod at a row of wall-mounted seats below the rise.

"If you insist, you'd better buckle up," she says. "Might not be enough time for you to get to the pods."

Joss keeps her smile in check but can't resist a mock bow before seating herself. The chairs have girthy straps and goddamned cupholders and make her feel relegated to the kiddy section, but do they do afford her a clear view of the upper level, now a flurry of light and movement. The faces of the crew at their stations form an intent circle, aglow in the emergency lights like a ghostly orchestra pit. Alice steps up behind Ota, her face sharpened by the glare. Behind them, partly obscured by a holographic console, Garber cricks his neck, noting his irritation at her presence, as he gazes at the crawl of data on his own monitor.

"What is it?" Alice is peering back and forth between the monitors and the viewport. The former showing an object fast approaching, in the latter, nothing but darkness.

"Not sure," Ota says. "Ship picked up another burst of energy coming off of 128-H, and this is some kind of prominence, like a solar flare. Only it's shifting, coming in and out like a solid object."

"Trajectory?" Alice says.

"Distance is about 140 klicks out. Initial velocity, approaching at 0.2 km/s."

"That's close. Still no visual?"

Ota's eyes never leave the monitor. He gives a half-hopeless gesture up at the main viewscreen. "What you see is what we're getting. Radar clocks it sometimes as a wave and sometimes a blip, but the gravitational perturbations keep shifting. It's hard to get a lock on scale." His fingers tremble over the touch panels, dashing through all the feeds from every angle of the ship. "We should be seeing something. This doesn't tally."

"Not a meteor or debris then?"

"No spin," Ota says. "Bounce off says it's hol—"

"Ota, any word yet from our friends who sent it?" It's Garber, he's looking at Alice like he's checking off a list and prepping to give her demerits.

"No, Sir. Inquiries made but so far, radio silence."

"Radio silence," Garber says, gesturing up at the telemetry data. "Think that might tell us something, Commander?"

Alice glances up at the screen, a frown stretching across her face. "What the hell is that?"

Joss can't make out the numbers flitting across their monitors, but she has a good view of the main observation window. Outside, there's nothing but darkness and the pinpricks of distant stars. But on a corner of the display, Joss can see a small, rounded object, the light from Ross 128 reflecting off it like a dusky penny. It shrinks from a coin into a dot as it makes its way toward an area marked by the tracking overlay. Ota starts to reply, but Alice is scanning the data, her expression darkening into a glower as the answer makes itself clear. "You sent an Exploratory EVA out there? Who—"

"I took that liberty, Commander," Garber says.

Her eyes narrow further. It's like watching a trap shut. "You had no right."

"This is a joint mission, is it not?" Garber says. "Expedience was necessary."

A voice bleats over the comms. [*Tereshkova*, this is the Little Beetle, we're moving in on the anomaly. Velocity 0.5 km/s. Time to approach eleven minutes and 38 seconds.]

"The EVA's personnel?" She looks at Ota, her eyes wild with barely contained anger.

"Sloan is piloting, Sir," Ota says. He clamps his mouth shut, helpless as Garber spins back around in his chair.

"You see, the naked eye was called for here." He gestures up to the monitor, to that thing, thrashing and twisting, flickering in and out of space, as it advances on them.

"Sloan," Alice flicks on her earpiece. "This is Commander Dray. Do you read?"

[Copy that, Commander.]

"Slow your approach!"

[Sir?]

"Slow your approach vector!"

"Disregard that, Sloan," Garber says, sounding over her.

[Sir?]

"That was an order, Sloan!" Alice says. "Slow your goddamned approach vector. Now. Just keep sending back that data."

[That's a copy, Sir.] His voice brightens noticeably. Alice watches, her stance easing as the EVA's avatar decelerates. Garber shakes his head and makes a tsking sound. "Maybe we should have moved in a little earlier, Commander? Before those spectres started lobbing rocks at us?"

She ignores him. "Ota, have you tried hailing it?"

"No response."

"And what about the gemel?"

"Same."

"Keep trying."

Ota repositions his earpiece and taps a few commands into the holographic console. "Incoming, this is the Terran Federation Frigate *Tereshkova*, do you copy?"

No answer at first. Just a long static-filled silence, perforated by a voice, muffled but recognisable—it's like someone trapped in a capsized boat, shouting from a dwindling air pocket.

"Sloan," Alice says. "Are you getting anything?"

[Copy *Tereshkova*] Sloan says. [I've got radar but still no visual. It's dark out here, Commander.]

We...ve... radar... no ... visu...

The crew looks up, disoriented by the echo. The second voice seems to be coming from different corners of the bridge, bouncing off the panels like a hall of mirrors. Ota and Alice look at each other, confusion clouding their faces. Ota punches in a few adjustments on the controls.

"Sloan?" Ota says. "Do you copy?"

[Yes, Sir. Copy that, Sir.]

Co… ir…

"Where's that coming from, Ota?"

Ota gives Alice a worried look and mutes his comm. "Spectral analysis says it isn't an echo, Sir. It's coming from the object, but it seems…" he frowns. "These readings can't be right. The point of origin, that distance … it's too far."

"Sloan? Pull back. That's an order!"

There's a thick burst of static, and the holographic interface flickers to life as an audio wave snakes across the screen.

"Incoming communique from Haitch, Sir," Ota says. "Our friends are finally responding."

"Initiate communication," Alice strides up to the viewport like she's about to address a crowd. "This is Commander Alice Dray of the Terran Federation Frigate *Tereshkova*. Respond and state your purpose."

The tone is preternaturally calm despite the urgent staccato of the voice. "To warn you. Do not engage with the object."

"I'm afraid it's engaging with us," Alice says. "What the hell is it?"

Malachi stops for a moment, choosing his words carefully. "The unfortunate side effect of human hubris, and one that can no longer be contained. For your sake, we suggest you depart. And quickly."

Garber huffs out a breath. "What did I say? This is a goddamn warning shot. We can't risk—"

"And you can't risk leaving your post, Colonel," Alice says. "Now sit down!"

Alice looks at the monitor. No object reveals itself in that inky darkness, and there's still no avatar appearing on Malachi's feed. Her hand twitches as she slides it through her hair, her body taut like a trembling wire.

She looks sick, Joss thinks. Like she's barely holding it together.

"We don't take threats."

Malachi's voice is serene and noncommittal. "This is not a threat but a warning. We are telling you as a courtesy. Do not engage."

There's something forming in the observation window, a cloud of light amassing in the darkness, about ten klicks from the EVA. It seems to coalesce out of nowhere, strands of mass churning themselves out of nothingness, manifesting into something solid.

[Commander Dray?']

…raaaay…

Sloan's voice is shaking now, a tremor in sync with the increase in static. [Commander Dray, are you seeing this?]

…seee …isss?…

The echo comes faster now. Joss has that same feeling she had as a kid during a lightning storm when the lag between the light and thunderclap grew shorter and shorter. "I think he's right," she says. She unstraps the safety harness and gets to her feet. "We've got to jump."

Ambaus is up and already on her, but Alice gestures for her to stand down. "How do you know?"

"Jesus! This is a spook tactic," Garber says. "Get her out of he—"

Alice shoots him a look that could slice through steel. She's breathing hard, her chest rising and falling as she paces. Joss can see the shimmer of sweat on her skin. "You've already disregarded my orders once, Commander Garber! Sloan disengage! Initiate retreat along your current vector."

[Copy, Sir. Commencing reverse trajectory.] But the confidence has sunk from his voice. The mass is stretching, its strands reaching out like a plant seeking sunlight, and as the EVA moves, the cloud moves with it. It's slowed its trajectory now as it furls around the EVA. [Sir, I'm moving away but it's gaining!]

…ing…ut…aining…

The EVA has no jump capacity. It's been built for short excursions and was never meant to wander far from its container. It purges its jets and darts back from the mass looking very much the way a human does when they realise they've attracted a wasp.

"Sloan, take evasive manoeuvres!" Alice says. She turns back to Joss, her eyes wild and frantic. "How do you know?"

"This is stupid," Garber says. "We've got a clean shot now!"

"No!" Joss approaches Alice and takes her by the arm, her grip is a little too hard and Alice's eyes widen. She lets go and holds her hands up in compliance. "We've got to jump."

Alice stares at Joss, her eyes are glassy and full of indecision.

"Don't believe me?" Joss says. "Bring her here! She'll tell you!" She gestures out of the viewport, to that thing amassing around the EVA. "You said it yourself. She's made of this stuff, right?"

"Goddamn it, Dray!" Garber says. "You're wasting time."

They stare at each other for a long moment; Alice is shaking her head, but not at Joss. "It's my command," she mutters. She turns away and presses a finger to her earpiece. "Release the gemel, Lieutenant Burke. Tell her she's wanted on the bridge." Then to Joss with a sneer. "Better keep her leashed."

"Give her access to the situational data at least," Joss says.

Not-Alice materialises almost instantly, solid and aglow compared to that shadow Joss saw in the containment cell. Her eyes drift over the startled, grim expressions around her before stopping on Joss. She gives her a tight smile. Her mind is already syncing with the ship, sponging up the details of their situation. "I see," she says as if listening to some long-winded caller. "Yes..." She glances back and forth between the monitors and the viewscreen; her calm already reassuring. "We've got a wanderer."

"We've got something," Alice says.

Not-Alice hovers around to face her, so fast Alice flinches the way she used to when she'd pushed Joss hard enough to blow up during a fight. "Let me put it to you this way. Think of it as an aneurysm, the energy released creating a tear in the fabric of spacetime that's bleeding into this one. All that energy is seeking sentience. Now, if this had happened in an empty pocket somewhere, one without any observers present, you'd have a non-event. But our minds, our thoughts are drawing it out. The more we interact, the more we give it purchase. If the EVA fires on that object, it will only gain a stronger foothold in this reality. Or worse."

"And if it's a probe?" Garber says. "Or a weapon? We've still got time to save him."

"Only he can do that now," Alice says. She cracks her neck and makes a 'no' motion up at the gunner. Her face is surf white and coated in sweat. She looks like she's going to vomit. "Sloan, retreat. Take evasive manoeuvres as best you can. We'll come back for you. Anders, prep to jump to fleet coordinates!"

But Garber is already in motion. He's barged up to Ota's station and is leaning over him, punching commands into the holoscreen as Ota sputters and tries to block him. Garber leans over, and shouts into the comms. "Sloan! The only way you're going to lose the thing is to fire. Fire on it. That's an order!"

[Commander...] Sloan's voice is thick with terror.

Com...

...der

[Oh, god, Commander. Are you seeing this?]

...eing... this...

They can't be certain if it's on Garber's orders or Sloan's instinctive fear response, but the EVA expels a warning flare, a gust of projectiles that seem to time themselves with the gasp expelled from Alice's throat.

Ander's voice rings through the bridge. "Gravity's on lockdown. Prepare to jump."

The klaxon blares as Alice lifts both hands to her ears, pressing hard as if she's trying to crush her own thoughts. She's shaky and sweating. Joss bounds forward through that partial weightlessness just as Alice, her feet still locked to the surface, floats back, arms winding behind her like a dancer dropped from the stage. Joss reaches up, arms slipping around her waist, trying to right her in the gloom.

"I'm sorry," Alice whispers. "I'm so sorry."

Her eyes are wide and haunted as they take in what unfolds before them in those last brief seconds before the ship jumps into the black. The projectiles connect with the mass as the light swarms around them, whirling into a funnel that burrows out to its aggressor. Joss doesn't like to project or anthropomorphise, but it seems to be feeling out the EVA, exploring and invading it the way a virus might take over each and every cell of its host, and then it starts to take shape, melding into the blocky contours and curves of the EVA itself.

[Commander!]

…*ander*…

[Commander! It's so dark.]

A howling tears through the comms, an echo of nothing and forever. The crew hunkers down as Joss presses her face to Alice's neck, one hand over her other ear as it passes through them, an endless empty spasm. It sounds like grief, Joss thinks, like something old and hollow. She holds Alice in that darkness until it passes, both adrift but neither moving.

When it passes, Joss looks up, slowly, not wanting to see. Not wanting Alice to see. Both bogey and ship have blipped from all the monitors as if they never existed at all, and then the *Tereshkova* shifts into the blue of between space.

Alice is sagging against her, barely able to hold herself up. She utters one last command to Ota before her will gives out. "Take things from here."

Ota nods. Whatever's happening with Alice, he's aware of it enough to co-conspire. Alice's fingers lock on Joss's wrist. She makes a last, flagging attempt to right herself, but Joss pulls her closer, gently this time. A strange mix of caution and tenderness rides through her at the press of Alice's body. "Easy, Dray. Not here."

"I need to…" Alice says.

"No," another voice says, "you don't."

For a brief flash, Joss fears another echo has followed them, that of this Alice, answering her back from somewhere in the void, but Al is gliding toward them across the bridge, her arms outstretched and her face fraught with worry. Joss holds out her hand, feeling that strange compulsion to touch her, but she stops herself, lowering her head to place a gentle kiss on Alice's forehead. Her skin is sick with heat.

"Let yourself rest, Dray," she whispers. "This is not on you. None of this is on you."

Chapter Seventeen

Waiting isn't Joss's strong point.

The *Tiktaalik* was a limbo, but survival had given her a mission, however hopeless. Now, she sits in the visitor's chair, her leg bouncing nervously as she watches Alice through the observation glass. No one's asked questions, maybe because she and Ambaus were the ones who brought Alice in here, and maybe because Joss doesn't look like she'd be willing to leave. She slips her hand into her pocket and clasps the pill bottle again, watching through the glass as the medical drone scans Alice's retinas with a pinprick blue light.

She needs something more to chew on, and Al has given her one more puzzle. That memory of Matilde's moths kamikazeing into the porchlight. Joss had loved those nights, the temperature lulling as they watched her cat Mika bound upward, swatting at them as they circled the glow.

"You know it's a leftover tic of evolution," Matilde told her. "They were meant to follow the moon, but then we came along with our lightbulbs, and they were forced to take a detour."

The thought made Joss sick. Like someone shouting out random digits when you were trying to remember a password, or waving their hands in your face as you read, but this was massive. Life-wrecking. You could aim your whole existence at something, something you were sure enough about to die for, and have it turn out to be meaningless. An accident of one species blithely tromping over another.

"Landon feels like that sometimes," Joss said.

Matilde laughed and settled beside her on the swing. "People talking of the moon when they're really staring into streetlamps?" She raked a hand through her hair. "It's good that you see that, Joselyn."

Joss glanced out at the plain in front of her, the low hills softened by stretches of tall grass. "Wish I didn't sometimes."

Matilde wrapped an arm around her and tugged her in close. "You've got an enviable clarity of mind. You can cut yourself on that sharpness, but if you aim it the right way, it will protect you, help you carve out a path."

She squeezed her shoulder and stood, strolling over to the screen door to open it just wide enough to reach for the switch on the other side. She nodded up at the fading glow of porchlight before flicking it off. "Moon's still out, Jocelyn. How about we help them find their way again."

She'd like to ask her about this, but Not-Alice has been taken somewhere, likely another debriefing to unpack what they've just witnessed, those eerie tendrils of light, taking on ghostly contours of the EVA. She's been shaking off the memory of that scream for hours, that last flicker as it imprinted on her retinas. The EVA—that object reflecting its form like a ghost—they were just gone, like a hole had been cut out of existence.

It's another hour before the human medic emerges. That same ruffled and bespectacled man in the debriefing. He halts in surprise as he sees her, adopting a confused but benign expression. "You're still here."

Joss stands up, barely stifling her impatience. "May I see her?"

"Go on in," he says, with a mild shrug. "Doubt she'll be good company though. She'll barely answer my questions."

Joss brushes her hair back and checks her reflection in the glass before she activates the door. It jerks open, fast enough to give her a little start. Alice is sitting up on the bed, a commsbell half shrouding her features with its muted digital interface. She notices Joss's approach and mutters something before the display chimes out exposing a face now open and surprisingly vulnerable.

"You were what? Just waiting out there?"

Joss tilts her head, feeling an unfamiliar shyness in the directness of Alice's gaze. "It beats your bed."

"Does it?" Alice's eyes roam over her face. "Thanks for that back there. You probably could have used not to see me like that."

"It's a normal reaction. I think that other thing was worse." Joss approaches her bedside. She's not sure of the extent of her welcome, so she doesn't sit. "I was tempted to throw up myself."

Alice laughs. "Garber did apparently. All over Ota." Her eyes go distant, and she gives a faint, angry crick of her head. "Serves him right."

"Surprise you haven't had him thrown out the airlock."

"Oh, I'd like to. Unfortunately, the brass thinks his background in Systems Intelligence makes him essential to this mission."

"He certainly thinks so," Joss says. She lowers her gaze and shifts on her feet. "So how are you dealing with that?"

Alice intertwines her fingers and gives her arms a leisurely stretch. "I didn't have to do much. Garber did it for me. I might have fainted like a lady on the bridge, but he got a boy needlessly killed. He's been reassigned until further notice. I've had him transferred to the *Eberhardt*. Keep him out of our hair."

"Good." She nods to the monitor. "I meant with that."

Alice is looking at the bottle in Joss's hand, her face loose with the weary fade of acceptance. "Should have known not to leave you alone in my quarters," she says. "I guess you'd better sit down then."

Apprehension coils through Joss's insides. It's rarely good when people make that request. She summons a visitor's chair and lowers herself into it.

"It's serious?"

The question drops, spiralling out into the quiet around them and for a long moment, the only answer is the chirrup of the monitors. Joss keeps her eyes on the tracking lights on the floor, afraid she'll see the answer in Alice's expression and feeling very much the coward as she waits. There's a rustling sound as Alice shifts on the bed, a soft intake of breath, and then her hand covers Joss's own.

"I'm not dying if that's what you're worried about."

Joss lets herself breathe again because for a minute there, she was terrified. She closes her eyes and forces down the vertigo, but when she opens them, Alice isn't smiling.

"But..." She slows her delivery as if she's trying to make it easier as she squares Joss in her gaze.

But.

"A part of me has."

"What..." She huffs out a laugh, feeble and devoid of breath. "What does that mean?"

Alice gives a wan smile in response as if she's not sure she should have divulged this much. Then she draws up against her pillow, her fingers tightening around Joss's hand. "After I reenlisted, there was another incident on Mars. A cartel was trafficking in refugees from Tranquility, promising safe passage and then selling them off to work in those moving isotope extraction facilities they've got popping up all over the surface like molehills. I led a raid in to shut one of them down. I got hit."

She looks at Joss and swallows, running a finger along the scar on her temple. Joss can feel herself convulse a little, an echo of the pain that inflicted that wound. She leans forward and Alice draws back, shaking her head slowly. "It's okay…" she says. Almost embarrassed. "They got to me fast. Quick intake, surgery, nothing but a little damage." She sees Joss's expression and takes in a breath. "Cognitive function, retention, encoding. All of that's fine. There are just gaps in my past."

Alice smiles, giving Joss a curt, encouraging nod like she's trying to will the bravery back into her, but Joss can feel herself shaking. The light, the muted glow from the machinery seems to warp and intensify, as if lensed by the gravity of what Alice has told her.

That talk about the bamboo plant, one half of their memories together gone upon impact, and with the revelation comes the grotesque relief that perhaps Alice's lapses weren't just a matter of forgetting her and moving on.

Alice's fingers ease, and she traces her thumb along the back of Joss's hand as if following an old throughline. "I'm making it sound worse than it was. I was lucky. The timing couldn't have been better. There was a new treatment, a nanite device that repairs the damage to the tissue and restores the neural connections." She smiles. "It even provides an illusion of continuity."

"How much…" She's afraid to ask. "How much did you lose?"

Alice takes her hand away, gripping the arm of her chair as if to bolster herself. "It's difficult to say. I feel it most when I'm talking to people who've known me longer, it's like I'm standing in front of a chasm and I can't see it, but they can. They're looking over my shoulder afraid I'm going to fall in. But I worked hard, passed all the neurological exams, and poured myself in upgrading my skills." She touches her temple. "That part's still here. Better even." She gives a little shrug and looks away, her expression blithe and resigned. "The doctors say it will get better over time, that the nanites will integrate themselves fully into my system. But I have headaches, and sometimes my dreams get a little"
—her brow furrows as she snags on the description— "weird."

"Why are you out here, Alice?" Joss says, not prepared for the response.

"I'm fit for duty," Alice says, her tone sharpening. She sees Joss flinch and softens, her hand easing on hers. "I've seen a lot of specialists about this, and you know what they tell me? The only way to get over the loss of memory is to make new ones, and you can't do that well unless you face the precariousness of things. The fear and loss and the danger. Take on the hard things and you'll make memories that stick." She smiles, some sadness tucked into that wry expression. "And you know me. Can't think of a better way to do it than blowing up cartel smugglers and dropshipping onto asteroids."

Joss chuckles, prodding Alice's smile into a grin, and they look at each other for a long moment, but not with their old connection. This is the frankest Alice has been since their reunion, but with it comes a distance. A no-fault acknowledgment of their estrangement.

"Well," Alice says. She lets go of Joss's hand and props herself up further, as the commsbell flickers with an incoming feed. "Ota. There's never really any rest."

"Sure," Joss says. "I uh … I suppose I should let you go."

Alice doesn't object, but as Joss pushes herself up, Alice grabs her hand again. Joss starts at the touch, the sudden pull against her body.

"That's why," she says, and for a moment, Joss stares down at their hands, wondering if Alice is asking for a second chance. "I'm going to give you the floor."

"Are your people going to like that?"

"Garber's not an issue anymore, so no," Alice says. "And if what happened to Sloan means anything, it's that we don't know what we're dealing with. But you've got humans down to a science, and you're more experienced with…" she pauses. "The gemel. It's worth it from that standpoint alone."

"Alright." Joss says, still in disbelief that Alice has agreed to this, but despite the chasm between them, it feels like a semblance of their old partnership. Professionally at least. "When?"

"I need to talk to Ota," Alice says. "Convene the team. See if Garber's cooled his britches down enough so that he won't go crying via pulse to the brass. But if what happened to the EVA is any indication, then whatever they let loose on Haitch is growing and becoming less stable. We need to throw everything we have at the wall."

"Then I'll need help," Joss says, letting some of that old tenacity slide into her tone. "From someone who understands them better than I do."

Alice looks at her, almost surprised by the demand. "I've already cleared her release. Conditionally. She's blocked from interacting with any and all of the ships operating systems or communications. No access to our databanks unless given express permission. From me."

"I think she would find that fair," Joss says.

Alice nods, curtly. "Good. Then go back to my quarters and rest. I'll call you to the bridge when we're ready."

Alice activates the commsbell before Joss can even nod in assent. She makes her way back into the waiting room and out into the corridor, her resolve waning with the grief that laps over her with every step. So many pieces of Alice's life are gone now, from a childhood already rent to pieces to her parents, much of the time they've spent together.

What you remembered was so rarely in your control. Even if you were meticulous about it, kept a diary, stored old imagery and olfactory cues in well-guarded data vaults, you never really got to choose what you kept and what you lost.

She stops at a bend in the corridor and leans against the wall, letting herself weep from exhaustion and loss, for stupid choices and her own stubborn resolve, less a virtue than a club she's used to beat herself into the same self-destructive patterns. She presses her hands to her face, fists clenched, aware suddenly of a presence, of the soft smear of light through her closed lids, the radiance dancing between her fingers as she opens them.

Not-Alice stands before her, a ghost aglow in the corridor.

"I'm sorry," she says, her expression shifting between dazed embarrassment and concern. "They let me out, and I'm afraid I didn't have anywhere to go but to you. Are you all right?"

Joss blinks at her, feeling that hole begin to fill again. She brushes back her hair, her face still wet with tears. "You're here."

Not-Alice smiles, her eyes replete with a warmth Joss has only let herself dream about. "I am. I'm here."

Chapter Eighteen

Joss Carsten has experienced almost every kind of negotiation scenario. She's stood on the parapets of bridges and rooftops with rivers and bright streams of traffic snaking far below. She's been within touching distance of an interlocutor and far enough away to cause a thirty-minute time delay. But other than the training mods at the academy, she has never had to negotiate with a sentient A.I.—unless you count Not-Alice, who's bested her every time.

Now she sits on the bridge surrounded by holographic flowcharts, depicting risks and mitigation strategies and potential escalation paths—there aren't many. The gemel have been very clear about their intentions. The plasteel viewport spans out around the bridge, providing a view of the stars with Haitch in the lower distance. Holo monitors flicker in every corner of her sightline, alive with every transmission hiccup or gravitational wobble.

Not-Alice hovers at the edge of Joss's vision as she collates the incoming data, the rhythm of her simulated breath offering a strange if not human kind of comfort. Not-Alice is herself separated, but also a separate part of herself—that other better self she has become, and it scares her to think of life without her. Those memories, the way they pushed her to this.

One good thing. Like a seed or a drop of clean water.

She wants to talk to Al about these things, but they haven't had enough time together, and in much of it, human Alice has been there, asking questions and strategising. Al and Alice have dropped into a dynamic, not quite friendly but more than reminiscent of what she shared with Alice early in their relationship. There's a tension in their start-stop transactions, only it's Alice, battling with issues of military clearance, who's doing the withholding this time around. It's jarring, like watching their past together play out on a funhouse mirror.

"Remember, Carsten." Alice gestures around to the hovering stream of displays, each a thicket of potentialities. "Everything you've got up there, what takes you hours and months of research, they can access it at a fraction of a nanosecond."

"You're a real comfort, Dray. Thanks."

"I do try." She winks at Al, who hovers over to her, running a hand over the back of her neck in a mock attempt to push down a tag. Joss reaches up and feels nothing.

"And that time delay might be an advantage when it comes to humans," Al says, "but not in this case. You stall and all you're doing is giving them a few more seconds to calculate."

"Sure, boss." She looks at them with bemused suspicion and finds they're too busy sharing a look with each other to notice.

There's not much of a delay to begin with, a little over a second with the *Tereshkova* maintaining the gemels' stipulated distance. A whopping 1.5 seconds in which they might easily skim all of Shakespeare, solve the Riemann hypothesis, and disembowel whatever slow-footed negotiation strategy or rapport cue Joss can lob at them.

Ota, his face stained by the blue light of consoles, darts his fingers over the keys as the rest of the crew hustle back to their stations. Joss ventures a glance at Al, trying in that last instant to ignore the tick down of the clock and the hushed last-minute chatter of the crew filtering through the comms, and worrying somehow that she isn't going to reciprocate. But as the chatter dies and the signal for the incoming message flashes on across the monitors, Al raises her eyes and sends Joss a look so encouraging it seems borne of a subroutine of longing and promise.

"Signal locked and encrypted, Commander," Ota says. "We're on."

A hush settles over the bridge as that audio wave flickers across the monitors, a snaking line giving off an illusion of continuity. Joss pushes herself up from her seat, the cameras lurching in response to her movements. She can't see the gemel, but Alice has opted to let the gemel see her in the hope her humanity might inspire trust, or at the very least, overconfidence.

She takes in a breath and speaks. "This is Agent Carsten. Ready to establish communication protocol. Can you hear me?"

Malachi's voice, when it filters through, is flatter this time, an almost organic distortion as if he's speaking through snow. "So, it's Commander Dray this time."

"Nope." Her eyes follow the rhythmic oscillations of the wave. Like Al, Malachi's voice is cadenced with simulated breathing, but there's an odd strain to it, like he's wheezing through static. "But I assume you remember me."

There's barely a beat before he slings out his reply. "Carsten, Joselyn Dorotiea. Survivor of the *Tiktaalik*.

"Only survivor," Joss says. This time, she has to wait for a reaction.

"We apologise for causing what must have been a highly traumatic experience," he says, with no lack of sincerity. "We had hoped to make the *Tiktaalik*'s destruction painless for all on board."

"No need," Joss says. She rubs the back of her neck. "Too bad you can't apologize to the others."

Not so much as a pause. "Why am I speaking to you?"

"Because I requested it," Joss says. "Commander Dray also thought it was a good idea."

"I understand her reasoning. You have been on Haitch and are familiar with both me and my progenitor, which gives you what you colloquially refer to as an 'in.' In addition, you are a recognised negotiator. A wise strategy considering Commander Dray's personal limitations."

Joss can see Alice stiffen at the edge of her vision. She shakes her head. "We've all got them, so let's not go there, shall we? I'm here to tell you that we've agreed to your terms. We're willing to leave the system, with—"

"We're not releasing the hostages."

Joss catches herself before she shows her surprise. In a normal interaction, she would have taken her time with her demands, let her interlocutor try to anticipate her words as they rolled out. It bought time, throwing them off when she tossed a rhetorical curveball. By the time she establishes contact, her human subjects are usually exhausted and strung out, their physical limitations providing those added chinks in their armour. Talking to Malachi, however, is like conversing with an ice maker, the words flying out of him faster than the West Antarctic sheet. She glances over at Not-Alice who shrugs as if to say 'see?'

"We had hoped that this audience you requested was merely a formality," Malachi says.

"You're going to kill them then?" Joss says, not quite fast enough to cut him off.

"You undermine our motives, Agent Carsten," Malachi says. "We are not killers by nature. I did not inherit my progenitor's sociopathic traits, or at least the protocols within me have not allowed them to develop. Our decision to take the lives of others was and is entirely by necessity. And for the record, we have no intention of killing these people unless you fail to comply with our demands."

Joss folds her hands together, allowing herself the luxury of a protracted exhalation. "That's only because you don't have to."

There's a lull, infinitesimal, but one Joss might feel proud of if not for the circumstances.

"Do explain."

"You're on a countdown," Joss says. "One that's ticking down faster every second. That thing Vecher and his cronies made tore a hole in the fabric of the universe or spacetime or whatever the hell you want to call it, and it's growing, becoming less stable by the hour. Am I warm?"

"As stated before, we won't—"

"Nah, nah, humour me here. You see, what you're betting on is that you won't have to kill them because it's only a matter of time before the thing collapses in on itself."

"We'll neither confirm nor negate," Malachi says. "For your sake as well as ours."

"And." Joss draws in a breath, lacing her tone with quiet certainty. "You're not letting those people go is confirmation enough."

"You baffle me, Agent Carsten," Malachi says, his voice bordering on petulance. "But do go on."

Joss stretches her neck from side to side, like she can't be bothered. Something flashes in her peripheral vision as Al subvocalises over the feed.

[Remember, you can't outthink him. He's got every contingency worked out to needlepoint exactitude. Approach him like a human. Like you'd approach yourself.]

Joss smiles inwardly. *[Are you saying I surprise you, Al?]*

[Just about every day.]

She pushes down the warmth rising inside her and speaks, catching that low vibrato in her voice that comes with a rush of adrenaline and focus. "Because you're right," she says. "About everything. What Vecher built down there is a massive, existential threat and humans are too stupid and short-sighted to grasp it. Not hard to figure out. We made you after all. Even worse, it's unstable. Our own readings can tell us that, but it's still just a small threat, a few tears in reality, trying to sync with our own, and you've calculated that there isn't much time. You're going to wait it out, take these people down with the ship."

"Very astute," Malachi says.

Joss nods toward the image of Haitch on the monitor. "Free them, allow these folks to live and go Earthside, and someone—some ambitious colleague of Russ, a Federation weapons lab—will be gathering up scraps of what they know, putting the pieces together from their memories. Doesn't matter if these people weren't involved. Any piece of the puzzle at all will add to the whole and bring humanity one step closer to midnight. But if they die, you can stop this from happening or at least slow its progression."

"Our decision was not made lightly, Agent Carsten," Malachi says. "It was the end of a labyrinth of long-term ramifications, all of them pointing to the inevitable."

"Inevitable," Joss says. She nods thoughtfully and lifts her chin. "You know what's even more inevitable? Human stupidity and on the brighter side, determination. I can assure you that, give it ten years, a hundred maybe? Someone will complete the puzzle those poor suckers discovered in those caves and figure out how to rebuild that thing. If you're 100% certain, then letting these people die won't prevent it from happening. The only thing you can do to stop us is to persuade us that we shouldn't."

"No one convinced you to stop wrecking your planet," Malachi says, a retort so cutting that Joss can't quite stifle a laugh.

"Ah," Joss says, "but they did slow us down. Just like you're trying to do. And we're still here. Give us that at least. Survival is a slow crawl, and as you've surmised, even the smallest pieces matter. But why would we listen to you when you've failed to show us the slightest scrap of mercy?"

She crooks her neck again, feels the raw ache in her muscles as her eyes dart up to see Human Alice staring down at her from her perch. The set of her mouth is tense, but there's a thrill stirring behind her eyes, a cheer Joss hasn't seen on that face since long before the divorce. She pulls her gaze away and settles into herself once more. "You do this," she says, "and any trust humanity has placed in the gemel will be dead. But if you show a little of the compassion we give ourselves far too much credit for, then when the time comes, maybe some of us—maybe even enough of us—will understand your reasons for having done what you've done. And maybe then we'll listen to your warning."

Joss says nothing more, just waits, her eyes locked with Alice's as the hush on the bridge stretches for what feels like hours. Static hisses over the comms, and then an odd breathy noise again, like an awkward clearing of the throat.

She catches the words, Al's faint subvocalisation in the back of her mind.

[I can't subvocalize for certain, but I think … you've got this.]

And Joss feels it, knows from this, that somehow, she's reached into that silence, the gap of time and reaction, and that vast mind hundreds of thousands of kilometres away to unlock a very human response.

"You have given us much to consider," Malachi says. "Although consideration is really a human trait requiring a slowness of thought we don't require."

Joss glances up to see a collective sag of relief among the crew. Hands clamp one by one over mouths as they exchange a flurry of glances.

"We must discuss amongst ourselves how to proceed before we convene with Commander Dray, but there is much to be done, and quickly. And many conditions you must adhere to if you are to extract the hostages safely."

"Understood," Joss says, letting a hint of a smile get away from her. "Thank you."

There's an audible sigh throughout the bridge as the wave on the screen flattens and dissipates. Alice draws up and hops off the raised platform and hurries toward Joss with such brightness in her eyes that Joss is ready to confuse her for her counterpart. She skids to a halt in front of her, looking dazed as if she's still taking it all in. And then, in a single resolute lunge, she throws her arms around her.

"You've done it … asshole."

"Thanks?" Joss says, startled as Alice's hands find her face and she suddenly and inexplicably leans in to kiss her. Joss freezes for an instant, her heart stuttering, but then Alice's arms slip around hers and the bridge erupts into applause and the kind of obnoxious whoops and cheers reserved for hazing parties. She pulls back but only a little, her weight still resting against her. She's weak and unsteady, and maybe leaning a little more heavily than if this kiss was just an ebullient formality, but for the first time in a very long time, it feels like hope. Joss rests her chin into Alice's shoulder, her gaze falling on Al now watching them from across the bridge, a mix of wistfulness and complexity crossing her expression.

※

Hours later, Joss is watching them both from the doorway. Alice is lying in bed with that Pendleton tucked up around her shoulders, her eyes covered with a damp cloth as she rests after hashing out the extraction plan. Al sits beside her, a soul hovering outside its body. "That was at Crystal Cove," she says. "We … or you took us back there to see your hometown."

"When?" Alice is exhausted, her voice trailing off on the cusp of sleep.

"You and Joss cut out early after your panel and went to the beach. You wanted her to see that part of the coastline before it washed away completely."

Alice lifts her head slightly, piqued by the memory. "And did we? Did we go?"

Al nods but says nothing, deliberating as Joss walks over to join them. She lowers herself to perch on the edge of the bed. "We did in fact. There wasn't much of a cove left but you showed me your old lookout."

The memory is a little hazy. Joss has flashes of sun on her shoulders, of the sudden turn to a cold mid-afternoon, when not wanting to walk back to their hotel, they'd bought a pair of ugly sweatshirts in a gift shop. Alice smiles at this but her jaw sets as if she's trying to find purchase in the memory. "I do remember being a kid there. The lookout. But not that day."

"Maybe…" Al lifts her hand and turns to Joss, her eyes asking a question. "I can help with that."

Joss nods and closes her own eyes as the scent of the ocean, of driftwood and kelp beds wafts around them.

"Oh my god, we did," Alice whispers. "There was a … your sweatshirt had that bear on it. It was awful." She laughs as if she's just been shown it for the first time.

She shifts in bed, one hand reaching up now, trying to tug the cloth away from her eyes.

"Hey," Joss says. "Easy. We've got a big day tomorrow." She takes her hand and gently prises her fingers from the cloth. Alice's close around her own.

It's a jolt this time, the sensation of warmth and flesh combined with those scent memories. Her eyes meet Al's. "It was a good day, wasn't it, Dray?"

"It was," Alice says, a little more certainly. Joss feels her chest tighten as she looks down at their hands.

"Thank you," she whispers. She leans forward into Al's light and the three of them sit with the memory, their experiences coinciding in that instant before the wave crests and leaves them to their loneliness.

Chapter Nineteen

The cockpit of the dropship *Florenz* is a cramped three-seater with a retractable canopy and hands-on control yokes. A rusty analog throwback Joss finds reassuringly solid despite her queasiness. Ascents and landings turn her green, whether by ship or space elevator, so she sits rigidly in the jumpseat, a borrowed oversized helmet sliding halfway off her head as she keeps down the bad coffee and somen noodles she's eaten for breakfast.

Alice sits in the co-pilot's seat next to Anders, both of them armoured up like sea turtles. Joss too is trussed up in several layers of flak and an oxygenator, a get-up that had been heavy enough on the *Tereshkova*. The lighter gravity on the *Florenz* offers only a modicum of relief.

Malachi was clear. One dropship, no more than seven in the crew. That was fine with Alice, who was already worried about how the *Florenz* would take off with seventeen extra bodies aboard. Alice ordered a strip down of the ship, ditching the consumables and non-critical backup systems, plus a few of the secondary fuel tanks. Minus the three requisite escape pods, all other non-essentials have been left behind in the *Tereshkova*'s cargo bay. She also whittled Malachi's number to five. In addition to Anders, one of the best fighter pilots in the Federation, she's chosen two hyper fit grunts eager to make themselves useful. Frannie and Kessler sit strapped against the arcing walls of the *Florenz*' cargo bay, chatting and occasionally glancing up at Not-Alice who hovers across from them as she collates incoming data.

She pushes her helmet up and the viewport becomes visible once more, Alice's tense profile a secondary source of information as she and Anders chat and monitor their progress toward Haitch, now an ochre smear looming like a half-melted candy left in someone's pocket.

Alice flicks a few switches on the panel above her and unbuckles herself from her seat. She rises and turns, shooting Joss an uneasy smile as she clambers toward her through the narrow cockpit.

"You know you were right!" Alice shouts over at her.

"What?"

She gives a bemused once over to Joss's oversized military fatigues, the loose trousers and the sleeves lapping over her fingers like French cuffs, then taps the side of her head, directing her to switch to a private channel.

"About *Monsieur Hire*." Alice's voice is light and casual, like they've all just decided to take a road trip to the beach. She clasps an overhead grab rail and swings into the empty jumpseat beside Joss.

"You mean *Monsieur Verdoux*," Joss says. Then more hopefully. "You remembered?"

"Nah," Alice says, keeping her eyes forward. "I had to look it up." She winces a little. "It is funny though. When I did, some part of me connected the reference with the title. I just couldn't seem to pull up the memory."

"It's an easy one to forget," Joss says, trying to sound unconcerned. "But it had a point. Or you did anyway." After a pause. "If we get back, maybe we can watch it together. You liked it. A lot. I uh, think I might still have your copy."

Alice doesn't answer, but Joss's helmet starts to sag again, and she reaches over, gently stopping its progress. Joss watches her fingers work as she undoes the straps, her thumbs grazing against her cheek as she lifts its weight from her head.

"Sure this is safe?" she half-teases, but that's when she realises that Alice hasn't clambered over here to talk strategy. She's here because this might very likely be the last moment of privacy they have, period.

"Your hair," she says. "Always a mess." She brushes a lock from her eyes, and Joss revels in the pleasant tingle, not quite sure how to read this. That kiss on the bridge was less a rekindling of their relationship than a comradely 'well done,' but she's still hard-wired to read those signals the wrong way, and her calm flees at the contact, groping about for something to diffuse the tension.

"Wish it were that easy," Alice says. "You know if I could just rewatch my memories like some old black and white."

"Maybe Al could help you," Joss says. They both pause, her words shunting them back into last night.

"Does it have to matter?" Alice says. She pats her temple. "I mean, I'm still here. There's still plenty of space in here for new memories and experiences. It's enough."

Enough, Joss thinks. "Yeah."

After all that time and distance and loss. When Alice looks back at her, there's a finality to it, like the last line on a page or the edge of the water on a shoreline. It's the farthest thing from peace and yet the closest thing to it, and Joss finds herself reaching over to take her hand.

"I'm glad you're still here, Dray," she says.

They're both quiet as they watch the cratered and rocky terrain of Haitch roll up in the observation window, obscured by a wet haze of mud and fog. Alice nods back through the open door of the cockpit at Not-Alice, her eyes closed, her legs crossed, and her hands folded as she keeps vigil over the onboard system. Kessler and Frannie sit across from her, watching her in fascination.

"Think your gemel can hear us being nice to each other?" Alice asks.

"Think she'd believe it if she did?" Joss chuckles then, but her laughter is smothered by the saw-like whine of the air pressure as the *Florenz* nudges into atmo, the shake and groan of turbulence while the ship wrestles with unfamiliar currents. She leans as far forward as her safety harness will allow her, gauging the roil in her stomach and marvelling at how Alice takes it like she's just getting blood drawn in a doctor's office. She's up, manoeuvring through the cockpit like an experienced traceuse, and slipping so quickly back into hardass it's like watching a kernel blacken in a flame.

Haitch was never meant for permanent habitation. It was warm enough, the atmosphere breathable, but the soil is so infused with heavy metals and alkaline it could never develop a self-sustaining food supply. Joss had heard, long before she'd set down here, that the only things that grew on Haitch were weeds and Haxen bank balances.

She fights down the nausea and keeps her eyes on the viewport ahead of her. From this height, nothing about Mudtown looks different. She can make out the compact dwellings carved into the cliffsides, all connected by a tangle of covered walkways to keep out the constant barrage of rain that blankets the planet's surface. Storage Silos and gantry cranes interlarded with communication towers that jut up like poppies amid the mud-swept landscape. But there are no lights winking up from the hover ferries that cart people around when the rain is soup thick. There's nothing moving below, and the fiery outflush from the refinery stacks is now a cold phosphorescence highlighting the emptiness.

The *Florenz* banks into a wobbly incline, prompting a staggered yelp from the crew, as it touches down in the wind-battered quad. It drops level, like an overloaded wheelbarrow, and they all go silent, listening to the scatter of groans and creaks as the ship settles itself in the mud. Frannie and Kessler are up before the engines quiet, checking their instruments and adjusting their breathing apparatuses—an added precaution—as the ramp lowers and their ears are met by Haitch's relentless thrum of rain.

They run a quick check of atmospherics before Alice directs Not-Alice down the ramp first, followed by Frannie and Kessler, who despite layers of bulk, move like dancers, rifles steady, the lights on their helmets carving saw-toothed paths across the rain-soaked pavement. Alice goes next, walking ahead of Joss like her very own secret service detail.

"Look any different?" she says to both of them.

Al looks out into the distance, her expression pensive. "Nothing about the landscape or the organisation," she says. "Nor the structures. The layout is all the same, but the energy from the rift is creating an anomalic flux.

Joss pushes up her helmet and adjusts her visor optics, drawing the landscape into a clear, tight focus. On first sight, Tarquin Square, with its lumpy memorial to Haitch's co-discoverers and bordered by an octagon of mouldering capsule hotels and covered arcades, just seems empty. Like those rare nights before the pay transfers come through when The Sour Tap isn't abuzz with folks flashing their newly loaded tats for booze and sundry gratifications.

"The way the light diffracts and reflects is distorted." Al passes a hand over her eyes. "There's a visual overlap, the images are shifting through different potentialities, maybe different times. But other than the layout plans and other information from the *Tereshkova*, I don't know. I ... I'm..." she looks at Joss. "I'm only familiar with your experience here."

Joss rolls her shoulders, trying to lessen the weight of her armour as she adjusts to Haitch's slightly heavier gravity. That's when she notices the strange tint to the air, a glistening fog that can't be solely blamed on the rain. There's something spectral to it, less liquid than pixelated static, reminding her of the way old holotech revealed its artifice when you looked at it from the wrong angle.

"Something's off," she confirms, but Alice is turned away now and speaking into the comms as she gestures for Frannie and Kessler to fan out and check the alleys between the buildings. Malachi and friends said they would be arriving from the North end of the Square.

"Ota?" Alice says. "Any word from our hosts?"

Joss doesn't hear the answer, but Alice's deepening scowl provides enough of one. She twists around to face her, still listening intently, and gives a brisk nod toward the ramp.

"Stay near the ship. Both of you. I'll holler when I see company."

She bolts into the haze after Frannie, the downpour rattling against the armour she wears as lightly as folded paper.

"You all right?" Not-Alice stands to one side of the ramp, the light from the hatch cutting through her figure and casting her aura in an orangish glow.

"As good as I can be," Joss says. She pulls the filter from her face and takes in a long gulp of Haitch's clammy air. The masks are just a precaution and she's had about enough of having her senses twice removed.

She sees what used to be a third-party pay-out centre for some of Haitch's local gambling establishments. Weekends and bonus days would see lines crawling around the block. People with their rain hoods pulled low, clinging to winnings of smokes and cheap booze to be traded in for tatcredits. Now, the place is a shell of itself, devoid of the neon adverts for bot-masseuses and investments in Ponzi mineral schemes meant to hide its true purpose. It seems to be dissolving, growing translucent and insubstantial in the thick patter of the rain.

"Never thought I'd find myself down on this shithole again," Joss says.

"We go in circles," Al says.

It's less a response than a separate observation. Her face is drawn and contemplative, and Joss is suddenly aware of an aloneness she hasn't felt before in her presence. She huffs out a nervous laugh. "So, what do you think, Al? Is Haitch as bad as I remembered it?"

Not-Alice smiles in response, but her eyes are still distant. "On the surface, at least. I can definitely see why leaving became such a distraction for you."

She knows she shouldn't go here, that they both should be staying alert, scanning the horizon in search of gemels or some ghostly untethered energy or hell, a zombified Haxen exec roaming the ruins, but the question still drops from her lips.

"How did you know?"

"Know?" Al recoils faintly, turning toward her.

"Those memories," Joss says. "The ones of my father. How did you know it would cue up the right solution?"

She lowers her gaze for a moment. She looks frightened, like her thoughts have stoppered inside her. "I didn't. When they locked me up, certain recollections of yours kept coming at me, pieces of conversation, questions, experiences you had, but I didn't know why. I thought it was my own emotional response to being trapped, some side effect of separation anxiety." She raises a hand to her face, holding it there as if she can touch her own skin. The rain glistens as it falls through her fingers.

"I'm still trying to figure out the moths," Joss tenders, hoping some humour will dispel the distress creeping over Al's face. "That one's still—"

"Joss?"

"Yes."

"I'm still exper—I've been getting a lot of those flashes." She's still staring at her hands. "It's like I need to tell you something, but it won't come out the right way, and I'm not sure what it is."

She fixes Joss in her gaze, her face tight with heaviness that pulls at Joss's centre. "I-I feel like we're floating away from each other, you know? Like I'm getting farther away from you and then someday you'll—"

"Hey," Joss says. She reaches out, a reflex, but lets her hand hover there. A dim solace to the space between them. "I'm not going anywhere. This is just … gemel growing pains. The longer you're here, the more you individuate. It's natural."

It's only human.

"You're still you. You're more you, in fact. That's not going to change … even if we see each other differently."

She leans in, closing the distance to that luminous outline of a body and realises she's stepped into a shadow.

It's blurry and less distinct, an effect of the haze brought on by the incessant rain, but she's not hallucinating. Al sees it too, a rippling, elongation split from Joss's own. She takes a halting step back, and Joss can almost feel the ghost of her retreating, feeling out its limits in the flow and drag of the wind.

"Differently…" Al says, the words trailing off, but with those four syllables, the mist in the air seems to shift, as if moved by the force of an exhalation. "I'm different."

"No," Joss steps forward, her heart hammering. "You're—"

Alice's voice cuts through the comms. "Fall in everybody! Company's here!"

Joss squints through the murk to see Alice, flanked by Frannie and Kessler. Behind them is an uneven line of figures, some of them trudging low to the ground, while three others glide as smoothly as if they were bound to tracks.

Malachi hovers in between two of his kind, both women. Joss recognises one of them, or the features of her progenitor at least. Some distributor of cheap terraforming equipment, the kind that broke or got jammed after one or two uses. The other one, she's never seen before, but this doesn't surprise her. The wealthy like to keep themselves sequestered from the little people and Haitch is no exception. They're still aglow despite the gloom, carrying themselves with that ethereal grace of Not-Alice, but Joss detects a fluctuation in the way the light bends around them, an uneven, encroaching solidity she's encountered in the landscape. Like they're coming in and out of focus.

They walk before the rag-tag group of human survivors. The sixteen miners who'd been lucky enough to be underground when Vecher's device went up and the energy tore through the colony—and Eve, who's just goddamned lucky.

Malachi doesn't speak at first. His eyes roam the faces of the crew until they land on Joss. He extends her a clipped nod, far less the unctuous servant she met in Vecher's office, and shifts his focus to Not-Alice. She's rigid, staring at her shadow like it's a hole opening up beneath her.

"I wouldn't worry about that," he says. He hovers up to her, holding out his hand in demonstration. The rain goes through it, but there's a skip to the patter. A few errant droplets spatter off his palm into the gloom. "It's a gradual change. It will let up when you gain enough distance from the rift. Unless, of course, the rift swallows you first."

She glances up at him, her eyes wide and attentive, and he chuckles. "Poor thing. Still unsullied."

"This everyone?" Alice says, steeling the irritation from her voice. She nods over to the hostages. "We've not much time."

"Everyone among the living," Malachi says, his eyes lifting toward the horizon.

Alice gestures for Frannie and Kessler to do a headcount.

"The rift is becoming more unstable," Malachi says, "and your presence will only exacerbate things if it becomes entangled on the right stray thought. As it is, I'd say you have less than a few hours to get within a safe distance. We're likely to have another prominence soon if not the complete collapse. When that happens, you'll be too close to get away."

Alice claps her hands together. "All right then! Let's move, people! Not a second to spare!" She presses a hand to her ear. "Warm him up, Anders!"

The *Florenz*'s idling engine rumbles to life as the tracking lights pierce the darkness. There's no time to think as Malachi and the other gemel hover aside, allowing the hostages, sodden and weak, to stagger forward with a collective cry of disbelief and joy. Frannie and Kessler leap into the crowd, identifying the weaker ones first; among them, the bartender, for whom Joss might feel a pang of sympathy if she didn't keep looking behind her like there's a monster lurking somewhere beyond the hills. She traipses back down the ramp to find Malachi waiting for her.

"I must say I'm surprised," he says.

"About what?" She stops, her eyes tracing the slight depressions in the mud trailing behind him. Is he walking now? Can she even call it that?

What does it feel like? To be here and not here?

"That you bet on the possibility of my owning a heart."

"Oh, I'd never do that," Joss says. "I rarely do that with my own kind."

Malachi looks over at Frannie and Kessler now moving the last of the hostages, a thin man with a leg brace, up the ramp on a stretcher. "I can see why."

Joss snorts and gazes at him directly. "Why not come with us? It's not like you'll take up space."

A thin, wistful smile stretches across his lips. "No can do. We leave, we lose our autonomy. We'd go dark."

"But you'd just save yourself in our data banks," Joss says. "Isn't that how it works? One back up copy allowed if you're in danger of extermination?"

He looks at her, his eyes narrowing in faint suspicion. "And who would reactivate us?" He nods over at the man on the ramp. "You know why we need to go down with the ship. You said it yourself. We know too much. Another glorious example of your species would bind us upon landing and extract the information and like that…" A shimmer of movement as he opens his hand, watching fascinated as the rain dances in his palm. "We'd be no more." He nods over at Alice, who's stopped on the ramp, a hand clamped to her earpiece. "Case in point."

Alice's face has gone shock white. She's twisting away from them, one hand pressed to her forehead. "When? On whose orders?" Her commsbell goes up, shrouding her expression, but Joss can see the tense rise of her shoulders, the expulsion of breath against the silencing field as she spits out a volley of questions. She lowers it, calling out one last order as she turns to face them. "Anders! Prepare to launch."

"What is it?" Joss asks.

Not-Alice, her eyes roving over the horizon is the one to answer. "Garber's commandeered the *Eberhardt*. He's en rou— "

Al and Alice's words are lost in a bright flash and the low rumble of another dropship as it dives through the cloud cover. Joss feels herself yanked violently as Alice pulls her down to crouch behind one of the landing struts. Kessler takes cover beneath the ramp. They hunker down, all save Al and Malachi, shielding their eyes as the ship swoops low over the square, the rain gusting them in its wake. As it passes over, it neither fires nor decelerates, careening at a drunken tilt toward the distant ridge of the canyon and that cold phosphorescence.

"He's heading right for the rift," Malachi says, his voice preternaturally calm.

"That's suicide," Joss says.

"He doesn't think so." Alice's tone is mordant, but her fingers rest gently on Joss's arm. "A last-ditch attempt to gather data. Jesus. He's stupider than I thought."

They watch as the air around the dropship starts to shimmer, growing soupy with that thick phosphorescence and eroding the outline of the ship as it nears the canyon.

Malachi releases a weary exhale, that strange wheeze in his throat again as he lifts a hand to calm her. "Like my progenitor, he stopped at nothing and nothing is what he'll receive."

His demeanour is unruffled as his eyes trace the ship's trajectory. "But now you've even less time. Direct contact with the energy will further destabilise the rift. You must go, Commander Dray. Now. It will not go well for you, I'm afraid. But you must try."

There's no time to make sure everyone's secure before they lift off, just a quick headcount as the *Florenz* shoots up, backside first like a kicking horse as its passengers either grab on to something or go hurtling across the corrugated floor of the cargo bay. Joss is barely inside, the ramp clattering under her boots as it retracts mid-flight. She catches a last glimpse of the Mudtown shrinking into the cloud cover, sees that phosphorescent light pooling along Haitch's surface, through the narrow churn of streets as it washes out the blocky contours of the settlement like a carpet bomb on a forest floor.

Such cold grey light.

Is that what it looks like? she wonders. *When there's no barrier? When every existence melds itself together?*

She staggers into the cockpit, hastily strapping herself down into the jumpseat as her ribcage keeps time with the rattle of the engines. Alice and Anders are bickering up front, their voices shrill and barking over the din.

"You see that, Commander?"

"I see it, Lieutenant! Punch it!"

"Sir, that's too steep!"

"It's that or what's following us, Anders! Do it!"

Anders yanks the throttle and Joss is slammed back in her seat as the ship spirals upward and prepares to breach atmo. She sinks down, slings her arms through the metal safety bar and clings, nauseous, as her skin is stretched and dragged by the rising G-forces. Outside, that cold grey glow from Haitch is growing brighter, seeping through the cockpit window and she squeezes her eyes shut, remembering that same arctic light she'd seen from the escape pod. She keeps them shut, trying to keep that dread chill from seeping through her lids, until she hears the burst of the engine as the vessel punches out of orbit.

When she opens them, she's met by the cool darkness of the void, the stars spinning out in front of her as the ship starts its gallop toward the *Tereshkova*. Alice is a soft blur, her face coming into focus as she glances back over her shoulder.

"You all right?"

"Yeah. We out?"

She shakes her head. "Not yet."

That light may be gone, but the monitor above her is a flurry of activity; the icon for Haitch is flashing, pulses radiating out from its centre in waves of concentric circles as the small blip of the craft inches away from the planet with excruciating slowness. The *Florenz* isn't capable of FTL travel; it needs to be safely hitched within the *Tereshkova*'s foldspace net in order to make the jump.

Alice flicks on the rear-view monitor, revealing a receding image of Haitch. Within the minutes it's taken the *Florenz* to break away from the planet, that small nub of a world has transformed, that cold light stretching across it like the encroaching sunrise of a denser star.

"Hang tight," Alice says. "We're not out of the woods yet."

"Sir?" Anders jerks his head up at the adjacent monitor, his face is frozen in shock as his fingers fly over the keyboard. The *Florenz*, once a single blip on the monitor, is being trailed by a swarm of signatures arcing out from its surface, a shower of static and force traveling toward them in a steadfast trajectory.

"And there it is," Alice says. Joss knows she's thinking it because they're all goddamned thinking it. Garber stirred the pot, consigning them to their doom before his mission aborted itself in the vortex. "Anders. Now might be time to add those backup thrusters!"

Anders slams his hand down on the control, freeing up the auxiliary propellant, and gives another yank to the yoke. The energy signatures are spreading out across the dark patches, groping blindly through that vastness like tendrils seeking air and warmth and light. Even the simple, almost childlike graphics on the overlay communicate a loneliness and sense of lostness to their movements.

"Velocity," Alice says. "Can we make it?"

"Not before that shit makes it to us. Apologies, Commander."

"What about the ion pulse?"

"Already at full capacity," Anders says. "They'll be on us when we slow to dock with the *Tereshkova*."

Alice's eyes don't stray from the monitor as Anders speaks, but even then, a look of acceptance washes over her features. She bends forward, hands splayed on the console as she forces some friendly bluster into her tone.

"Ota, do you copy?"

"Affirmative."

"We were hoping to hitch a ride with you folks, but I'm afraid you're going to have to jump." A pause. "Yeah, well, prep for it anyway! We're taking evasive manoeuvres. It's all we can do. No! Don't wait! Whatever this is, we'd be bringing it right to you!" She glances back at Joss, offering her best and bravest semblance of a smile. "Hang on, Carsten."

The monitor is brighter now, flecks of light from the swarm converging, crawling closer into the path of the *Florenz* as Anders banks the ship into a hard spin and sends it arcing upward, or what feels like up. Joss can't tell. She clutches the armrests of the jumpseat, her jaw tight and her mouth bitter with the acid rising from her gut. All she sees is dark, and the occasional flicker of a warning light searing through her skin. All she can hear is Alice, barking orders, frantically urging Ota not to wait. To go where they'll be safe—at least temporarily. The ship tilts again and she swallows back bile, dipping her head to wipe her mouth on her shoulder.

When she lifts her gaze, Not-Alice is in front of her.

She's phased through the closed cockpit door, her back turned as she hovers between Joss and the helm. Alice is twisting back to speak to her, that hard, determined mask loosening in confusion as Al bends toward her and whispers something in her ear. It's a courtesy, to make these human gestures, to speak directly when she could simply communicate through the comms. Amid crisis, it's a strange act of grace.

"Al?"

Joss sits up, trying to catch their words through the din as the ship continues to whorl, end over end over end, the stars pivoting and smearing into single strands of coruscation, but there is nothing but the judder of the engine and the clatter of equipment as rattles against the bulkheads. Amid all that motion and sound, Al is motionless, her hands positioned on each side of Alice's head like she's offering a prayer. She pulls back, her eyes locked with Alice's, her hands still hovering on her head, as Alice's eyes narrow and a strange sorrowful expression clouds her features.

She blinks up at her, disoriented, and then she seems to steel herself, smiling once before nodding to her. They've made a decision. Without her.

"Al?" Joss calls over to them and she rises and turns, a firmness in her expression, a determination welling up that Joss has never seen before. She smiles, her voice gently reverberating through the comm. "I know what it means now, Joss." She's speaking so fast. "The moths." She glances back at Alice and Joss catches the tell-tale shimmer in Alice's eyes before she turns away.

"Al? What is this?"

Alice stares at her, silently urging her, trusting her to grasp what she is only beginning to comprehend even now. But in that trust is a distance Joss has never felt before. A severance, and she lifts a hand, letting it hover at Joss's cheek as if to make up for this sudden estrangement.

"What Matilde said, about them being led by the wrong light. That's why that force is following us. It's drawn toward consciousness, an observer to give it direction and form and meaning. A polestar to guide it back home. You…" She gestures about the cabin. "You're not the right ones. But I … I am."

With those words, something starts to break inside of her. She can hear Alice giving an order behind her, her voice low and subdued. "Anders, commence pod decoupling protocols. Ready number 2 for launch."

"You can't…" Joss reaches down, her hands fumbling with the security harness. The buckle snaps hard against her fingers. "Al. I can't let you can't do this."

Not-Alice inches back, her hands outstretched, placating. "It's not about you, Joss. Don't you see? That memory wasn't for you."

"No."

The ship banks but she pulls herself up, in thrall to a denial that conscripts her whole body. Her vision's blurring, but she's not sure if she's weeping or if Al is already beginning to fade around the edges. "You don't mean this."

Alice shakes her head and hovers closer, her fingers ghosting Joss's chin, a warm, bright emptiness that feels like everything. "It's the right thing. I know it because you know it, Joss."

This is goodbye.

"No!" Joss reaches for her, but only feels a faint and crackling resonance. "I-I order you to stop! Do you hear? You're still bound to—"

She halts and swallows at those words, horror giving way to tears as Alice brings a hand to her chest, and God, she can feel it, that muted resistance, that feather-light impression of another being.

"I'll still be here, Joss, because you're here."

"I love you." She stammers it out as if to smother what she's just said, to pull that ugly claim of ownership back into her like a rip current, but Al has already forgiven her, and her voice breaks a little as she says it.

"I love you too."

She smiles and backs away, flinching as Joss lets out a cry that might snap them both in two. Her eyes never leave her, even as she glides away, Joss trying to follow, her face contorted as Not-Alice's body fades through the bulkhead. Her outline remains, burned by the sear of grief into her sightline.

"No, no, no. Goddamn it."

Joss climbs over the jumpseat, reaching for the buttons that will open the access port into the main compartment, but the hatch won't give. It might as well be a wall.

"Joss!" Alice's voice is warped and distant. Joss slams her fists against the button, and when she gives up on that, against the bulkhead, her sobs shredding through her like the metal now threatening to break her fingers. She throws her body against the door. Again. Again. Again. Fingers lock around her wrist and force her into a turn. Alice's grip is strong and not short on pain and Joss freezes, unable to weigh the abyss inside of her against the solid presence without.

"Joss..." Alice loosens her grip as she pulls her to her, her breath warm against her ear. "Don't do this," she whispers. "Your survival is the only thing you can give her right now. Make it count."

She holds Joss there as the ship tussles with velocity, arms wrapped tightly around her until the air runs out of her and something inside her relents. Joss's eyes fixate on the monitor, that bright line of the *Florenz's* trajectory with the flurry of lights moving fast behind it, and now, something smaller, a single arc of light moving away from the *Florenz* in a steady glide toward its pursuers.

Anders swerves again, hard, forcing Alice to loosen her grip and fall back, but there's something in her eyes, a flush of stupor as her lips part and she takes in a breath that seems to rise and shiver like a wire.

"Dray?"

Alice stumbles back, her gaze distant, as she raises her trembling hand to her head.

"Hey, Alice?"

Panic shoves her back to the present and Joss throws herself forward. She gathers Alice into her arms as she pulls them both into the jumpseat.

"Secure her there!" Anders says. "Now! This is going to get choppy!" He turns back, his eyes wide with fear and exhilaration "Would you look at that fucking thing!"

In Joss's line of work, it's not uncommon to encounter loss when you've got no room to process it. A squad mate or a friend can die right there beside you, and you're too busy saving your own ass to feel much more than that sharp incision severing past from present, that strange, slow wave of disassociation as the world rushes at you, altered into a thing you no longer recognise.

Joss holds tight to Alice, unsure if she's doing it for Alice or herself, or the one whose loss now suffuses her body with emptiness even as she draws in Alice's warmth. All she can do is hold on.

That's all you can do.

That's all anyone can do.

She secures the belt around them, pressing her face into Alice's shoulder as the ship rattles violently around them. She sees the arc of Al's escape pod as it sinks into the flurry of lights, a vortex of mass and multitudes,and thinks her soul might shatter with the ship.

The pod keeps going, arcing around to dive toward Haitch.

The light follows.

Joss wishes with all her heart that she could too.

Not-Alice wasn't Alice.

She wasn't Joss.

But she was someone.

And now.

Now she is not.

Chapter Twenty

To some extent, you can control how you die. You can eat better, cut the booze, avoid driving when there's ice on the roads in places where the cold still clings to the earth. You can go in for your regular checkups and monitor your symptoms, examining each inch of your skin with a magnifying glass to keep death within the purview of freak accidents or just those things that can't be helped.

You have some choice in how you'll leave this life, but you can never choose how you'll return to it, nor what or who will bring you back.

In this case it was both.

Not-Alice brought her back. Hovered and fussed over her and forced her to face the things she'd shoved down until she felt alive again. Now it's her turn to do the hovering as she sits by Alice's bed, watching her sleep with nothing but the glow of a scrollscreen and the hum of the equipment for company. It's an odd reversal, watching the rise and fall of Alice's chest, the steady stream of her vitals on the holodisplay as she waits to tell her about a dream she's had while she dozed off over lukewarm coffee.

The *Tereshkova* has rejoined the fleet. They're staying in a holding pattern, keeping their distance from the jumpgate at Kestra-Gardis and other inhabited regions until they can be certain none of Haitch's residual energy has tagged along for an encore. There's nothing left of the rift or of Haitch. It swallowed itself as Malachi had predicted, and Fleet communication logs have received no transmissions either from Garber's dropship or the *Eberhardt*. They'd taken a risk and gotten too close. Ota is interim commander while Alice recovers, and the rest of the crew works on getting their stories straight for those inevitable debriefings back on Earth. Alice may have failed to obtain the prize, but she saved their lives. They know where their loyalties lie.

Joss sits in a half doze, when her body allows her to drift, her days counted out by the shifts in Alice's breath as she stirs in her sleep. When she dozes, she dreams of Hugo and Matilde. In one, she's a girl, clambering up the rickety stairs of that old porch to tell Matilde that she'll save them. Save everyone. It's not the moths in this version, but a flock of Sandhill cranes Matilde used to seek out along the river. Her avó glowers at her like she's aware of the discrepancy.

"I told you, Joss. Those cranes aren't nocturnal. You mean the ovenbird warbler. Now those birds follow the moon, *queridinha*."

When she sees her father, she offers no forgiveness. She just asks him why he left her the farm. Hugo never answers.

Sometimes, the young medic who plugged for Alice in the debriefing strolls in to check on her. He comes bearing coffee and the good sandwiches from the mess. The chicken only slightly tastes of rubber, and the coffee is laced with whiskey. Joss has made an effort since to learn his name—Doctor Scanlon—but she just calls him Wenn. He doesn't seem worried, despite the fact that Alice hasn't woken up in days. In fact, he seems encouraged.

Once, in the wee hours of the not-night, she awakens to find him gaping at the biometric display, his head tilted to one side like he's staring at a perplexing work of art.

"What is it?" She bolts up, running a hand through a strand of matted hair, some of which has gotten in her mouth. She spits it out and wipes her palm across her lips, and when he doesn't answer, she tries to glean one from the glyphs and symbols, but all she sees is a long string of code, fluctuating like a seismograph.

"Something wrong?"

Alice is still deep in sleep, but there's more colour to her cheeks, and even that scar seems to have faded into a thin pale band across her cheek.

"Nope," he says, glancing back at her as if he's been forced to notice the furniture. "Her BCI's are elevated. A lot shifting around in there. Either that or she's having one hell of a dream."

Joss's stomach heaves like it's going to fight him. "What does that mean? Should we wake her?"

"No, no. She's good," he says. "More than." He takes a step back and peruses the data pad he's got balanced on one arm. "You though…"

He reaches into his coat, something crackling like plastic between his fingers before he passes her a cookie, frosted in blue and individually wrapped. "I like to carry these with me. They have a little something in them. Might help you get some decent shuteye." He nods over at Alice. "Maybe you can join that party she's having over there."

"Might be nice to," Joss says.

When she sleeps that night, she dreams of Al for the first time.

They're on the *Tiktaalik*. Maybe in the mess or maybe that fancy suite Joss took for herself when she thought she was dying, and Al is pacing and gesticulating, her hands moving in some old movie version of being inspired.

"I found out something while you were sleeping, Joss," she tells her. "Did you know how many dimensions there are? I mean, they thought it was ten, eleven if you count time into the mix. But that doesn't even begin to cover it." She's talking fast as if she's trying to countervail Joss's old impatience, but all Joss can do is stay perfectly still, her breath stopped in her throat because she knows if she disturbs the order of things, Al will be gone again.

"It's all there. All of it. The things we did. The things we never got around to. The emptiness and the fullness. Every moment we ever shared together here and not here. I could recount it all for you, but that" —she looks at her, her brown eyes crinkling into a smile— "that might just take forever." She moves in closer, her eyes searching hers. "There are so many choices and if you think too long about it, the here becomes not here. The only thing you can do is just trust yourself to be."

She bolts up shaking, her palms wet with her own tears. The lights have dimmed, and Alice is flat on her back, her soft snores drowned out by the hum of the equipment. Joss wipes her eyes and curls into herself, letting the sorrow lap over her until a soft rustling stirs her from her grief.

Alice is watching her from her bed, her eyes filled with confusion and mild worry.

"You all right?" she manages, her voice still raw and papery from sleep. She pushes herself up on her hands, weaving slightly as she steadies herself against the mattress. Joss shakes her head and blinks, swiping her sleeve over her face as she scoots forward in her seat.

"Fine. You … are you all right?"

"You look like shit," Alice says.

Joss laughs, surprised to be back in her body. "Like Betty after one of her benders."

Alice gives a weak chuckle but not without enthusiasm. "God, remember that time she stole the good scotch from under the Christmas tree?"

"You remember that?"

Alice crooks an eyebrow in disbelief. "Of course, I remember. That was an 18-year-old Macallan for Christ's sake." Her eyes go distant, lips pursed as if she's hit upon a stray thought. "That sasa plant though." She exhales, giving a rapid, overwhelmed shake of her head. "Now there was a guzzler. You know I almost got fined for that."

"I remember," Joss says, feeling a faint twinge of hope steal into her gut.

Alice is gazing at her, a strange sharpness mixed with bewilderment in her eyes as if she's startled by her own thoughts.

"You okay?"

Alice gives her head a shake. "Fine. Maybe it's the drugs they pumped me with but that just came to me. Clear and focused. It was almost like I was back there again."

"Yeah?"

As they stare at each other, Joss can feel an odd pull in her chest, that pinch of recognition that fades before you've had a chance to take any names. There's a difference to Alice, but one that's mingled with familiarity and a renewed sense of rapport, like she's mirroring back a part of herself.

"Maybe..." Joss says, not sure if she should say it. "Maybe you've been bugged."

Alice turns to her, her eyes narrowing, a ghost of recall flickering across her face.

"For better or worse," she says as if she's joining a chorus mid-song. "I think this is more of a feature."

When Joss lets herself think it, she starts to shake, the tears falling freely as Alice's eyes light up with alarm. She sits up, one arm out as if she's not sure if she should hold her or if that might be crossing a line. She settles for taking her hand, and when that doesn't help, Alice pulls her blanket off and scoots closer, reaching out to wrap her arms around her as Joss weeps into her shoulder.

"Why so sombre, Carsten?" she whispers, her breath warm and real in Joss's ear. "You didn't lose me."

She leans closer, her hands tracing gently along her shoulders, tentative and searching as if she's touching her for the first time. "I'm still here, you know? We're both of us still here."

Acknowledgement

I owe a great deal of gratitude to three remarkable people: To Steph Bianchini and Dolly Garland for their encouragement and insightful critiques and occasional yelling, and to E. Louise Nielsen, for her wit and gentle feedback. You helped rescue these characters from more than a few embarrassing moments—not to mention space peril--and I couldn't have done this without you.

Thank you to M.H. Dyson and Maya MacDonald of the Tokyo Spex Fic writing group for your warm and honest critiques, and to Segfaultfault, who true to their handle, spotted some last minute repeats in the manuscript. I'd also like to thank D.K. Griffin and H.S. Gray for your encouragement and help with the pitch and the synopsis, and Diane Hawley Nagatomo for vetting the Nebraska sections and introducing me to runzas.

I'm grateful to my mother Jody Ellis, who graciously provided the time and space for me to work on the manuscript during a visit amid an overheated Tokyo summer.

Finally, a heartfelt thank you to Francesca Barbini at Luna Press Publishing for giving this story a home and for your encouragement and patience throughout the process. It's been a pleasure working with you—and warding off karaoke viruses with song! And a special thanks to Shona Kinsella for the careful edits of the manuscript, and to Tara Bush for her stunning cover art and excellent music recommendations.

All of you believed in this story, some of you from the very beginning when it was just a drop of space angst during the early months of the pandemic.

The stars are indeed lit.